BONUS GAME

CHICAGO RED TAILS
BOOK 6

SUSAN RENEE

Bonus GAME

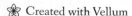

PROLOGUE

Riley...Dude...pro tip:
Stop leaving your fleshlight in the shower.
Your poor sister is going to need
years of therapy.

"**A** FLESHLIGHT? Are you serious, Landric?" I shout as I step out of Milo and Charlee's guest bathroom. "You have a fucking FLESH-LIGHT sitting out in your guest shower?"

"What are you doing peeking in their shower, Miller?" Dex challenges from the dining room table where the rest of the group is seated for game night. Looks of surprise and snorts of laughter fill the room as I gesture inside the bathroom trying my best to rein in my own humored shock to no avail.

"Dude, the shower curtain was wide open when I went in there and Milo's got his fleshlight standing tall on the shower shelf like it's a statue on a goddamn living room mantle!"

Rory pulls an Uno card from the ones in her hand and places it on the discard pile. "Who keeps a flashlight in the shower?" She glances with a narrowed eye at a blushing tight-lipped Charlee. "Does Milo shower in the dark?"

Tatum leans over and whispers to her, "Not a flashlight, Ror. A *flesh*light."

Rory's brows pinch. "What's a—"

Hawken clears his throat, covering his mouth to hide his smirk as he performs a quick hand gesture for Rory.

She finally catches on and nearly chokes on a laugh. "Oooh. *Flesh*light..."

Colby shakes his head. "Poor Milo. Not even in the room to defend himself."

"Where'd he go?" I ask.

Charlee squeaks. "Changing Amelia's diaper."

Still horrified and amused I take my seat at the table next to Charlee. "My poor eyes. He could've fuckin' warned a man before leaving something like that around."

"Why? You want to give it a whirl, Zeke?" Dex laughs.

"Shut up, Asshole." I turn to Charlee. "What the hell does he even need that for? Do you not let the poor guy in or what?"

She bursts out a laugh, shaking her head as she plays a yellow SKIP card. "What can I say? That last trimester was a bitch so I bought it to keep him occupied while my baby factory was working overtime." She stands from her seat. "Plus, he showers in there when he gets home late at night and I'm already asleep, though I wasn't aware he had it on display. Sorry Zeke. I'll go get it. Oh, and you're skipped by the way."

"I got it, Goldilocks." Milo comes down the hall with a tiny bundle of joy clothed in pink footed pajamas on his shoulder, his large hand practically palming her entire body. "Don't get up." Charlee watches him lovingly as he holds their precious little girl against his body.

"It's perfectly normal for guys to have toys too." Kinsley pulls a yellow six from her hand and the play continues around the table. "Guys aren't exempt from having a little pleasured fun once in a while."

Charlee smirks. "Why do you think none of the other guys at this table have said a thing about Milo's fleshlight?"

Tatum snickers. "Because they all have their own fleshlights just like that one in their own homes." She bumps Dex's shoulder with her own. "Dexter included."

"Ooooh!" Kinsley sits back in her seat, glancing at Carissa, Charlee, and Tatum. "Did you three—"

"Yep." Carissa pops her P as she tosses a blue six onto the discard pile.

My brows furrow as I look around the table making the realization myself. "Wait. Hold up. You guys all got your own toys?" I gesture to the ladies. "From them?"

Colby and Dex try to hide their embarrassment much to Milo's amusement.

"We went shopping together and bought them at the same time," Carissa explains, playing a blue nine when it's her turn. "Sex is great and all, but when you're the size of a whale and your ankles are swollen larger than your forearms..."

"And all you want to do is sleep," Tatum adds, tossing a WILD card onto the pile. "Green."

Charlee adds, "Yeah. And you horny lot have a good game and need to fuck the energy and adrenaline away so you can sleep at night when you get home..."

Kinsley's jaw drops and she turns to Quinton. "So that's the secret! Sounds like I need to go shopping!"

"Wait." Quinton's eyes grow and his cheeks pinken.

"What's that supposed to mean? You trying to tell me you don't like when I—"

"Uht, duht, duht, duht, duht." Kinsley silences Quinton with a finger against his lips. "Let's stop you right there because yes I always love it but good Lord you guys are horny as hell at two in the morning and my body does not need to be bending that way between the hours of about midnight and six A.M."

Everyone at the table laughs, including me, though deep down I know I'm not nearly as happy for my friends as I am jealous. The guys all found their happy-ever-afters. They're all with the women of their dreams, and deservedly so, but me? I'm the loser whose wife left him—unexpectedly leaving me to raise Elsie on my own.

I should've been first. It should be me living a happy life. I was with Lori before Colby ever met Carissa. Before Charlee knocked on Milo's door several years ago. We were happy and starting our own family, but she was gone before our Key West trip that year. She was gone by the time Dex found Tatum. She was gone before Hawken and Rory finally fell in love. She was gone before Kinsley and Quinton got together. Now, instead of being a happily married man and world's best father I'm the guy who skips the hang outs at Pringle's after our home games so I can say good night to my kid who hasn't seen me in two or three days. I'm the guy who's waking up at the ass crack of dawn to get everything ready for the day before dropping Elsie off with my parents for God knows how long. I'm the guy who has to take his daughter to her grandparents several nights a week in order to do my job because there's no mom at home to help me.

I'm the guy who wonders if I'll ever get to be genuinely happy the way the rest of these guys are now. The one who wishes he had time to even consider meeting another woman let alone fall in love with her.

"Listen, I'm just going to say this once and then I promise I'll shut up and stop being a Debbie Downer. But you guys all have it incredibly lucky. You have each other to come home to. You have each other to help out with parenting woes." The play finally gets back around the table to me so I play a card and hold up the only other one in my hand. "Uno. Just...I don't know..." I shake my head. "When things get tough, and I promise they'll get tough, remember how blessed you all are. Talk to each other. Yell it out if you have to, though not in front of the kids, of course. Do whatever you have to do to keep the spark alive and remember why you love each other, because it's no fun when the spark snuffs out and you're alone."

Silence falls over the table.

"Uh...Miller?" Hawken cringes.

"Yeah?"

"You alright over there? You haven't said something that deep since...uh..."

"Ever." Quinton finishes Hawken's statement.

"Yeah." Hawk nods. "What he said."

Slouching in my chair, I look around the table at everyone's pitying and concerned faces. "Yeah. Sorry guys. I promise I'm fine. I really am."

"You know you're allowed to not be fine, right?" Colby throws a Draw Four card onto the pile and calls out, "Red."

"It's not that I'm not fine. I am. Truly. Elsie is fine. She's a happy kid who doesn't know any different than the life she has, but..." I sigh. "I'm not going to lie. It sucks having to take her to my parents all the time. It's like they're raising her and I'm the fun uncle that shows up from time to time. I love my parents. I do. And I very much appreciate that they've stepped up and been willing and able to help out, but let's be honest here, they should be enjoying retirement. They should be enjoying being the grandparents that get to come over and spoil their granddaughter from time to time. Not the ones putting her in time out or making sure she eats a balanced meal several times a day. That's my job."

"But you can't always be there." Charlee shrugs. "It's the nature of the career. Everybody knows that. Certainly, all of us. Nobody blames you at all for the way you parent your kid, Zeke. You're doing the absolute best you can. We love Elsie to pieces."

"Am I though? Am I really doing what's best for her? She barely lives in her own home for Pete's sake. How is that good for her? And she starts preschool. Someone has to be available to pick her up mid-day."

"What do you *want* to do?" Colby asks me. "What does the perfect life with Elsie look like to you right now?"

I scoff lightly. "I'm not sure the perfect life can exist for us right now. To her, the perfect life is one where both of her parents are around every moment of every day. I mean this summer has been magical because I've been home with her more often than not. We've spent so much time together these last couple of months, but the regular season is about to get into full swing and that means we're back to several days and nights a week away from each other. I just want to be able to come home at the end of the day and be a dad, you know?"

"And maybe date again?"

"Hmph." I roll my eyes. "That'll be the day. With our schedule? Who's going to want to date me when I can't commit to anything for a good nine to ten months out of the year?"

"There are good women out there, Zeke," Rory states. "Women who understand the business and would support it. I mean look at all of us."

"Is there a list out there or something?" I tease. "A list of promising hockey wives and girlfriends? That might make things a hell of a lot easier."

Rory smiles. "That's an innovative idea. I'll have to do some internet research."

"What about a nanny?" Carissa suggests. "Someone who could help with Elsie in your home so when your workday is done, you don't have to spend time traveling to the opposite side of town to pick her up only to bring her home and put her to bed and do it all again the next day? If you had someone at the house with her, you could be home in fifteen minutes and have more time to spend with her."

"I've thought about a nanny." I nod. "But you're talking like, a full-time live-in kind of deal?"

She shrugs. "Yeah."

"And that isn't weird? Asking some random person to pick up their lives and move into my house?"

"It's not like you don't have the space," Quinton reminds me. "You have more than enough bedrooms in your house. The nanny would have plenty of space so it's not like you would be on top of each other all the time."

"I mean...unless he wants to be on top of her," Dex jokes. Hawken shakes his head at the absurdity of Dex, but he laughs just the same.

I roll my eyes. "Dude, that's gross. I'm not going to fuck the goddamn nanny."

"You say that now," he smirks, "but have you met the nanny yet? I mean, maybe she'll be hot. You could add that as a requirement." He gestures up in the air as he calls out his headline. "Full time nanny for hire. Hot as fuck is a must."

"Fuck you, Dexter." I finally laugh. "I can only imagine the kind of people that would be lined up for that interview."

"Right? It's genius if you ask me. And they'd all be lucky as hell. Man or woman, cause you're a catch, Zeke." He winks.

"Thanks, I think."

"Think about it." Carissa smiles. "If you want some help coming up with a job posting or a list of responsibilities, we're happy to help any way we can. You deserve to be happy just as much as the rest of us."

"Yeah. Thanks." I nod. "I'll definitely give it some thought."

A full-time live-in nanny. I gave some thought to the idea of a part-time nanny as a glorified babysitter before, but never the idea of having someone in my home full-time. That could take some getting used to.

But if it's in Elsie's best interest...

There's nothing I wouldn't do for her.

She's my world.

"Missessss..." Dex looks down at the resume in front of him. "Fahrtinga? Did I pronounce that right?" He makes a guttural noise with his mouth trying not to laugh out loud at this poor woman's name. As annoyed as I might be at Dex's immaturity, I'd be lying if I said I was taking any part of this interview seriously. I should've just said thanks but no thanks, but Tatum and Carissa thought her resume looked good and that I should overlook the odd last name.

Seriously though, am I really going to live with a woman whose last name is Fahrtinga?

Please let someone else's interview be better than this.

For the love of God.

"Yes, that's correct." The stout older woman nods with a stern scowl.

I give her a polite smile and shake her hand, taking notice of her firm, confident handshake. "Thanks for coming in today, Mrs. Fahrtinga. It's lovely to meet you. Please allow me to introduce you to a few of my colleagues." I gesture down the table. "This is Dex Foster, Milo Landric, and Colby Nelson. They, like me, have children so they know the rigors of the job and what might be needed for my daughter, Elsie, so I asked them to help me out with the interview process."

"Fair enough," she answers.

I spend a few minutes explaining what I'm looking for from a full-time nanny and then give the guys a few moments to ask questions so that I can sit, listen, and watch. More than anything I really want to get a good feel of who these potential hires are and what their personalities might be like when they're around my kid all day.

"Mrs. Fahrtinga," Colby starts. "Do you have children of your own?"

"Four grown children, yes." She nods without as much as a smile. "Two of my daughters work at the Color Me Happy salon on the southeast side of town. And one of my sons works for the sanitation department."

That's three...she said four.

"And the fourth child?"

Her face remains neutral as she answers curtly. "Incarcerated."

Jesus.

What the hell for?

Drug possession?

Theft?

Murder?

Rather than ask further questions about it, Colby continues on. "And what was your parenting style as they were growing up? Did you have strict schedules for them to follow or were they free to do a lot of whatever they wanted?"

But more importantly, why the hell is your son in jail?

Mrs. Fahrtinga opens her mouth to answer Colby but I interrupt her because my gut won't let me not ask. "I'm sorry, Mrs. Fahrtinga. I don't mean to interrupt with such a personal question but would you be comfortable telling us why your son is incarcerated?"

She rolls her eyes slightly and I can't tell if she's annoyed with me for asking or her son for getting himself into trouble.

"They accused him of taking part in a child pornography ring online."

"Oookay." I stand with force almost knocking over my chair and step to the door. "Thank you for coming in Mrs. Fahrtinga but I won't be needing anymore of your time. I'm certain this job is not going to be the right fit."

She pops up from her chair, her eyes wide.

"But—"

"There are no buts, Ma'am."

Like hell if I'm going to let anything like that even remotely close to my child.

"We're done here, Mrs. Fahrtinga. Have a lovely day."

"So, you said you have kids of your own Ms. Silverman?"

"Yes," she answers with a smile. "Six kids. Three different fathers. Will they each be getting their own bedrooms when we move in? I'll especially need to make sure Nico and Nash are separated. They don't always get along and tend to end up fighting. And Jennica, she sleepwalks a lot so she'll need to be on the main floor so she doesn't fall down the stairs."

Next.

"Oh, I do have a list of allergies I should go over with you if I'm going to be in your home," our next interviewer adds after our round of questioning. She's a middle-aged woman, petite, with long brown hair and silver wire-rimmed glasses she pushes back from the bridge of her nose. So far, her interview has been great and her disposition completely opposite that of Mrs. Fahrtinga. Thank God. The more I get to know her, the more I think Elsie might like her.

"Absolutely. I want you to be as comfortable as possible in my home."

She hands me her list of allergies and I read down through the extensive file.

Carrots
Beets
Watermelon
Green grapes
Wheat bread
Flour
Milk
Feathers
Cats
Dogs
Goats
Gerbils
Hamsters
Grass
Maple trees
Pine trees
Oak trees
Ragweed
Marigolds
Dandelions
Garlic

Pesto

Rosemary

Cotton

Dust

Mold

Mildew

I'm also sensitive to most scented soaps, perfumes, and candles.

I hand the paper back to her and nod kindly. "Thank you for your time, but I don't think this will be the right fit."

"Ms. Bendit," Milo begins, glancing down at our next applicant. "Can you explain the three-year gap in your resume between your last job and now? Did you go back to school...or..."

"Uh..." Her face pinkens and she shifts in her seat. "No. I didn't go back to school. I've actually been gainfully employed these past three years making a very solid income."

"Oh, great." Milo clicks his pen. "Can I ask what you do for a living currently then?"

"I sell my panties."

What. The. Fuck?

All of us look up from the table, speechless.

Milo clears his throat, his brows furrowed. "I'm sorry?"

"My panties," she repeats. "I sell my panties online."

"Do you design underwear or something?" I ask her with morbid curiosity.

She shakes her head. "Oh no. I wear them for the day and then I package them up and send them out to the next buyer."

Dex leans forward in his chair. "You sell...used panties?"

She nods. "Yes."

He cocks his head. "How does that work exactly?"

Oh my God, I can't believe he's asking this.

What am I saying? It's Dex, of course I believe it.

"It just depends on what clients want. Sometimes they'll ask for one day of wear. Sometimes they'll ask me to wear them for two or three days. I've had a guy ask me to masturbate wearing a pair and I even had one who asked that I pee on them before sending."

She cannot be serious.

Dex smiles like a goofy teenager. "Fascinating. And what do they do with—"

"Thank you for your time, Ms. Bendit," Colby says for me as I'm still trying to pick my jaw up off the floor. "But I think we're going to go in another direction."

"I apologize for my frankness here, Ms. Wiltzer, but before we get any further into this interview, I need to ask if you sell pictures of child pornography online or if you send out used panties to willing buyers?"

The young woman, who can't be a day over twenty, laughs. "Good Lord, no."

"Thank Christ." Dex sighs with relief. "It's been a day around here."

"But I do run a podcast called Orgasmic ASMR."

The fuck?

Milo chuckles, shaking his head. "Aaaand thank you for your time."

When the last applicant walks out of the room, Carissa and Kinsley walk in with our lunch delivery.

"Lunch time gentlemen." Carissa smiles, lifting several bags filled with pasta and breadsticks from one of our favorite Italian restaurants. Time to carb-load before afternoon practice. "Any luck? Did you find someone good for Elsie?"

"That's a huge negative." I scoff, exhausted already and it's just barely noon. "Are there seriously no good people in Chicago who love kids and are, I don't know, normal?"

"Uh oh." Kinsley cringes. "That doesn't sound good."

Colby chuckles, his face half cringing, half smiling. "I would've never believed it myself if I hadn't been here listening to some of these whack jobs."

I slump down in my seat, opening my container of pasta. "Something tells me this is going to be harder than I thought. I won't let just anybody around my daughter twenty-four-seven. I have to find the right person, or I have to figure out a plan B...and C...and D."

Kinsley tips her head to the side, chewing on the inside of her mouth. "You know, I might know someone."

"Really?"

I would trust Kinsley's taste in people. She's fun. Energetic. Nice. Friendly. She's been a great fit for Quinton.

She nods. "Yeah. Great girl. She works at the animal

17

shelter. She's the one who introduced me to Nutsack, and we kind of clicked right away. Her story is...well, I should let her tell it. But I know she's been looking for something a little more full-time than what she's currently doing. And she actually used to be an elementary school teacher."

"Well that sounds promising," Milo says, taking in a huge mouthful of his spaghetti.

"Yeah. Maybe."

"I'll call her and see what she thinks. If she's interested, is it okay if I pass along your contact information?"

"She doesn't sell feet pictures online does she?"

Kinsley smirks. "Not unless they're the boudoir pictures I took of her last year."

"So, she's married?"

"Uh, no." Kinsley shakes her head. "Not married. Again, I should let her tell her story. It's not mine to tell. But trust me, she's as normal as normal can be and has a great personality. Aaaaand she's hot."

Dex sits up, his brows peaked in interest. "Oh yeah? How hot are we talking?"

"Uh, like I'd do her if she swung that way. Her boudoir shoot was fire."

Dex claps me on the shoulder. "Just what our man Zeke needs! A hot nanny! Let's bring her in."

I roll my eyes at Dex but give a nod to Kinsley. "Alright. I trust you. Thanks Kinsley."

"Sure. Anything I can do to help."

2

ADA

"That's it, Purrito. Let's hear that purr, purr, purr. You like the scritchy-scratches don't you?" I say to one of my favorite long-term residents of the Paw Palace Animal Shelter. His orange and white tail swishes back and forth as I scratch his back. "I know you do, bud."

Purrito has been at the shelter longer than I can remember off hand. It's definitely been all spring and all summer. My heart breaks for so many of our furry friends who spend their days and nights here waiting for their forever families to waltz in and pick them. I chose Purrito to be our office cat for the day because even cats need a change of scenery from time to time.

"Let's see if we can find you a treat, Purrito." I step over to the back cabinet where some of the treats are stored, making kissy noises for him to follow me. "Come on."

I drop a few of his favorite catnip flavored treats on the floor at his feet for him to enjoy as my phone dings in my pocket. I pat a noisily purring Purrito on the top of his head and then pull out my phone to check my text.

KINSLEY

Hey Ada! I have a quick question for you!

ME

Hi Kinsley! Okay, ask away. Everything ok with Nutsack?

KINSLEY

Do you mean besides the fact that Quinton has trained him to give high-fives and play hockey on the kitchen floor with a water bottle cap? LOL!

ME

HAHA OMG That's amazing. At least Nutsack loves his Quinton and Quinton seems to love his...uh...Nutsack. Sorry I guess I set myself up for that one.

KINSLEY

He does indeed love his Nutsack. LOL!

ME

So, what can I help you with?

KINSLEY

Ummm, so what would you say if you had the opportunity to be a full-time live-in nanny for a little girl and live in a pretty swanky house with an extremely hot (and single) man?

ME

HA! I would laugh and ask you what fairytale you pulled that idea out of! 😉

KINSLEY

I know right? But what if I said I was dead serious?

I don't even bother responding to Kinsley's text. Instead, I hit the button to call her immediately. I need to hear this explanation.

"Did that pique your interest?" Kinsley laughs when she answers my call.

"Uhh, damn right it did. I needed to hear this, whatever this is, straight from your mouth instead of a text, so please, explain."

"Okay, so Zeke Miller, are you familiar?"

I scoff. "Am I familiar with the star goalie of the Chicago Red Tails hockey team?"

"Okay, I'll take that as a yes." She giggles. "Anyway, you know he has a little girl. Her name is Elsie."

"Riiiight." I nod slowly, remembering having seen Zeke in a few pictures with his daughter. "I do remember that now."

"Yes! She's a super spunky and fun little kid and he's looking for a full-time nanny for her during the season and I think you would be a fantastic fit for the job!"

My brows furrow. "Wait, full-time nanny. Where is his wife? Or I guess maybe ex-wife?"

"Definitely an ex-wife as she's been gone for three years now. She up and left not long after Elsie was born," Kinsley explains.

"Oh man. That's rough. So, he's been taking care of her on his own?"

"Yep. He's a great dad with her and he hates having to

21

get her a nanny. His parents have really stepped up and helped out but he knows they're not getting any younger and they deserve to enjoy retirement. He wants that for them. He wants them to be grandparents, *not* parents. Sooo he's looking for someone."

I'm a little taken aback by the notion she thinks I would be a good fit for this kind of a commitment. "Why me? What made you think I would be good for this?"

"Well, your teaching background for one. I know you haven't taught since, well, you know, but you're obviously comfortable and good with kids. It's very generous pay and you would have your own living space there to come and go as you please on your days off. I mean seriously, it's way better than a one-bedroom apartment in the middle of Chicago's finest."

I know she's teasing me because I live in a not-so-great part of the city. There are five locks on my front door, and I still lean a chair up against it when I go to sleep. I don't dare walk down the street alone at night, which means I rarely go out unless I'm staying with someone. What can I say though? When the price is right, beggars can't be choosers. And I know it's not my forever home.

"I suppose a comfy upscale home would be a nice change from where I am now," I chuckle.

"And did I mention he's hot? And obviously very single?"

I cringe shaking my head even though she can't see me. "Okay first of all, you know I'm not looking for anything like that. Sleeping with my boss would be hella-weird. But also, does that mean he has loads of women coming in and out of his house?"

"Are you kidding?" She scoffs. "Since I've known Quinton, Zeke never goes out with the team because he always runs home to his kid. I don't think he's done the dating or the hook-up thing at all since his wife left."

"Interesting."

Don't know if that's a good thing or a bad thing, really, but I suppose I can't judge the man given my lack of wanting to put myself out there after Luke. At least we would have something in common...as morbid as that is to think about.

"Let me schedule you an interview with Zeke. He's really down to earth and between you and me, I think he and the guys didn't have a great interview experience this morning. He's feeling kind of down about finding someone good based on the riffraff he spoke to earlier."

"Uh oh."

Kinsley laughs. "Yeah something about some woman who sells her used panties online and another woman with a son in jail for kiddie porn and—"

"Oh, my God!" My jaw drops. "Where did he publish an ad for this job? Weirdos R Us?"

"Right? Ugh!" she answers. "I felt really bad for him because he just wants to find the perfect person for his kid and that made me think of you."

Phew. Moving in with a celebrity who is still a stranger to me and taking care of his kid all hours of the day? That's a lot to take in. That's a big life change. A commitment I really want to take time to think about before giving an answer.

"Can I think about it?"

"Of course. It would be weird if you didn't. If it sounds

like something you think you might want to at least discuss, I'll contact Zeke and set up an interview for you. And if you decide you're not interested, no harm, no foul. I'll just tell Zeke his little beautiful baby girl will have to raise herself because nobody wants her."

"Okay, Bitch!" I huff out a laugh. "I highly doubt she's a cute floofy puppy you can just walk away from at the shelter. She's a human being. She's someone's world. That's a lot to commit to."

"I'm just teasing you. Seriously though, think it over. Let me know what you decide?"

"Yeah. Of course. And thank you. Truly. I'm touched that you even thought of me for something like this."

"Zeke is a really nice guy who was handed a shit deal when his wife left him. He hasn't put himself out there because Elsie is his world. He lives and breathes for her. We just want to see him happy. And Elsie too. And you too, of course."

"Thanks Kinsley. I'll call you later?"

"Absolutely. I'll be around."

"Great. Talk soon."

"Bye."

I hang up the phone and notice Purrito weaving in and out of my legs as I stand along the hallway wall.

Full-time, live-in nanny.

I'd be raising someone else's kid.

The kid I never got to have.

Thoughts of Luke roll through my mind and my chest tightens for a moment.

I miss him.

It's been three years for me too.

Three years of loneliness.

Three years of feeling like my life has no purpose.

Luke would tell me to do this.

"You're meant for this," he would say.

By the time I get home for the day it's nearly sunset. I still can't get my mind off Kinsley's phone call. The opportunity she shared with me. I can't help but wonder what the details are. What kind of guy Zeke Miller is off the ice. I've seen the man play. I don't know how he still has knees. He's a beast out there. To see him be a monster on the ice and then know he goes home at night to a little girl makes me smile.

I bet he's the coolest daddy to her.

I should talk to the guy.

Talking to him doesn't mean I have to take the job.

Okay. I can do this.

Before I can stop myself, I'm pulling my phone from my back pocket and texting Kinsley.

ME

> If the position is still open, I'm interested in an interview.

KINSLEY

> EEEEEEEEEK!! OMG! I'll set it up ASAP and get back to you.

ME

> Thanks.

Within minutes she's texting me back.

KINSLEY

> Tomorrow at the arena. Nine o'clock.

25

ME

Perfect. Thank you.

KINSLEY

You're going to be great! I just know it!

ME

We shall see.

I didn't sleep a wink last night.

I slid down the Zeke Miller rabbit hole and spent hours internet searching everything I could about him. I've seen his stats as a player. I studied his career path and know he's been with the Red Tails for seven seasons. I've seen more pictures of him than I can count. Even some of him and his daughter. She's super cute and from the looks of everything I saw, he lives to please her and she loves the stuffing out of him. I learned that his wife of two years, Lori, left after Elsie was born but nobody says exactly why. There's a lot of speculation, but I assume the only ones to really know what went down between Zeke and Lori are Zeke and Lori.

And that's how it should be.

I found no evidence of him bad-mouthing her in public or online, which made me feel good. Not that she doesn't deserve it if she did something wrong. His feelings either way are valid, but it's nice to know that no matter what, he seems like a stand-up guy. He spends a good deal of his time visiting kids at the children's hospital and gives to their charity every year. He's helped out at one of the local elementary schools a few times too. He's clearly a man who is comfortable around kids.

I wonder for hours what life might be like if I were to get this job. What it would be like moving into a man's house when there's nothing between us but a professional relationship. How awkward it might be if he brings a woman home. How weird it might be if or when I might have a new love interest. Not that I'm planning on that any time soon.

I know Luke would be disappointed that I haven't moved on yet. Three years is certainly long enough to mourn his loss. If he were still here, he would be telling me to stop putzing around and go have fun. Live a little. But then again, if Luke were still here, he wouldn't have to tell me to stop putzing around because I would have him. And we would be having all the fun in the world.

"I'm gonna do it, Luke," I whisper to nobody in the darkness of my room. "I'm putting myself out there. I'm going to meet Zeke Miller tomorrow. It's time to do something new."

By eight-forty-five I'm showered, dressed in my favorite black jeans, purple blouse, and black flats, and walking into the arena for my interview. A petite woman dressed in black jeans and a Red Tails sweatshirt meets me inside the door.

"Ada Lewis?"

"Yes."

"Oh my God, you're perfect," she says with a sigh of relief and a huge smile.

"Uhh..."

She offers me her hand. "Sorry. Forgive me. Hi. I'm

Carissa Nelson. I'm a friend of Zeke's and I work for the team. I told him I would come up and meet you when you got here since he had a morning team meeting."

"Oh. Great. Thank you. It's lovely to meet you."

She cringes. "You know what, before we go any further would you mind if I asked you a few super weird questions?"

I chuckle but shake my head. "Don't mind at all."

"Do you uh...sell panties online?"

"Ew!" I almost snort. "I can't believe people actually do that. Oh, also, that's a no, by the way. I don't sell anything online...except my soul when I jump down those social media rabbit holes."

Carissa laughs. "You and me both, girl. And I do social media for a living."

"Oh, you poor thing."

"Sometimes it's not so bad." She winks. "I started the team's best ass competition you know."

"I'm actually familiar." I laugh with her. "I may have watched the latest just last night."

"Ah, doing your homework, I see. That'a girl. Sooo do you have any felonies?"

"Nope." I grin.

"Allergies?"

"None that I know of."

"How about kids? Do you have a gaggle of children that you're hoping to move into a celebrity home?"

My smile falters slightly with her question and I shake my head. "No. I don't have any children."

She stops walking and touches my shoulder. "I'm so sorry, Ada. That was probably too personal of a question."

"Not at all. Totally valid. I'm a fur-mommy to many animals at the shelter."

"That's right!" Carissa smiles. "Kinsley told me you're the reason she has Nutsack."

"That ornery cat." I snicker. "He was the perfect choice for someone like Kinsley."

"Right? I totally agree with you."

"Can I ask you a question now?"

"Oh yeah. Totally."

"Why did you ask me those questions specifically."

She giggles and rolls her eyes. "Let's just say that should give you a clue as to what yesterday's interviews were like."

I cringe. "That bad, huh?"

"Very much so. But lucky for you they were, because Kinsley thought of you when she heard they hadn't found someone yet."

Shaking my nervous hands at my sides, I confess to Carissa. "You know, I've never actually been a nanny."

She stops and looks at me and for a hot second I fear she's about to tell me to hit the road. She doesn't. Instead, she smiles and gives my upper arm a soft squeeze. "And that could very well be why you might be perfect for the job."

"What?"

"Trust me."

Carissa leads me down the stairs to one of the small meeting rooms where several of the guys are hanging out.

"Gentlemen, I'd like you to meet Ada Lewis."

"Miss Lewis." One of the men stands from his seat

smiling at me politely. He shakes my hand as his eyes quickly give me a once-over.

Oh, okay, a twice-over.

And now he's staring into my eyes with a starstruck look on his face.

Hope he likes what he sees.

He hasn't stopped shaking my hand, but he also hasn't said anything besides my name. Of course, I know who he is because I spent hours studying him last night.

One of the other guys at the table behind him clears his throat, which seems to pull Mr. Miller from his trance.

"I'm Zeke Miller. It's a pleasure to meet you."

I smile back at him. "Likewise."

The first thing I notice is how soft and warm his hand is. It's not at all calloused like I would've expected for someone who wears gloves and holds a wooden stick all the time. Not that I've spent a great deal of time wondering about a professional hockey player's hands. Maybe they squirt moisturizer into their gloves for all I know. At any rate, yeah soft hands—er, hand. The rest of him isn't too shabby either.

What am I saying? Kinsley was right. The man is beautiful.

Light ginger colored hair that's neatly faded around the sides, the rest slightly longer and wavy.. Like it's all business on the sides but a party on top. It's a great look for him that makes him appear slightly younger than I know him to be. Not that thirty-two is old in my book. Not at all. His perfectly manscaped beard is slightly darker in shade and covers up his square jaw. I can still see the distinct line of his cheek bones though so the beard doesn't cover everything. Unsurprisingly, he has a crooked nose that has probably seen a few punches in his tenure. It gives him an Owen Wilson vibe. It's cute. His Red Tails t-shirt doesn't hide his broad shoulders nor his strong arms. I have to imagine he has tremendous thighs hiding under the workout shorts he's wearing. If nothing else, the thickness of his calves tells me he spends a lot of time in a squatted position. He's muscular and fit that's for sure.

Speaking of squats, I wonder what his ass looks like.

Not that I should be looking at my potential new boss's ass.

But if I take away the potential boss part, he's a pro hockey player with a potentially nice ass.

"Let me introduce you to some of the guys."

Rather than let him introduce me formally, I smile at each one individually and shake their hands. "Milo Landric, Dex Foster, and Colby Nelson."

"Wow, Zeke," Milo says with an impressed smile. "This lady must know her hockey."

"I guess this is where I should admit that I swear I'm not some crazed fan who spends her days and nights watching hockey and memorizing everything about you," I explain. "Sports runs in my family so I'd be lying if I said I didn't watch from time to time. And it *is* pretty cool to be meeting you all."

"Sports runs in the family huh?" Zeke smiles. "Did you play?"

"Me? No. But my brother plays baseball in the minor league. He's hoping to make it to the majors someday."

"No kidding? That's cool. Then you have a little bit of an idea what kind of schedule we have during the season."

"Oh yeah. I get it. You're busy and on the road a lot."

Zeke nods. "A lot."

"Hope you don't mind us sitting in," Colby says. "We promised Zeke we would help him find the world's best nanny for his kid."

Zeke leans over and murmurs, "Between you and me, Ada, I didn't get much of a choice in the matter."

"Right." I laugh. "Every parent needs a village, right? It's very admirable and I don't mind at all."

Zeke gestures for me to take the seat at the end of the table while the guys spread around on either side.

"So, first things first," Milo starts. "Do you sell panties or feet pictures or anything else on the interwebs that we should know about?"

My eyes slide to Carissa who is standing in the doorway. She laughs and gives me a wink. "Told you. Yesterday was an odd day. I'll see you later fellas."

I look back at the guys and shake my head confidently. "I promise you I do no such thing. My internet activity consists of baseball stats, hockey fights—that one with you and Jared McClacken a few seasons back was outstanding by the way—and the rest are puppy and kitty videos."

"Jared McClacken can eat a bag of dicks," Dex mutters under his breath much to the guys' amusement.

"Agreed."

"Can you tell us what you bring to the table in terms of this job, Ada?" Zeke asks me. "What qualifications you have?" He looks down at my resume. "I see you were an elementary school teacher?"

"I was when I lived in North Carolina, yes. My

husband was in the military so he was gone a lot and I spent my days molding the minds of tiny humans."

"My wife and sister are both elementary school teachers," Dex adds. "It's a thankless job much of the time. You folks deserve a lot of praise."

"Thank you. Yeah, kids are fun. They're never the same from one day to the next. They're always learning new ways to express themselves, which can be fun, funny, or sometimes downright challenging, but in the end, meeting them where they are and letting them know you love them no matter what...that matters to them. I really enjoyed teaching."

"Why aren't you doing it now?" Milo asks.

"Uh..." My face heats and I swallow the knot in my throat. "My husband. He um, passed away unexpectedly while overseas."

Milo hangs his head. "Shit. I'm sorry, Ada. I didn't mean to sound—"

"No, no. It's okay. It's been three years. He would laugh at me if he thought I couldn't talk about it after all this time. Anyway, after he passed away I left the military base and moved back home for a while. I taught there, but I couldn't shake the feeling that everyone was staring at me like the poor lowly widow, you know?"

God, should I even be explaining all this?

Am I saying too much?

"SOOO I knew it was time to move away and get out on my own. I chose Chicago to be a little closer to my brother. He plays in Indianapolis so it's not that far. And I've always loved the city. Rich in culture. So much to do. I needed to get out of the stifling small town. I moved here mid-school year though so I subbed in a few districts until I got a part time job at the Paw Palace animal shelter."

Zeke passes me a friendly smile. "What's your favorite? Cats or dogs?"

I narrow my eyes playfully. "Oooh wow. I don't know if I can answer that. Man, I love a big floofy dog so much, but on the other hand, cats are so entertaining to watch when they play. And they're typically minimal maintenance. Dogs are a little harder to own when you live in the city. You don't have to walk a cat."

"Elsie, that's my daughter, she would tell you that cats reign supreme. I think if she had her way, she would gladly be a four-year-old version of a cat lady."

"Well, she clearly has good taste. You should take her to the shelter sometime. She'd make about fifty new best friends in a matter of minutes."

"Right." Zeke laughs. "Except then I would have to be the bad guy who says no when she asks if she can have them all."

"Hmm. You're right," I chuckle. "Maybe you could just appease her with six or seven."

His eyes brighten as his smile widens. "Yeah. Something like that."

3

ZEKE

Holy shit, Kinsley wasn't lying when she said Ada was fire. She's breathtakingly beautiful. She looks pretty in her purple shirt and black jeans. Her shoulder length light brown hair is half up in a clip behind her head, the rest hanging down in loose waves. Her make-up is subtle, which I like. She's not trying to overdo it and doesn't come across as a diva type at all. She seems relatively fit which I also like for Elsie. My daughter needs someone who can match her energy most days so she doesn't feel like she has nobody to play with. It's nice to feel like we're just having a conversation instead of a formal interview. She's comfortable, easy to talk to, and so far, doesn't give off any weird vibes. After the hot mess of yesterday's applicants, I have all the appreciation in the world for someone like Ada.

"So, if you'll humor me for a minute, I should probably explain the nuts and bolts of the job," I say.

"That would be great."

"First of all, Elsie has preschool three days a week in

35

the mornings, so she'll need someone to pick her up at eleven-forty-five."

"Alright." I nod. "No problem."

"Most nights, when we don't have a game, I'm home in time for supper and have no problem relieving you so you can be free to...you know..."

Date?

Does she date?

Is she seeing someone?

Is that a weird question to ask her?

I don't think I would want some other guy around Elsie right now.

My brows pinch and I boldly ask, "Are you uh, in a relationship or you know..."

"Dating?" she asks.

"Yeah." I shake my head and hold up my hand. "And please understand it's none of my business except to say I'm not sure I'm comfortable with other men hanging out around Elsie right now. Men I don't know, I mean. And certainly not in my house, but you're more than free to, you know, see people."

Ada shakes her head and smiles reassuringly. "No, that's a perfectly valid question and the answer is no. I'm not..." She takes a breath and I inwardly cringe remembering what she said about her late husband.

Fuck.

"I'm not in a relationship of any kind. I'm embarrassed to admit my social life is not at all what it probably should be for a thirty-year-old woman. Give me a book, a blanket, and a comfy chair and I'm happy."

"Ah, so you're a reader?" Milo unsurprisingly pipes in. Milo and Charlee are the definite book nerds of our group.

"Yeah." Ada smiles. "I'll read pretty much any chance I get."

"Can I ask what your last read was?"

She blushes and squirms in her seat a little. "Um, well, I like to read a bunch of those gushy romance stories. I guess I'm always cheering for the girl to get her happy ever after."

Milo smiles back at her, nodding approvingly. "You and my wife should meet. She edits romance books for a living and she could talk your ear off about any one of them."

"No kidding?"

Dex scoffs teasingly. "Don't act like you don't also read them, Landric." He gestures to Milo with a hitch of his thumb. "When this guy isn't on the ice you'll almost always find him with a book in his hand."

"He's right," Milo confesses. "My mama didn't raise no dummy."

Ada laughs and something in me warms. She has such a lovely disposition and seems to have a well-balanced sense of humor. Her voice, seeing her smile...I think she could be perfect for m—Elsie. Perfect for Elsie.

"Daddy looooook!" The voice of my favorite four-year-old screams from just down the hall as she comes running into the room, my mother not far behind. Some days Elsie loves coming to *"Daddy's work"* so my parents will pick her up here and take her back to their place or sometimes my house. I realize it may be an inconvenience for them, but they also respect my love for my daughter and that I want to spend

SUSAN RENEE

as much time with her as I possibly can whenever I can. Even if that just means a morning drive into the city for work. Plus, she likes being Miss Christy's helper in the daycare when the guys bring their kids in from time to time. When she runs into the room where we're all seated, she's holding what looks like a Mister Potato Head in her arms. Her smile is wide and her eyes are filled with excitement but as I'm about to remind her not to run, she gets tripped up and falls, the pieces flying off Mister Potato Head and landing on the floor.

"Whoa! Slow down sweetheart." I jump from my seat and round the table to help her, but Ada, being at the end of the table, beats me to it.

"Hey," she says softly, already crouched down and helping Elsie up off the floor. She instinctively checks her for any cuts, scrapes, or growing bumps. "Are you okay?"

"Mhmm but look." She holds out the Mister Potato Head. "His face fell off and he was gonna be Daddy."

"I'm sorry, Zeke." My mom reaches the room almost out of breath. "She really wanted to show you her Mister Potato Head before we left."

One thing my mother never needs to do is apologize for my kid wanting to see me. I'd have her next to me all hours of the day if I could.

Okay, maybe not all hours.

A man needs his privacy every once in a while.

I shake my head, waving my mother's worries away, and gasp playfully as I watch Ada's interaction with Elsie. "Oh no!" I pat my own face with my hands. "My face fell off? Where's my face? I can't find my face!"

Elsie giggles. "No, Daddy! Not your daddy face! Your Mister tato face."

"Oooh." I hold my hand to my heart. "Phew! I was afraid I would never be able to use my eyes to see you again. Or smell your sweetness with my nose. Or hear your beautiful giggles with my ears."

I'm about to help Elsie scoop up the fallen pieces when she takes her potato head to Ada and hands it to her. "Can you help me?"

Ada smiles kindly at her. "Of course I can." She lowers herself to the floor and Elsie sits in front of her. "My name is Ada. What's your name?"

"I'm Elsie."

"It's nice to meet you, Elsie." She picks up an eye from the floor and says, "Hmm where do you think this goes?" She pushes it on the top of the potato head where the hat goes. "Does it go here?"

Elsie shakes her head. "Nooo."

"Oh ok. Does it gooo..." She puts it on the side where the ears go. "Here?"

"Nooo." Elsie giggles. "It goes right there." She points to the two holes in the front where both eyes go and Ada pushes them in for her.

"Great job. What part should we do next?"

Elsie grabs the ears and shows Ada how good she is at pushing them into the holes and Ada showers her with praise until every piece is back in place.

"High five, Elsie!" Ada raises her hand so Elsie can slap it. "You did it! And do you know what? I think it looks just like your daddy."

"Yeah!" She squeals. "Daddy look! You are a tato head!"

"Perfect likeness, Lil' Squish," Dex says to Elsie. "That's exactly what your daddy looks like."

"Yeah! Uncle Dex, look!" She jumps up and takes the potato head to him. The guys on the team have been honorary uncles to Elsie since the day she was born. I couldn't be more grateful for every single one of them for stepping in and being there for us when Lori left. Now that several of them have had kids, it'll be my turn to repay the favor.

"I especially like the abnormally huge nose," Colby says with a wink. He reaches out his hand to give Elsie a fist bump. "Good job, Squish."

"I'll show *you* a potato head!" I tell her right before I pounce and snatch her up into my arms in a fit of giggles, showering her with kisses. "And now you have a face full of potato head kisses from potato head dad."

Her belly laughs are my favorite sound. "Daddy!"

I give her another big daddy kiss and then lower her back down to her feet next to my mom who is waiting patiently near the door. "Thank you for showing me my amazing potato face, Els. Now how about you tuck him in for a nap back in Miss Christy's room before you leave with Nana okay?"

"Okay Daddy. Bye"

"I love you, sweetheart."

"Love you, Daddy."

"Bye, Squish!" Milo calls out to her.

She shouts "Byeeeee" as she runs back down the hallway.

My mom apologizes again for the interruption but I place a kiss on her cheek too and reassure her. "Mom, she's my kid. If she wants to see me, she gets to see me. End of discussion. One day when she's a teenager she'll hate me, so I'll take all the snuggles I can possibly get now."

I wave them both goodbye, watching Elsie try to skip down the hallway toward the daycare. Once they're out of sight, I turn back toward the room where Milo is helping Ada up off the floor. She smiles at me and laughs softly. "She's really sweet. And very smart. You're a great dad."

I can't seem to form any other words at the moment except, "You're hired. When can you start?"

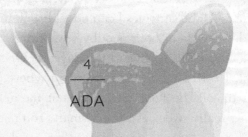

"Okay, do you have everything you might need?" Kinsley looks around my very tiny apartment. I don't own much, and the place is quite small, but it's been a reliable home for me since I got here. A couple boxes are packed and stacked by the door and I have all my clothes packed in two suitcases and my shoes in a large duffle bag.

"Yeah. I think so. This is enough to get me started anyway. If I need to come back here on an evening or day off to grab something, I can do that."

"It's very nice of Zeke to continue paying your rent so you have a place to hang out if you need it."

I nod. "He paid it out through the end of the contract. He told me he would've felt terrible if I had left here and moved in with him and Elsie and then hated it but had nowhere to go back to. Though he also promised me if I end up not liking the job and I want to leave, he's happy to rent me out a new place up town. In a safer area, I think is how he put it."

"I am not the least bit surprised by this," Kinsley tells me. "That man is a class act. Super nice guy." She looks around the apartment and gestures out the window. "And he's not wrong. I would not want to be a single woman living here at night."

I shrug and open the door, hoisting my duffle bag over my shoulder and grabbing one of my suitcases. "Meh. That's why my door has five different locks on it and I set booby traps at night, so I'm relatively safe."

A curious grin spreads across Kinsley's face and she spits out a laugh. "Booby traps?"

"Yeah. You know...a chair against the door. That kind of thing. But I put empty bottles on the chair so if the chair falls, the glass breaks. With any luck, I'll hear that and maybe have a minute to jump out my window or hide or call 9-1-1."

She shakes her head in disbelief. "Good Lord, Ada. I'm really glad Zeke hired you. At least I know I'll never need to worry about your wellbeing ever again."

"I'm glad you feel better." I snicker. "So, you're certain I'm not moving in with an axe murderer?"

"Positive. In fact, I'd be surprised if he even owned an axe. Now let's get your stuff into the car."

Kinsley spends the next five minutes helping me load my car and then gives me a big hug. "I really am so happy for you. I think you're going to love this job. At least, I really hope you do."

I shake out my excited nerves and give my friend a smile. "I'm cautiously excited. Just have to get through the awkwardness of tonight, you know?"

"Elsie is a darling. She's going to looooove you.

Honestly, I think once you settle into a routine you guys will be just fine."

"What do you think I should do once Elsie goes to bed? Is he going to expect that we'll just...I don't know...sit on the couch and watch television or what?"

"Is making out, out of the question? Because I'm just sayin' if Zeke Miller wanted to make out..."

I laugh. "Kinsley! Let's not start that now. I haven't even been with the man a whole hour yet."

"Okay, okay, you're right." Kinsley shrugs. "I don't really know what Zeke does when Elsie goes to bed so you'll have to sort of take his lead and just go with the flow. Maybe he'll just want to talk and get to know you a little. But definitely text me later tonight and tell me everything. And you know I'm here any time for whatever you need."

"Thanks, Kinsley."

"Sure thing. Do you want me to follow you to Zeke's and help get your stuff in?"

I shake my head. "Nah. I should probably do this part on my own. Show him I'm capable and all that."

"Right." She smiles and waits while I lock my apartment door. "Well, be safe and text me later?"

I cross my heart with my finger. "I promise."

I pull up to the address Zeke gave me trying to keep my jaw from falling completely off my face when I take in my surroundings.

"Holy shit. He lives here?"

44

I didn't realize his address was this close to the country club but here I am pulling into the gated community like I live here.

"Holy shit...*I* live here?"

The light brick house sprawled out in front of me when I turn into the drive looks like a castle. There are two turrets along the front of the house boasting long windows that clearly let in an abundance of natural light.

I bet it's gorgeous inside.

There are four different garages attached to the right wing of the house, the left wing extended by decorative fencing. There's no doubt the house looks inviting, but wow.

Just wow.

From my apartment to this?

What is this life?

I swallow back my nerves, throw my purse across my body, and make my way to the front door. I don't even have to knock because the Ring Doorbell has already alerted Zeke to my presence. He opens the door before I step up to the landing and greets me with a killer smile.

"Ada." His smile is contagious.

"Hello!"

"You made it."

"I did." My brows shoot up as I take a deep breath. "It's beautiful out here. I've never been this far out of the city."

His smile falters. "Oh, I'm sorry. I hope you didn't have trouble finding us."

"Oh no." I shake my head. "No trouble at all. Your directions were perfect."

"Great." He nods. "Good. Well, come in, please." He

45

moves out of the way and gestures for me to come inside. When I step past him into the foyer I get a whiff of his scent. A mild cologne or aftershave. Whatever it is, it's pleasant and I notice.

Not that I should be noticing how good my new boss smells.

I hear the pitter patter of little bare feet running down the hallway.

"Please stop running, Elsie Jane," Zeke calls out to her as she gets closer, her light brown hair bouncing behind her. She slows and comes to a stop right as she gets to her dad. Her little arm wraps around his leg and her chocolate brown eyes peer up at me.

"Hi," she says with a shy smile.

I return her smile and crouch down so I'm at her level. "Hi Elsie. I'm Ada. We met yesterday."

Zeke bends down, his hand on Elsie's back. "El, remember when I said Ada was going to be living here with us so she can help take care of you when Daddy's playing hockey?"

Her eyes light up a little more and she turns to me, hopeful. "Do you like to play mermaids?"

My eyes grow wide to match hers. "Oh, my goodness did you know playing mermaids is one of my very favorite things in the whole wide world?"

She jumps up and down. "It is?"

"Mmhmm." I nod happily.

She grabs my hand without fear and squeals, "Come on, Ada! Let's go play mermaids!"

"Whoa, whoa, whoa. Hold up, Els." Zeke stops her. "We should probably show Ada around the house first and let her know about our schedules before you play mermaids."

Her shoulders fall. "Is that grown-up stuff, Daddy?"

Zeke huffs a soft laugh. "Yeah it's grown-up stuff. But I promise I won't take long, okay? Why don't you finish your show while Ada and I finish talking and then you can play mermaids before bed."

I raise my hand up to get a high-five from her which she gives me excitedly. "Can't wait!"

"Yay! Yay! Yay!" Elsie exclaims as she skips back to wherever she came from. Zeke and I watch her, both of us smiling.

"Well, I'm going to go ahead and say that went perfectly fine." Zeke laughs. "Do you have stuff you want to bring in? I could help you."

"Oh, no, it's fine. I mean yes, I do. Just a few bags and a couple boxes but I can grab them after Elsie's in bed. No hurry."

Zeke nods. "Alright. Can I show you around then?"

"Please."

We spend the next several minutes going through the downstairs portion of Zeke's palatial home. I've seen the kitchen, the dining room, an office of sorts, the library, Elsie's playroom, the gym, two bathrooms, two living rooms, an enclosed sunporch, several garage spaces, and what I'll label Zeke's pride room as it's filled with all of his hockey awards, mounted team jerseys, and other memorabilia.

"Bedrooms are upstairs." Zeke gestures and starts up the oversized staircase. "All of our rooms are on the same floor. Elsie's room is this one here in the corner," he says, opening her bedroom door and revealing a beautiful space decorated in soft shades of blue, pink, and white. Her white toddler bed sits along one wall, the others holding a dresser, a bookshelf, and numerous pictures of her and Zeke or her and the guys I recognize from the team.

"Is she close with the guys on the team?"

"Oh yeah," Zeke says, smiling. "They're all fun uncles to Elsie. To be honest I don't know where I would be without them."

"That's so sweet."

There's a closet door on another smaller wall and in the corner of the room near the oversized windows stands a white teepee on a pink shaggy rug covered in white sparkly lights.

"Oh my gosh, Zeke, this is so beautiful."

"Thanks," he says behind me when I walk in to look around.

"Did you do all this yourself?"

"I had some help from Rory, Dex's sister, when Elsie's mom left. I wanted to give her something new to be happy about. Not that she has any memory of her mom really. She was only about a year old at the time."

I want so badly to ask him about his ex-wife and what happened between them. Part of me wants to justify knowing since I'm working here so closely with his child, but then again, I don't always love having to rehash my memories of Luke for mere strangers so I get it. Maybe he'll tell me when he's more comfortable.

"Well, it's spectacular." I take a quick peek into the teepee and note the pile of throw pillows and blankets inside.

"She loves to sit in there and read," Zeke tells me.

"Ooor you know, just lay in there and talk to herself or whatever imaginary friend she might have in there with her at any given moment."

"So cute." I smile.

He points out the bathroom that Elsie uses next to her room and explains that she's usually pretty good at using the bathroom. Understandably, he had left this task up to his mother since Elsie was with them most of the time... until now.

"I'm so sorry she's not uh..." He scratches his head. "Well, sometimes she still..."

I nod knowingly. "She has accidents."

"Yeah."

"Totally get it," I assure him. "And I would be surprised if she didn't. It's no big deal and I'm happy to help out."

He stops for a moment and gives me a look. His maple-colored eyes staring at me with...what is that? Relief? I wish I knew what he was thinking and just as I'm about to ask he says, "I might forget to say this a lot, or I might say it way too much for your liking as we go forward, but I am so grateful you came in for an interview." He smiles, shaking his head and sliding his hand through his tussled ginger hair. "I was losing any hope of finding someone...uh... normal. A nice person, I mean. You know? Ugh. Good nannies are harder to find than I thought."

"Were you expecting Mary Poppins?"

"Perfect in every way?" He smirks.

"Yeah."

"Maybe not perfect and certainly not with a never-ending bag of furniture like she had, but you know...the spoonful of sugar and all would be nice." I catch his eyes as they trail down my body and back up. "You certainly come across as a spoonful of sugar and a big ray of sunshine so that is a relief."

I laugh. "Well, I'm usually a pretty sun-shiny kind of person. I like to see the glass half full and all that, so I think I can guarantee a spoonful of sugar. But I should probably tell you now, I can't fly or jump inside sidewalk paintings."

"No chimney sweep friends either?" he muses as we leave the room.

"Nope. Don't even know one."

He turns back around, stopping in front of the next door. "Really though, thank you, Ada. I'm really glad you're here."

"It's my pleasure. I get that it's hard to find someone you can trust with your kid so for what it's worth thank you for hiring me."

"That room there is mine," he says, pointing to a room next to the laundry room with a closed door. "And this one here is yours." He opens the last door, holding it open as I walk inside. "I'm sorry it's kind of plain." He stuffs his hands in his pockets. "I've never really done much of anything with this space so please, feel free to make it your own. I want you to be comfortable."

The room may be stark white from ceiling to wall, but the room itself is gorgeous. My entire apartment could fit in here. Soft gray furniture lines the walls and a tall white and silver lamp stands in the corner near the balcony doors.

Holy hell I have a balcony!

"Wow! Zeke this is..." I walk over to the balcony and open the door, admiring the view of the lake. "It's breathtaking." I glance over to the balcony next to mine and notice one of Zeke's shirts hanging from a chair.

Our rooms are pretty close.

"That's your balcony, I presume?"

"Mhmm. I like to sit out here sometimes and just... breathe," he says. "The view takes the stress of the day away, you know?"

"Yeah. I'll have to remember that."

We take some time downstairs to go over Elsie's daily routine and how things have been in the past when Zeke has games or late-night commitments. After he's shown me where everything is written down, Elsie interrupts once again to pull me away for some mermaid time. This time I don't say no.

"Can we talk more after bedtime?"

"Yeah, of course," Zeke says, watching me being pulled away by an excited four-year-old. "Have fun."

I turn back to Elsie and squeal with her. "It's mermaid time!"

ME

Phew. First night down. Not too awkward. You were right when you said Zeke is a nice guy. And Elsie is the biggest cutie pie I think I've ever met! 🩶

KINSLEY

See! I told you! Yay! I'm so glad everything went well. What did you do after bedtime?

ME

I helped clean up the kitchen after dinner and he helped carry my stuff in from the car. We made small talk but then he said he had some game tapes he needed to watch before tomorrow and left me alone to get situated in my room.

KINSLEY

Sounds like you're off to a great start. I think you're going to be perfect for this job! He needs someone like you. (And he's not bad to look at either, no?) 😉

ME

Oh Jesus. Are you really going to make me answer that?

KINSLEY

Nope. That was all the answer I needed. Sweet dreams Ada!

ME

Night Kinsley. Kiss your Nutsack for me.

KINSLEY

LOL! It's funny every time. *picture of sleeping Nutsack*

ME

My favorite hairless kitty.

KINSLEY

Mine too. 🤍

I lay my phone down on my nightstand and pull the covers up around me. I don't know what kind of heaven he got it from but this mattress is to die for. Firm but so soft I melt into it. Closing my eyes, I inhale a deep breath and play back my day, smiling at the memory of playing mermaids with Elsie, listening to her giggle at the dinner table, and reading with her before bed. Talking to Zeke tonight was nice too. He's amazingly easy to chat with and if I'm being honest, it's a refreshing change to have someone—anyone—to talk to in person rather than just me, myself, and I all the time.

And yeah, Kinsley is right. He's not bad to look at. Not at all.

5

ZEKE

When I open my eyes there's way more light outside than there usually is at this time of the day. I pick up my phone to see the time and, "Shit!"

I'm late.

Why the hell didn't my alarm go off?

Why hasn't Elsie been in to wake...

Nanny...

Ada...

I've got to get to the gym before practice.

Jumping out of bed I don't bother to shower. I'm going to work up a sweat this morning anyway so I'll shower at the arena. I pull on a pair of joggers lying at the edge of the bed and grab a fresh t-shirt. The smell of coffee wafting all the way up here awakens my senses. Fuck, I wish I had time for a relaxing cup of coffee, but I'll need my pre-workout drink instead and I'll have to gulp it down before I get into town.

I run a toothbrush over my teeth, tussle my hair a little

so it doesn't have that oh-my-God-I-just-woke-up-like-this look and fly down the stairs. When I get to the kitchen, Ada is making scrambled eggs.

"Daddy!" Elsie smiles.

"Good morning, baby girl." I kiss the top of her head. "Did you have good sleeps?"

"Mhmm. I only waked up two times."

Two times?

She woke up twice?

And I didn't hear her?

I meet Ada's gaze and she winks at me before saying, "She woke up to use the potty, right Elsie?"

Elsie gives an overdramatic nod. "Yep!"

"That's right and she did a great job and went right back to bed."

Trying to rein in my guilt for not waking up to help her, I give her an overexcited smile and a high five. "Alright! That's my girl! I'm so proud of you."

I turn back to Ada and my shoulders fall. I whisper to her, "I'm so sorry. You could've woken me up."

"It's no big deal. I heard her shouting and went to help her."

"Shit, I'm sorry, Ada. I forgot to mention that she doesn't always sleep through the night without waking up at least once. Plus, the whole potty-training thing. Sometimes she just can't sleep or has a bad dream or her blanket falls off the bed...it's any number of things. She usually calls for me."

Ada looks at me sheepishly. "She did. Call for you, I mean."

A knot forms in my throat. "What? Seriously? I've never not heard her before."

I've also never slept in like I just did either.

"Don't worry about it. I handled it. She was fine. First time was the potty and second time she just had a dream she didn't like and I talked her through it."

I slide a hand through my hair. "Thank you, Ada. I didn't mean to make you have to wake up with her."

She smiles at me and touches my forearm. "It's really okay. I hope you slept well. I made coffee if you want some."

"I would love some," I tell her, reaching over her for my favorite blue water bottle, my chest rubbing against her shoulder. "Excuse me. Sorry. But Iiiii sort of overslept accidentally and now I'm late for morning work-out."

Ada's eyes grow and she cringes. "Uh oh. I hope I didn't keep you up last night unpacking."

"No, no," I assure her, filling up my bottle with water and adding a scoop of my pre-workout mix. "I guess uh..." I huff out a soft laugh. "I guess I went to bed last night relieved for the first time in a long time."

"Relieved?" she asks, scooping some scrambled eggs into a bowl for Elsie.

"Yeah. Relieved. Because Elsie and I have you now, don't we El?"

"Yep! And we're gonna play mermaids and puppy school and Ada said we can have a tea party!"

I catch Ada's gaze when she hands the bowl of eggs to Elsie. Her eyes look different today. Yesterday they were brownish in color, today they hold more of a green hue. "Last night was the first full night's sleep I've gotten in three years. You clearly have something to do with that. You're lifting a little stress from my shoulders and I appreciate that more than you know."

"Well, thanks, I guess. And that's what you pay me for." She smiles.

Her cheeks blush just a little and I'd be lying if I didn't think it was cute. I noticed the spattering of freckles across her nose and cheeks last night. This morning though, with her honey brown hair tied up on top of her head and several missed tendrils hanging down around her face. Her blue sweatpants and baseball t-shirt that I can only assume is her brother's team. The way she smiles at my daughter like they've known each other forever.

She looks comfortable.

Like she belongs here.

Like she's been here all this time.

"I should go. Coach is going to have my ass for being late."

"Daddy...what's ass?"

Ada and I both spit out a laugh as I grab an apple from the basket on the counter and place another kiss on Elsie's head. "Ada will explain it to you, sweetheart. Daddy's got to go."

Ada drops her spatula into the sink and gives me an incredulous laugh. I wink at her with a guilty smirk and wave to them both. "See you later ladies. Have fun today. Love you!"

"Love you Daddy!"

"What the fuck, Miller? You're never late," Coach Denovah says when I literally toss my bag into my locker and pull out my work-out shorts. "Everything alright?"

"Yeah, Coach. Sorry. New nanny," I explain. "It's her first day."

"Ah. Well, that explains enough. You're never late so no harm no foul. Make sure you get those stretches in with Wilson this morning. We don't need any muscle strains today."

"You got it."

I tie my tennis shoes tightly and grab my sweat towel and head to the gym only to be immediately lambasted by the guys.

"The fuck, Miller?" Colby smiles wide. "You're never late, man."

"What happened to you?" Milo adds.

"Uhh..." I shrug my shoulders. "I'm going to blame the nanny?"

A sneaky smirk grows across Dex's face as he jogs on the treadmill. "You sly dog! Did you—"

"I absolutely did not fuck the nanny, Dexter."

He gasps. "How did you know that's what I was going to say?"

"Because all you think about is sex. That's how."

Hawken laughs. "Facts. He's got you there, Dex, eh?"

"Fuck you, Malone." Dex gives his best friend the middle finger and keeps jogging.

"Did everything go alright with Ada?" Quinton asks. "Kinsley said she texted with her last night and everything seemed fine."

"Yeah. It was great, actually. She fit right in and Elsie

loves her already. Honestly, it went so smoothly I fell asleep without a worry. It was like all the stress I had been holding in my body just kind of dissipated. I slept hard and when I opened my eyes the sky was well awake." I chuckle. "I've never slept in in my entire fucking life, but I've got to tell you, it felt good."

"Soooo what's she like?" Milo asks. "Is it weird having a woman in your house again?"

I hit the power button on my treadmill and push the appropriate settings. "You know, I didn't even give it a thought. But clearly my subconscious did if I slept as hard as I did. Ada said she woke up twice last night and I never heard her."

"So does that mean Ada managed it?" Quinton asks.

I nod. "Yeah. She said once was a potty break and the second time was a bad dream. I couldn't believe I never heard her shouting for me."

Colby does his set of squats and then adds, "Well, maybe that's a sign of good things to come. She knows what she's doing. You can trust that she'll be able to help."

"Yeah. I think you may be right."

"Did you see what she sleeps in? Is she hot?"

"Dexter, for the love of God, I am not sleeping with the nanny."

He laughs. "I'm just saying, man. She's the first woman you've had around in what? Three years? How can you not at least notice?"

"I..." I let out an exasperated sigh. "I don't know what she slept in. But yeah, I noticed, alright?"

His brow lifts and a cat-ate-the-canary smirk spreads across his face. "Aaaand?"

"And..."

Fuck.

"She's pretty," I admit. "She's pretty in that very natural kind of way. And she seems comfortable in her own skin. I did notice that her eyes change color. Last night they were kind of brown and this morning they looked green."

"Uh huh..." Dex says, waiting for more.

"That's it. She's a pretty woman. That's what I noticed. I didn't lay in bed and think about her. I didn't touch her or kiss her or hit on her in any way. That's your game, dude. Not mine."

"Mmkay." Dex laughs. "We'll revisit this conversation in a month or two."

I roll my eyes. "Pretty sure my answers will be the same, but okay Foster."

"Okay, Miller."

Our first week together has gone so smoothly it's as if Ada has been Elsie's nanny all along. Elsie seems to be Ada's little shadow, doing everything she does. If Ada cleans, Elsie helps. If Ada is cooking dinner, Elsie wants to help too. And now the girls have their very own secret hand shake that Elsie loves to make me watch at least six times a day. I've come home to several dance parties in the kitchen at the end of the workday and listen to them giggling together when I'm working on charity stuff. Every now and then I get a tinge of jealousy that Ada gets to spend so much time with my kid, but then I remember she's doing all this for me. So, I can keep Elsie here in her own home. Her own place of comfort. So, on my days where I'm not so busy, I can easily spend time with my little girl.

After a grueling morning workout and a hard practice this afternoon to prepare for tomorrow's game, I'm excited to get home and see Ad...Elsie.

Elsie.

I'm excited to see Elsie.

Hopefully, the ladies have made it through the day without any issues.

I open the front door and step into a relatively quiet house.

"Helloooo?"

"Daddy!" Elsie calls out. "We're havin' a tea party!"

"A tea party?" I ask excitedly, taking the steps two at a time, still feeling the burn of the new stretches Wilson had me doing earlier. "Well, I must've gotten home just in time because I've always wanted to have a—" I stop abruptly when I make it to the kitchen and catch the sight in front of me.

Don't react.

Don't react.

Don't react.

Ada greets my shocked face with an overexaggerated smile and a quick glance at Elsie. "Hi Daddy! Would you like to join our tea party?"

Her face.

What happened to...

"Wow!" I say, my eyes growing by the second. "You look..." Shaking my head slowly, I watch as Ada slides her eyes toward Elsie again, who is anxiously beaming at me. "Ada, you look beautiful!"

If beautiful meant every hairclip Elsie owns in Ada's hair, bright pink lipstick rimming her lips like a clown high on meth, eye shadow up to her forehead, and purple blush on her freckled cheeks. The yellow one-shoulder dress is a nice touch too.

"Thank you so much. Didn't Elsie do a beautiful job on my hair and makeup? She worked *really* hard on it."

I look at my daughter in her pink tutu dress, her hair expertly braided in a pattern I don't recognize and could probably never master. Her nails shimmer with alternating pink and purple colors. The pride on her little face melts me.

And there's a swell of warmth in my chest I haven't felt in a while.

"She did a magnificent job!" I step over to Elsie and take her hand, twirling her around. "I'm so proud of you, Sweetheart. You both look so beautiful. I think I'm underdressed for this tea party. You gals are stunning."

Ada nods appreciatively. I can tell she's grateful I didn't say anything about her hideous makeup job. "Well then you'll have to change so you can join our party."

"Yeah, Daddy. Daddies need a tie."

"That's right," Ada agrees.

I grin at them both. "Well alright then. I'll run upstairs and change. I'll just be a minute."

On my way up the stairs I hear Elsie say, "Oh no! We forgot our hats, Ada!"

"Are they up here?" I call down from the staircase.

"Yeah," Ada answers. "They're sitting on the desk in my room. Would you be willing to grab them?"

"Sure thing."

I change my clothes quickly, sliding into a pair of gray pants and a light blue shirt with a matching tie. Anything for my baby girl. Though I'm freshly showered after practice, I squirt a little cologne on for good measure and head to Ada's room to grab their hats.

"Hats, hats, hats," I whisper to myself, trying to remember where Ada said they would be. "Desk."

Spotting them both on the desk, I step over to grab them but when I do I knock the book that was underneath them to the floor.

Oops.

I toss the hats to her bed and bend down to pick up the book that appears to be a photo album or scrapbook of sorts. Other than the two boxes I carried in for Ada last night, I haven't seen anything of hers, but curiosity has me wondering if maybe there's a picture of her late husband in here. By all means her past is none of my business, but here I am opening the album and, "Hooooly fuck..."

This is not a photo album of her late husband.

It's an album of her.

A sexy photo album.

I look back at the front cover and notice Kinsley's photography logo.

Holy shit. These are the photos Kinsley was talking about?

The entire book is filled with pictures of Ada I should absolutely not be looking at but fuck me, I don't think I could look away at this point if I was offered all the money in the world.

I swallow hard and turn the page, my chest tightening and my eyes glued to the stunning photos of Ada, one after another. Dressed in next to nothing, posing in positions I would die to be able to witness in real life, she is a goddamn goddess. Her long, toned legs poised in the air, her ankles crossed and her feet covered in a pair of red heels. Her body, wrapped in the sexiest piece of lace I've ever seen rests on a plush white bed. Her head tilted back, elongating her slender neck. One of her hands lies on her chest as the other pushes through her feathered brown hair.

Yeah. She's downright sexy.

Hot as fucking sin.

Her face though. I feel my dick stiffening in my pants as I focus on her beautiful face. Her eyes closed in ecstasy and her mouth in that perfect O shape that I'm certain she gets right before she comes.

This is definitely a permanent entry in my spank bank.

Shit, why am I looking at this?

I need to stop looking at this.

Fuck that.

I want to keep looking at this.

"Did you find the hats, Zeke?" Ada calls from downstairs.

Shaking myself from the hypnosis that is Ada's sexy body, I nearly drop the album on the floor again. "Yep. Got 'em! Be right down!" Before I get myself in any kind of trouble, I shut the album and set it down quietly on her desk and then take a deep breath.

Picking up the hats for the ladies, I close Ada's door

behind me and take one more deep calming breath, making myself count to ten and willing the chub between my legs to calm down before I have an embarrassing moment in front of my daughter and her nanny.

But I can never unsee what I saw.

It's there forever etched in my brain.

Her body.

Her passion.

And hell, if I'm not going to spend the rest of this night and every one after this wishing I could see more of Ada Lewis.

"You're really great with her." I grab the dish towel hanging from the stove and dry each dish as Ada washes them before putting them away. "Elsie's always been a creative and playful kid but she's very different with you than she is with my parents."

She turns her head and smiles and I have to break eye contact because the moment she looks at me I see her in the red lacey number from her picture upstairs.

Except for the ungodly makeup still on her face.

"Really?"

"Mhmm." I clear my throat. "I mean you *are* probably close to thirty years younger than my parents so there's the whole age difference thing. You have more energy and imagination than both my parents combined."

She chuckles. "Imagination is one of the things I love about kids. Their brains at this age can literally come up with any scenario without fear of judgement. It's dragons, castles, and princesses one day and it's cowboys and bank robbers the next. Kids are so much fun."

Ada finishes washing the last dish from our tea party and leans against the sink with a clown-like smile on her face and I laugh, shaking my head.

"What?" She looks around. "Did I miss something?"

"I'm sorry," I tell her trying and failing to hide my amusement. "Your face."

She cackles covering her face with her hands. "Oh God! I totally forgot what I looked like! I'm so sorry!"

"No, no, no. Don't apologize at all. You're a Godsend. My mother would never have allowed her to do it in the first place. I bet she was giddy as hell."

"She was." Ada nods with her hands on her cheeks. "Which reminds me, I should thank you for not saying anything when you came in earlier. Elsie was so proud of her accomplishment after giving me a quote-unquote princess make-over."

"I'm pretty sure I'm the one who should be thanking you for letting her do it and for not changing it once she did."

"Oh, I would never change her work. I'm a firm believer in letting kids do their own work no matter what it looks like in the end. It's how they learn. Plus, kids grow up fast enough on their own. I see no need to make them grow up even faster by stifling their creativity and expression. And before you even ask, yes, I took several pictures."

"That's great," I laugh. "Well, for what it's worth, it was quite the tea party."

"That it was. And I'm glad you got to join us."

"Me too." I put away the last dish and rehang the towel I was using. "Can I get you anything? A beer? Glass of wine? I think you've more than earned it."

And I'd love to get to know you better.

"Thanks, but I should probably..." She gestures upstairs. "Go, uh, you know, get out of this dress and wash my face a few hundred times in the shower before my pillowcase looks like a stained-glass window."

A pang of disappointment shoots through my chest.

She turned me down.

"Right. Yeah. Of course."

She crosses her arms over her chest. "Thanks again though for a fun evening, Zeke. She'll be talking about tonight for days."

She really does look pretty in that dress.

"My pleasure. Any time. Well," I shrug, "I guess I mean mostly any time."

"Right." She smiles and slides her hair back behind her ear. I follow the movement of her hand wondering just for a moment what it would feel like to do it for her. To feel her silky hair in my fingers, her warm skin under my palm.

Shit. Cut it out Miller.

She's not yours.

"Well, good night," she says with a nod before heading upstairs.

"Goodnight, Ada." I watch her walk out of the kitchen and into the foyer to the stairs. Once she's out of sight I slouch back against the counter where I'm still standing and blow out my breath, relieved in a way. Now that she's gone she can't see how awkward I feel.

Maybe she didn't notice at all. I could be so lucky.

"God, what am I even doing?" I whisper to myself, rubbing my forehead between my thumb and forefinger. Seeing her in those photos is doing something to me and I wasn't ready for it. It's been so fucking long since I've been with a woman. Not just intimately but emotionally. I'm relatively good at making small talk with anyone, but when it comes to Ada I feel a bit tongue tied. The more I watched her tonight the more I thought about her playing a different role in my life.

She's pretty.

She's smart.

She works hard.

She's creative.

She's fun.

She loves Elsie.

These are all wonderful traits.

Fuck.

What am I doing?

Pushing away my immediate thoughts, I turn and reach for a small glass from the cupboard and the whiskey bottle from the corner cabinet. I pour myself a small drink and tip it back, swallowing it in one gulp. I wince slightly at the burn as it slides down my throat and then pour a second glass.

With any luck this will help knock me out so I can sleep peacefully and not have a night filled with thoughts of a scantily clad nanny invading my dreams.

6

ADA

"Good night stars. Good night air."
Elsie whispers with her eyes closed, "Good night noises everywhere."

I close the *Good Night Moon* book Elsie chose for her bedtime story as she yawns and pulls the covers up to her chin. Placing a kiss on her forehead, I wish her all the sweetest dreams and then close her bedroom door and make my way back downstairs to clean up from our day.

The dishes are done, the toys are put away, and Elsie's watercolor painting from this morning is hanging on the fridge waiting for her dad to see it when he gets home. She also colored me a super cute picture of a cat that, of course, I named Mr. Purrito even though she doesn't know who that is just yet.

Hoping to catch at least some of Zeke's game on television, I scroll through the channels until I find it, excited that it just started and they're only in the first period. My phone dings on the coffee table and I reach for it wondering who it could possibly be.

Can't be Zeke. He's on the ice.

> **KINSLEY**
> Hey! Is Elsie sleeping?

> **ME**
> Hey! Yeah just put her to bed about thirty minutes ago.

> **KINSLEY**
> Watching the game?

> **ME**
> Of course! Wouldn't miss it!

> **KINSLEY**
> Great. Then open the door! We're outside!

My brows furrow at her last text as I stand up and run to the door. "What...?"

I quietly open the front door and am greeted by four smiling women.

"Hey friend!" Kinsley smiles and steps forward for a hug. "I thought to myself, why should Ada sit at home alone to watch the game when we can keep her company? So, I brought some friends. These are the wags."

"Wags?"

"Wives and girlfriends of the hockey team. Well, starting lineup anyway."

She gestures to the woman next to her. "Ada, This is Charlee, Milo's wife. Charlee, Ada."

My heart warms and my smile grows when I realize who all these women are. "Oh, my gosh! Charlee, it's such a pleasure to meet you!"

She shakes my hand and returns my smile. "The pleasure is all mine, Ada. I've heard wonderful things about you."

"Wow, already? It's only been a couple of weeks."

"Good news travels fast." She winks.

"And this is Rory, Hawken's wife and Dex's sister, and also Tate, Dex's..." Kinsley's brows furrow. "Uh..."

Tate steps forward and shakes my hand. "His girlfriend slash baby mama slash would be his damn wife if he would just get his shit together and slap a ring on me already."

"Well tell me how you really feel, girlfriend." We giggle together and I swing the door wide open. "Please, come in. Make yourselves at home. If I had known, I would've done some extra shopping so we had—"

Rory holds up the bag in her hand. "Snacks?"

Charlee holds up a six-pack. "Beer?"

Shaking my head, I laugh softly. "Wow you guys thought of everything."

"Not our first rodeo," Tatum laughs with me.

"I guess not! I'm so glad you're here!"

Growing up watching baseball, it took me several years to really respect the game. To appreciate each player and his role on the team. As my brother got older and moved up the ranks, I learned more of what it took to be a professional player. The drive, the determination, the literal blood, sweat, and tears of trying to make it into an extremely competitive league.

Now, as I sit here watching Zeke do what he does, the

way he makes everything about hockey look so absolutely effortless...he amazes me.

"How does he not fall on his ass every time he goes down for the block like that?"

"Giiirl we need to get you to a game. Have you seen the man's stretch routine on the ice?" Rory asks, referring to Zeke.

I shake my head. "Nope. When I turned on the game tonight they were already in the first period. Why, does he do something special?"

She snorts. "Something like that."

"What? Is it hot?" I cringe and cover my face with my hand. "Ooh sorry. Pretend I didn't just say that about my boss."

"No, it's okay," Tate says. "And yes, it's hot. It's hot when any of the guys do it, but when Zeke does it?" She fans her face. "I think we all blush. It's like his very own Magic Mike show."

"What? How so?"

Rory hops off the couch and stands in front of the television. "Because he does this. Watch." She lowers herself to her knees, spreads them as far apart as she can and then with her hands on the floor in front of her she stretches out and pulses her hips up and down like she's—

"Oh, my God! And he does that on the ice?" I ask. "Like, in front of everyone?"

Rory nods with a sultry smile and Charlee giggles tossing back her drink. "Yep. And then they all do it. The whole team."

"And we can't lie," Tate says. "It's hot as fuck every single time."

"Oh, my God." My eyes grow as my imagination starts to run wild. "That is not how I've ever pictured the game of hockey."

Kinsley winks next to me. "Trust me girlfriend, if you're paying attention, these guys will show you a whole new side to the game you never saw coming."

"Wow. This is something I'm going to have to see."

"So, spill the beans, Ada. What's it like living with Zeke?" Rory asks, tossing a handful of popcorn into her mouth.

Charlee leans forward on the couch. "Yeah, does he run around here with his shirt off all the time?"

Kinsley wags her brows. "Does he do those stretches right here in the living room for your viewing pleasure?"

"Do you guys have secret rendezvous in the middle of the night?" Tate asks with a wink.

I nearly spit out my drink. "Oh, my God! No!" Nervous laughter falls from my lips. "Why would you think that?" My smile falters. "Oh, shit. Does everyone think that?"

The girls laugh and Rory pats my knee. "No. Not at all. But come on, you have to agree that Zeke Miller is hot as fuck."

"Wait..." I cock my head. "Aren't you all dating one of the other guys?"

"Some of us are even married to them," Charlee says, raising her hand. "But that doesn't mean we don't appreciate all the guys on the team."

"Oh." *Wait...* "Oooh." I look at each of the ladies. "Do you mean like...is this like...do you all..." I circle my finger. "Together?"

"What? An Orgy?" Rory crinkles her nose. "Fuck no. My brother is on the team." She snorts.

"Oh. Okay. Sorry." I shake my head. "I guess I just misunderstood what Charlee was saying."

"What she's saying," Rory starts. "And I think I can say this as well as we've both known Zeke the longest, is that we appreciate all the guys on the team for who they are. And Zeke, well, first of all he's hot as balls, no doubt. Any woman would be lucky to score him, but on top of that, he's also a super nice guy. Like...he might even be nicer than Milo and we all know he's like a goddamn golden retriever."

Charlee smiles lovingly. "He is. I'm very blessed. He's like every book boyfriend you've ever read all rolled into one."

"Book boyfriend?" I ask.

"Oh yeah. Sorry. I'm a romance book editor. That's my day job."

"Right! I remember Milo mentioning that to me the day I interviewed. Didn't know they were called book boyfriends. That's cute."

Tate circles back around to our previous conversation. "So, you and Zeke have never...?"

"No." I shake my head adamantly. "Never. I've never thought of Zeke as anything other than the man who hired me for a job. I mean, I won't deny that he's an incredibly attractive man but I don't think he would ever look at me as a potential love interest if that's what you're asking. And I certainly would never do anything to compromise what I have going for me here with Elsie. She's such a sweetheart."

The last thing I need is these ladies who are undoubtedly loyal to the team, running to their men and telling them I fantasize about my boss or try to hit on him or anything of the sort.

Tate goes to the kitchen to grab herself another beer. "So, have you thought much about what it might be like if he brought another woman home? Like a date?"

My chest tightens and a stab of disappointment hits my heart.

"Uh, no. Does he do that?" I clear my throat and try to act cool, calm, and collected. "I mean...often?"

They all shrug. "Not that we've heard," Rory answers. "But I guess none of us can really say for sure. Zeke's been relatively private since his wife left."

"What do you know about that?"

"She left right before Milo and Charlee got married." Rory rolls her eyes. "Some bullshit about not wanting to live the life of a hockey wife where he's gone a lot. Like she didn't already know what she was getting into."

I narrow my eyes. "So, she just walked out on her husband and her own child?"

"Yep." Rory pops her P, annoyed with the very idea of Zeke's ex-wife. "I heard she left the house one day with Elsie still inside and never came back."

"What the fuck? Who even does that? Jesus."

"It couldn't have happened to a nice guy either," Charlee explains. "He was heartbroken and then he was pissed. As far as we've heard he wants nothing to do with her."

"Damn. Poor Zeke. I hope I never have to cross paths with her. I don't know if I could bite my tongue."

"Fat chance you'll ever cross paths. She left three years ago and hasn't been back since."

"Good riddance then," Kinsley says, raising her glass and looking at me with an ornery wink. "And you...never say never my friend."

"You can say that all you want." I smile. "You can wish it every day if you want. But no matter how attractive he may be, I cannot sleep with my boss."

"Cannot...or will not?" Rory winks as the rest of the gals erupt in laughter.

7

ZEKE

We're losing this fucking game and it's all my fault. I've let two pucks into my net already and we're not even done with the second period. What the ever-loving fuck is my problem? Why am I even asking myself this question when I know exactly what my problem is? Or rather, *who* my problem is.

Ada Lewis.

Elsie's fun-loving, sweet as sugar, hard-working nanny. The woman who has literally been saving me from sleepless nights and endless stress as a single father with a demanding time-intensive career.

Fuck, everything was great. Smooth sailing for me, for Elsie, even for Ada.

Until I opened that damn photo album.

Until I saw Ada Lewis posing for the camera wearing nothing but satin, lace, and leather and simulating the most provocative poses. I couldn't have dreamed them up if I tried.

Now I can't get her out of my damn mind. Everywhere I look it feels like she's there even when she's not. She's invading my every thought and I'm allowing it to happen.

Get your head in the fucking game, Miller!

I watch down the ice as the guys fight for control of the puck. Malone tries twice to get it in the net, but even with an assist from Nelson they're unsuccessful. Foster has it now, swinging around the net but then it's stolen by Louisville's right wing, Olaf Mackleson. The River Frogs now have control and are headed toward me once again, only this time I'll be damned if I'm letting that puck past me.

Mackleson shoots to Simon McCray, who narrowly avoids being checked by Quinton, and passes to their team captain, Patrick Donoghue. He pulls his stick back on my left and sends a slapshot directly toward my chest.

"Miller!" I hear Quinton shout but it's all good. I saw the shot and readied my hand to catch the flying puck. It lands in my mitt and the crowd is on their feet cheering for the save...

Until I open my hand to make sure I indeed have the puck and it's not there. It's on the ground.

"Shit!" I drop to my knees to save the shot once again, only my pads knock the puck back toward my feet and when I try to move to find the damn thing, my own foot pushes it over the line into the net effectively scoring a third point for the Louisville River Frogs.

"Son of a fucking bitch!" I scream as the River Frogs celebrate my blatant stupidity.

The siren blows signaling the end of the second period and I'm the first one off the ice. I slam my gloved fist into the door and stomp inside, ripping my helmet from my head and throwing it across the room.

"FUCK!"

The guys follow behind quietly knowing full well that this game and it's inevitable loss is my fault and mine alone. I'm supposed to be the best fucking goalie in the league. Nothing gets past me. I'm good at my job, but today I'm a fucking sack of shit in a Chicago Red Tails uniform.

"Hey," Colby says, storming into the locker room. "Calm your tits, Miller. An outburst like that on the ice isn't going to win us this game."

"Yeah? Well, you may as well put Remi in the goddamn game instead of me for all the good I've done tonight because I'm certainly not doing you any fucking favors."

Hawken scrunches his face in confusion. "Dude, we're only down by one. We can make that up, eh?"

"Yeah well, we're down by one because I've let three fucking pucks past me today."

"Meh." Dex shrugs. "We've all had bad games. And we've come back from worse. Just...you know..." He shakes his finger at me like a scolding mother. "Don't do that again."

Hawken steps up to me, cupping my shoulders in his hands. "You know what Lasso would say?" He smirks. "He would say be a goldfish. So, fix your shit and go back out there and be a goddamn goldfish Zeke."

I slump to the bench, hanging my head in frustration. "I wish it were that simple."

"Uh oh," Milo mutters. "This doesn't sound like game talk anymore." I glance up at him with a reddening face. My hair dripping with sweat.

"I think you might be right, Landric," Colby says, lifting a brow. "You want to tell us what's going on?"

"Not particularly."

"Alright then I guess we're just going to take the loss, gentlemen, because Miller here doesn't have his fucking head on straight and is too much of a pussy to talk about it."

"Leave it alone, Nelson."

Quinton leans over. "Something going on at home? Things with Ada aren't good?"

I let out a resigned sigh because Quinton is my friend and these guys are my family and I hate that I got here today and didn't say anything to them and now I'm not just fucking myself over, I'm fucking them over too.

"Ada's fine. More than fine. She's...perfect."

"Oh shit." Dex huffs a laugh but his brows shoot up and he has a goofy smile on his face. "Are you telling us we're losing this game because you finally fucked the nanny and she's got you by the balls now?"

I shake my head. "I didn't fuck her. No."

All heads turn toward me. All eyes on me expectantly waiting for further explanation.

With another heavy sigh I tell them, "But I did open a photo album of hers a few days ago expecting to see her late husband and they were definitely not pictures of her late husband."

"Oooh" Quinton sits back with an understanding grin. "I think I know where this is going." I shoot a glance to Quinton and with a cautious smile he asks, "Were they pictures Kinsley may have taken?"

I nod silently.

"Boudoir photos?" he asks.

I nod again.

Dex laughs. "Oookay so you didn't fuck her but now you *want* to fuck her. You want to fuck the nanny."

My elbows on my knees I push my hands through my hair. "I...I don't know what I fucking want at this point but those pictures...they were...fuck...she was..."

"Yeah." Milo chuckles. "We all have pictures of our women that Kinsley took last season. We know exactly what you're talking about."

I sit up, glancing at each one of them, relieved at their understanding expressions. "Oh, thank fuck because I think I'm going crazy here you guys. Every time I look at her I see...a different side of her. It's all I've been able to think about. I struggle to talk to her now. Like she'll see that horny teenager inside of me who so desperately wants to tell her how insanely hot I thought she looked in those pictures. How am I supposed to keep looking at her like I haven't seen them? Like I don't know what she looks like under her normal clothes?"

"Does she know you saw them?"

"What? No way." I shake my head. "I was just grabbing something out of her room for her while I was upstairs and I accidentally knocked the book off her desk. And then once I saw them I couldn't *un*see them. But I don't want to unsee them, so what the fuck am I supposed to do now? Am I supposed to fire her?"

"Fire the nanny because *you* saw pictures of her she didn't intend for you to see?" Quinton scowls. "How's that fair?"

He's right. It's not fair.

Colby takes a long gulp from his water bottle. "Is she doing a good job?"

"A spectacular job. Elsie would be heartbroken if I asked Ada to leave."

"Then you have to get your shit together and put it behind you. Seems like she just knocked you off your game."

"Oh, he's so far beyond the game right now," Dex adds. "Maybe you should just scratch the itch."

All the guys scoff at Foster who doesn't seem to know when to leave the subject of fucking the nanny alone.

"What?" he asks with a shrug. "I'm just saying if he can't get her out of his mind, then he should fucking do something about it."

My blood pressure starts to rise as my anger and frustration grows. "Like what, man? You think I should walk through the front door when I get home tonight, bend her over, and fuck her brains out whether she wants it or not just because I saw a few sexy pictures of her?"

"Maybe not tonight, Zeke." Quinton smiles. "The girls all went over to your house to keep Ada company and watch the game."

"Oh, great. So now she's at home watching me play like a complete fuck nut."

Dex cocks his head. "What does it matter how you play in front of her? She's just the nanny."

"It doesn't. I know. I'm just—"

"Do you like her?"

"I barely know her!" I shout. "It's not like we sit at home at night and share our deepest darkest desires, Dexter. She's doing a job for me. She's taking care of the most important part of my life and I'm paying her to do it."

"I understand that but let me ask you something." He turns to me. "When was the last time you got laid?"

"Why is that even relevant? We have a game to win."

"When was the last time, Zeke?"

"I don't..." *Ugh.* "A long time ago. Before Lori left."

Dex's eyes practically protrude from his face. "You haven't—?" He starts to say before I glare at him with a don't-fuck-with-me-right-now expression. He holds up his hands in defense. "Okay, okay. So, it's been a while."

"Yeah." I nod, feeling even more pissed off than I was when I walked in here. "It's been a damn minute."

"So, she's your dangling carrot."

"What?"

"That part of you, the sexually active part of you, has been dormant for years and yesterday you opened a book that reawakened you a little. You haven't as much as looked at another woman since Lori left. Why not?"

"Because technically we're still married and I'll be damned if I willingly give her the chance to call me a cheater."

"Okay so first of all, that's a load of shit and you need to cut ties with her because until you do you've put your personal life on hold and that is completely unfair to you."

"How am I supposed to do that when I don't know where the fuck she is?"

"You call your lawyer, man," Colby says with a scoff. "Or are you hoping she comes back?"

"Not in a million years. It's not just me. I gave a damn that she left me three years ago but she went way too far by walking out on Elsie and that is unforgiveable to me. She doesn't deserve to walk back into Elsie's life whenever it's convenient for her. Fuck that."

"Okay." Dex nods. "Then Colby's right. It's time to contact a lawyer and finish what she started. And as far as Ada is concerned. She's like a dangling carrot. Something you didn't know you wanted until it was dangled in front of you. It's completely normal to be attracted to a pretty woman, Zeke, but you have to decide how you're going to manage your thoughts. If you like her and you're attracted to her, then maybe you should do something about that."

For the first time today, what Dex is saying is beginning to make sense.

"So, you have choices," he says. "You can fantasize about the nanny and jack-off all you want in privacy, you can watch some hot porn and try to erase the pictures from your mind, you can go find a puck bunny after the game and get some action, or you can literally go after the dangling carrot and see if it's a snack you enjoy."

Hawken leans over on the other side of me with a smirk and whispers, "I can have your very own fleshlight delivered via Instacart tonight if you want one, Zekey. It can probably be here before the end of the game if you need to relieve some pressure."

His question breaks the tension in the room and we all laugh. I bump his shoulder with my own. "Fuck you very much, Malone. I think I can handle it."

My fist will work just fine.

In the end we pulled out the win. I blocked every single goal attempt made and Quinton and Milo both scored in the final period, thank God. I took a long cold shower after the game relieved that my teammates came through for me, disappointed in myself for needing them to come to my aid, and determined to put my thoughts of the sexy nanny behind me.

She's just a person.

There's nothing between us.

She has no idea I've seen her pictures and that's the way it should stay.

I pull up to a darkened house after trying unsuccessfully to dismiss an invite to Pringle's with the team. I promised Ada I would be home before midnight, but after what happened between periods tonight and then pulling out the win, the guys insisted I go with them for a drink. I texted Ada earlier and told her I would be later than I thought so that she knew she didn't need to wait up but when I walk past the foyer towards the kitchen I stop short at the sight before me.

"YAAAASSS! GO! GO! GO!" Ada whisper shouts with two arms up in the air, a beer in one hand, as she cheers in front of the television. She's a fucking sight for sore eyes in her extremely short black sleep shorts and pink tank top. The way the lamp light illuminates her body from the side of the room, I can see the outline of her breasts through the sheer fabric of her shirt.

Fuuuuck me. She's not wearing a bra.

My dick stirs in my pants but I refuse to allow it to embarrass me further. Squeezing my eyes shut, I tell myself,

She's ugly as hell.
Looks like Nanny McPhee.
She smells bad.
Her breath smells like tobacco and onions.
And the braided armpit hair is definitely a turn-off.

None of those things are true, but a man has to try, right?

"SAFE!" she shouts as quietly as possible, doing a little happy dance in front of the television. She turns herself around in celebration until she spots me in the entryway. With a huge smile on her face, she skips over to me and puts her hand up for a high five.

"Hey! Congratulations Zeke! Awesome game tonight! That was quite the comeback."

I don't know how she does it, but with one smile, and one sentence, she breaks me away from my intrusive thoughts and reminds me that she's just a woman. A super cool, seemingly fun woman.

And she watched my game.

"You watched?"

She furrows her brow. "Uh, yeah. Of course I watched. "Elsie will be excited in the morning to hear that you won. She was talking about it when she went to bed." Her eyes grow and she points to me excitedly. "Oh, I almost forgot the best part of the night! Kinsley brought the girls over to watch the game so I could meet everyone. I mean not Carissa, obviously, though I've obviously already met her, but I met umm, Charlee, Tate, and Rory. They were all so sweet and so much fun!"

"That's great. I'm glad you got to meet everyone. Sorry I played like a fucking loser tonight."

She cocks her head with a scowl. "Okay first of all, you did not play like a loser tonight. Did you *see* you in the third period? You were on fire! And besides, everyone has a bad game. You came back in the end and won so chin up." She elbows my side. "You want a beer?"

She walks toward the kitchen and I follow her every move, watching her perfect ass sway with every step she takes. "It's twelve-thirty in the morning."

How does she have so much energy for this time of night?

She pulls a bottle of beer from the fridge and opens the top with the bottle opener attached to the cabinet. "Yeah but it's only ten-thirty in California and my brother's also playing tonight and it's one of his last games of the season and it's been a fantastic game so far! He hit a grand slam at the top of the sixth and I bet he's flying high right now and I wanted to wait up for you anyway so two birds one stone, you know? Carter's game is keeping me awake and also I maaaay have had a little too much caffeine about an hour ago but now here you are and the game isn't over so you should relax and watch it with me."

That was a lot of words she just rattled off. But also, her excitement for her brother is heart-warming.

And also, "You wanted to wait up for me?" I ask, dropping my duffle bag and taking the beer she offers me. "I told you, you didn't have to worry about it."

"Of course!" She beams. "You won tonight. You fought the good fight. I wanted to be able to congratulate you so I found my brother's game on my app and streamed it to the television while I was waiting for you. Come on." She plops down in the middle of the couch and pats the seat next to her. "Come watch." She stops and looks at me with huge round eyes. "Oh, unless you have some kind of strict schedule you keep. Especially after a game. I totally understand if you have—"

"Nope." I shake my head and kick off my shoes, taking the seat next to her on the couch. "We're off tomorrow before our away games start next week."

"Great!"

This might be an actual first in my life.

Lori never waited up.

Lori didn't give a damn about sports of any kind.

Lori hated what my career demanded of me.

And now I'm sitting next to someone who not only watched my game tonight, she waited up to talk to me about it. And now we're relaxing on the couch together with a beer and a baseball game.

And her shoulder is touching mine.

And she's not wearing a bra.

And if I don't stop thinking about that, I'm going to need to hug a pillow for the rest of this game.

The eighth inning has Carter's team, the Indianapolis Bobcats, trailing six to five. Ada has been on the edge of her seat, literally, for the last several minutes praying the game has a positive outcome for her brother. Admittedly, I've very much enjoyed watching her get all worked up. She's a loyal fan of not only the game of baseball but also of her brother. I'd like to think, in time, she'll be a devoted fan of mine as well. And I'm grateful she appreciates the lengths athletes must go through to be good at their sport.

"They cannot piss on his grand slam. He's having a

great game. They have to pull this out. Come on gentlemen! There's still time."

I'm so fucking relaxed. After the two beers I've just downed, I couldn't be happier sitting here with Ada watching baseball after an evening of playing hockey. This is quite literally a dream come true. The night could only get better if it ended with some wildly fun sex.

Not that I'm relying on that or anything.

Ada's hot, there's no question. And at least twice tonight, I've enjoyed watching her tits bounce up and down when she jumps up to celebrate her brother's team. I am a guy after all. I can look even if I can't touch.

"Fuck YES!" Ada jumps up again when Randall Simon hits a double at the top of the ninth. "Come on Carter! You can do this! Just one home run and you're all in."

She holds her hands in front of her mouth like she's praying as her brother comes up to bat. Even I find myself on the edge of my seat. Ada's energy for watching the game is contagious. The pitcher throws his first pitch and it's a strike for Carter.

"Shit!" Ada whisper-shouts. "Come on Carter. Eye on the ball."

"He's got this," I reassure her.

"How can you be so sure?"

"Look at his eyes. You can always see the focus and determination in someone's eyes. I know the look well."

The next pitch is good and Carter has a strong hit.

Ada throws her arms up in the air and it's like watching her do an aerobic workout. She circles her arm like a base coach telling their runner to keep going.

"Yes! GO! GO! GO! RUN CARTER!"

He taps first base and runs for second but he doesn't stop there.

Holy shit.

How's he going to play this out?

One of the outfielders throws the ball to the pitcher who sees Carter stuck between second and third base.

"Fuck," I mumble.

Carter pretends he's running back to second causing the pitcher to toss the ball to the second baseman, but it's a fake out as Carter shuffles his foot just as I would my skate to change directions and runs to third. The second baseman chases him until he gets close enough to toss the ball to the third baseman in hopes he can tag him out. But he drops the ball and now Ada and I are both on our feet watching the intense finish.

"OH MY GOD! CARTER GO!!"

The third baseman scoops the ball and chases after Carter when he shuffles back toward second but then he shuffles again and tries to get back to third. The pitcher moves toward third base but Carter dives in and taps the base with his hand before the ball is caught and he is—

"SAFE! OH MY GOD! THAT WAS IMPOSSI-BLE!" Ada jumps up and down.

"That was fucking amazing! I beam back at her. My hand in my hair, I blow out a huge sigh of relief and laugh in astonishment as she gives me a joyous high five, jumps into my arms, throws her arms around me excitedly, and kisses me.

Full. On. The. Mouth. With. Tongue.

Hooooly shit.

Her tits.

Her tits are brushing against my chest.

Fuuuuucking hell.

I haven't kissed a woman in an extraordinarily long time.

Please God, do not let me forget how.

I'm just about ready to believe she really wants to be kissing me when she stops suddenly and jumps away from me. Her eyes are like huge round saucers and she gasps, bringing her hand to her lips and shaking her head. "I...Oh, my God, Zeke. I'm...I'm so sorry. I don't know what..."

"It's okay," I try to reassure her and play it off. "I figured maybe that's how you celebrate in baseball. Thought maybe hockey could learn a few things."

She laughs and I'm grateful to have broken the tension a little. "I..." She brushes her fingers over her lips and I wonder if she's thinking about that kiss the way I'm thinking about that kiss because that kiss was the start of something amazing and she hasn't stopped staring at me.

Her soft lips moved against mine.

Her tongue was in my mouth.

I tasted her.

And now I can't stop picturing her in that red lingerie laid out on the bed. A feast for my eyes and a vivid memory for my dick.

Fuck, where's that pillow when I need it?

"I'm so sorry. I just got—"

"Caught up in the moment," I finish her sentence. "Don't worry about it. I kiss the guys all the time when I'm excited."

She laughs again and throws the nearest throw pillow at me. "You do not, jerk."

"You're right, I don't." I grin. "But if I wanted to, I'm pretty sure Dex would be all too willing."

"You're probably right," she laughs.

"But pick me first, alright?" I tease even though I'm so not teasing. "Don't kiss Dex. His breath smells like pork rinds. Just kiss me instead. I'm the far superior kisser anyway."

She blushes. "I'll keep that in mind."

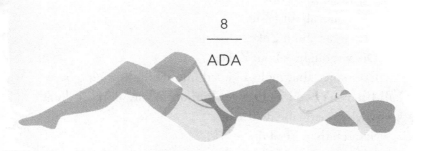

8

ADA

My first month and a half as Elsie's nanny has flown by. It's a job I never in a million years would have chosen for myself but it has been more fun than I could have ever anticipated. Elsie is an amazing little girl and so full of life and love. She's a cuddle bug when she wants to be and she's a spitfire ball of energy the rest of the time. She keeps me on my toes and she makes me laugh and seeing her with Zeke makes my heart so happy. He's such a lucky man to be her daddy.

Sometimes I lay awake at night and feel guilty for where I am.

Living in a huge house that isn't mine.

Sharing space with a man I am not married to.

Being a mother to a little girl who isn't my own.

Luke and I wanted to have a family. It was our dream when he was done in the service to settle down somewhere comfortable and raise a large family. Kids were a huge part of our future plan.

But life had other plans for us both.

There's not a day goes by that I don't think about Luke or where we might be if he was still alive, but now, three years later, new thoughts are starting to weave themselves into my mind more often than not.

Thoughts about Elsie.

Thoughts about Zeke.

Dirty thoughts about Zeke.

Ever since that night I kissed him while watching baseball I haven't been able to get him out of my mind. I don't know what made me do it.

Scratch that. Yes I do.

Luke and I would kiss when we were excited and celebrating Carter's wins. It's just something we did and there I was watching his game and what a moment it was. Zeke wrapped his arm around me, holding me against him like we'd been kissing forever. His lips were soft and gentle. His tongue was strong but tender.

Did he want to be kissing me?

I don't know.

But I do know one thing.

Zeke is an excellent kisser.

Ugh, I know, I know. I should not be thinking about my boss in such scandalous ways, but damn. When the hot hockey player with a body that would give Thor a run for his money comes into the kitchen a shirtless and hot sweaty mess because he was mowing the lawn or working out in his gym, what's a single girl to do?

It would be a waste of sheer masculine beauty if I didn't look and appreciate.

If not for me, then for every single woman or man across the globe.

My boss is hot as fuck and if I'm supposed to just not notice that or not think about what it might feel like if he were to take me in his arms, push me up against the wall, rip my clothes from my body and thrust his thickening mammoth-sized velvety soft—

"Ada?"

His voice tears me from my relentless daydream. "Hmm? What?"

"Did you not hear me?"

"What? Were you calling me?"

"Twice yeah." He chuckles. "Literally standing right here. You okay?"

I finally turn and see him and holy hell he looks every bit as delectable as he did in my dirty little thoughts just now.

Shirtless.

Chugging his water as sweat literally runs through the sinews of his abs. Yep. Even down those sexy alleyways.

What do we dirty minded women call those?

His happy trails?

His sex lines?

Apollo's belt?

The V-line?

"Uh..." I clear my throat and take a sip of water as a means of stalling to come up with a better answer than 'yeah I was just picturing you fucking me against the wall in a hot and steamy daydream because what normal single or married woman wouldn't fantasize about that if she were in my shoes'?

"Yeah, I'm fine." I smile and shake my head. "Sorry, I don't know where my mind went just now."

That's a lie.

"I must've been daydreaming or something."

"Day dreaming?" He smiles. "Anything good?"

"Scoring."

Another lie.

His brows peak. "Scoring?"

"Yeah." I shrug with a laugh. "Just wondering what it would be like if I did what you do. You make it all look so easy. Who knows, maybe I'd be good at it."

A broad smile grows across his face. "I have no doubt you'd be great at it. Maybe one of these days I'll put you in front of the net and let you try it out."

"Are you kidding me?" I scoff. "No fucking way. I don't want those big ass rubber disks flying at my face at a hundred miles an hour!"

Zeke cackles, a sparkle in his eye as he meets my gaze. "Oh, but I thought you'd be good at it."

"Good at losing two eyes, a nose, and probably all my teeth, you mean."

He grabs the towel that was hanging from his shorts and wipes the rest of the sweat from his face. I have to bite the inside of my cheek to keep from drooling.

"It would certainly be cute watching you try."

Sign me up, Coach!

"Anyway, I was just finishing my workout. I'm going to grab a shower quickly before I have to pack for tomorrow."

"Right. Yeah. Okay." I check the time on the microwave. "Elsie should be up from her nap soon and then she can help me make dinner."

"Great. I'll be down soon."

Though my days with Elsie and Zeke have been mostly smooth sailing, this morning was a bit of a sad one watching Elsie say goodbye to her dad as he left for the team's three-day stretch in Canada. Usually for games that aren't too far away, the team flies home the same night. Though he gets home rather late, Zeke is here when Elsie wakes up. A day here or a night there is one thing for a four-year-old kid, but knowing her daddy is going to be away for three whole days and she can't be with him is hard. It wasn't easy for Elsie to watch her dad drive away, but she was such a trooper. She cried for about ten seconds as we waved out the window and then I luckily saved the day by offering to take her to the Paw Palace to introduce her to all my puppy and kitty friends.

"Elsie this is Winston." I crouch down next to her and hold my hand out to the six-year-old deaf golden retriever in front of us so he can smell my scent. His tail wags and I give him a few scratches behind the ears. He turns to Elsie and licks her outstretched hand, making her giggle.

"Ew. He licked me."

"Those were just his doggy kisses." I hand her a small dog bone. "Here, would you like to give him a treat? Winston loves his crunchies."

Elsie takes the dog treat and I help her guide it to Winston in a safe manner. He sniffs it and licks it out of her hand, wagging his tail again as a thank you. We shower him with love and affection and then move on to a few of the other safe and gentle dogs in the shelter. Once we're done saying hello to some of my favorites and passing treats to as many of the dogs as we can, I take Elsie's hand and lead her to the kitty rooms to meet my favorite shelter cat.

"And this big old guy is Mr. Purrito."

In true fashion, my favorite orange and white cat saunters over to us, rubbing himself on the bottom of my leg before doing the same to a giggling Elsie. He flicks his tail and bops his head into Elsie's hand.

"Aww, I think he likes you, Else."

"Yeah. He likes me!"

I sit down with Elsie next to me and Mr. Purrito jumps willingly into my lap. His purrs loud enough for both of us to hear. Another little kitten, this one white with a few gray spots, playfully trots over to Elsie and paws at her foot. It meows and crawls into Elsie's lap.

"Ada look!" she says, beaming. "This kitty cat likes me too!"

"It sure does! Now be very gentle when you pet it okay? We don't want to scare our kitty friends."

"Do these kitties live here?"

"For now, yeah." I nod. "They're here to find new homes. They want to live with families who will give them lots of love. Like how your daddy gives you lots of love."

"These kitties can come live at my house. They can play with my toys too. I would share with them."

I rub my hand down Elsie's back. "That is extremely sweet of you, Elsie. These kitties are going to stay here for now, but maybe one day we'll be able to give one a very nice home." I lean over and whisper, "We should probably let your daddy decide that though. He's the boss."

"Yeah. We can show Daddy these kitties one day and he will like them all."

"You think your daddy would like all the kitties?"

Her eyes grow huge. "YEAH!"

Slipping into my pajamas after a long hot shower, my bed has never looked so inviting. Elsie will be awake in probably less than eight hours and if I want to be ready to hit the ground running with her, I need to get some sleep.

I set my alarm on my phone just as it dings in my hand with an incoming text.

> **ZEKE**
> Heyyyyy Sunshine.

Seeing his name pop up on my screen makes me smile.

> **ME**
> Sunshine huh? 😊

> **ZEKE**
> You happy always.

> **ME**
> Thanks, I think? I try. Congratulations on the win!

> **ZEKE**
> Thinks

> **ZEKE**
> I men thongs

ZEKE

Shit. THANKS.

ME

Uh, you're welcome. You okay?

ZEKE

Yep. I like you drunk.

ZEKE

No.

ZEKE

mmdrink. Drunk.

ME

I like you too Zeke. 😊 And I'm sober.
Enjoying yourself I see?

ZEKE

You know me.

ZEKE

I throw my pans up in the air sometimes.

ZEKE

Hawk says our world needs more corn so

ZEKE

Pretty sure he said corn.

ME

Totally get it. Corn for everyone. I'm glad
you're relaxing.

ZEKE

How's my girl?

My heart does a little flutter seeing the words *my girl* in his text. I know he's not talking about me, but my face flushes as if he is.

> ME
>
> We had a fun day visiting the animal shelter and I think she loved it.

ZEKE

Uh ooooh.

ZEKE

Dex wants to know how many pussies I own now?

Pretty sure if you asked nicely I would let you own mine.

Okay, you don't even have to ask nicely.

You could be a caveman about it if you want to.

ZEKE

He just snorted, cause I typed pissy.

ZEKE

possy.

ZEKE

LOL. PUSSY.

> ME
>
> 😂 We made it out with zero new friends if that's what you're asking. But I'm sure she has a list ready for you.

ZEKE

mmkay. Wow. I can keep you.

ME

You're funny when you're drunk Zeke. 😊 I should probably let you go. If it's late here it has to be even later where you are and maybe you need some water? And Advil? And sleep?

ZEKE

No! Don't go. Hafta tell you something.

ME

Okay...

ZEKE

Sort of a confesh

ZEKE

Feshion

ME

Confession?

ZEKE

Yeah

ME

Ok let's hear it.

ZEKE

Member when El forgot her tea party hat?

ME

Yeah.

ZEKE

I got 'em.

ME

Lol. Yeah you did. Thank you for that. Was that your confession?

ZEKE

Nope. But you're pretty.

ME

Uh, thanks, Zeke.

ZEKE

Wasn't snooping.

ME

Okay...snooping where?

ZEKE

Promise. Fell on the floor. Fuuuuck.

ME

You fell on the floor? Just now? Are you okay?

ZEKE

I'm good, Ada. How are you?

"Oh my God." I cackle into my pillow so I don't wake Elsie. "Drunk Zeke is killing me!"

ME

How have I been in this job for over a month and only just now see how funny drunk Zeke is?

ZEKE

LOL. Never give me Tikeela.

ME

Noted! HAHA! So, you were saying something fell on the floor?

ZEKE

In your room.

> **ME**
> My room? Did something break?

I do a quick survey of my room even though the only light on is the lamp next to my bed. Everything looks like it's in its place. I don't see anything missing.

> **ZEKE**
> Almost my penis. No biggie.

> **ME**
> What? LOL. I don't understand. Are you confessing to me that your penis is no biggie? You might be a little too drunk for this conversation, Zeke.

> **ZEKE**
> LOL! 😂 No way. My penis is not a lil' guy.

> **ZEKE**
> Q says it's Norman.

> **ME**
> Do you mean enormous?

> **ZEKE**
> Yep. Wanna see?

"Oh my God!" I laugh "Is he seriously offering me dick pics right now?"

Yes.

I mean...if you're offering...

I would be stupid to turn that down!

> **ME**
> Uh... You better not. You are my boss after all. I'll just take your word for it.

ZEKE

K.

ME

And don't send dick pics to anyone else.
Uh...I'm just reminding drunk Zeke that
he's a pro hockey player and probably
doesn't want pictures of his manhood out
there for anyone on the internet to see.

ZEKE

Ok Mom. 😊 Wanna know my favorite?

ME

Favorite what?

ZEKE

The lace one.

"What could he possibly be talking about?" My brow furrows as I try to translate Zeke's texts.

The lace one...fell on the floor...my bedroom...tea party hats...the lace one...What is he....

I gasp. "Oooh shit. Did he...?" My fingers fly across my screen as I type out my next text.

ME

Zeke?

ZEKE

And the red one on the Hed.

ZEKE

BED.

Oh God!

SUSAN RENEE

> **ME**
> Zeke are you talking about pictures?

> **ZEKE**
> mhmm

> **ME**
> You saw pictures of me?

> **ZEKE**
> Yep. HOT! 🔥

My boss has seen my boudoir photos and thinks they're hot! What do I say to that?

> **ZEKE**
> Sorry. Didn't mean to. Saaaaamn

> **ZEKE**
> I mean Daaaaaamn. 🔥👀 Sorry. Tikeela.

> **ME**
> Shit. I'm so sorry! 🙁 I was unpacking a box and I must have left them on my desk.

> **ZEKE**
> Nope. My bad. I confesh.

> **ZEKE**
> very sexy.

> **ZEKE**
> You kissed me.

> **ME**
> How are you drunk but you can still remember what happened weeks ago?

> **ZEKE**
> It was hot.

ZEKE

You can kiss.

ME

Umm...thanks?

I shake my head with a blushing smile because what am I supposed to say to my drunk boss about anything let alone pictures of me wearing next to nothing?

ZEKE

Does it smell like cheese where you are?

9

ZEKE

Damn, it's been a while since I've woken up with a hangover this nasty. My head pounds and my mouth is dry. My stomach feels queasy and my muscles are sore. Coach is going to have my ass if I don't figure out how to fix it before tonight's practice.

My phone dings on the nightstand beside me so I slowly roll myself over to see who the text is from.

COLBY

Wheels up in one hour gentlemen.

"Wheels up? Fuck." I sigh. "I cannot have a hangover on the plane."

ME

What the fuck did you guys make me do last night? I feel like shit.

MILO

Like sick? Did you catch the flu or something?

QUINTON

Nah. Zeke's got himself a hangover, I'm sure of it.

ME

Because you force fed me Tequila all night long?

HAWKEN

Dude, he may have force fed you one tequila. The rest you downed on your own.

DEX

It was pretty impressive. I was just about to come pound on your door to make sure you were awake.

ME

Please for the love of God do not POUND on anything around me. I need to fix this hangover.

COLBY

Drink a shit ton of water and take a few Advil. Carissa said she has some if you need them.

ME

Thanks. I'm good.

MILO

You need carbs. Lots of carbs.

DEX

Eat a burrito. You need greasy food. Or even a big ass burger and fries.

ME

Ugh. None of those sound appealing right now.

COLBY

Suck it up, Miller. Can't have you sick for practice and Coach will have all our asses for letting you celebrate too much last night.

QUINTON

Aww, give the guy a break. He needed the liquid luck.

My brows furrow at Quinton's last text. *Liquid luck? What for?*

ME

Why liquid luck?

QUINTON

looks at Hawken

HAWKEN

looks at Dex

DEX

Uh...ok. I guess I'm it. Sooo do you not remember texting Ada last night?

"What?" I close my text chat with the guys and find my text with Ada not at all remembering what we've talked about in the last twenty-four hours other than how Elsie has been doing since I left. I slowly read through the last several texts I sent her and spring up from my bed.

"Shit!"

"Ah, fuck!" The pain in my head explodes with my sudden movement. I palm my forehead and will the thumping agony to go the hell away while drowning in an overwhelming sense of guilt.

ME

Fuuuuuuuck.

DEX

I'm sure it's not that bad. Don't worry man.

ME

Not that bad? I fucking offered her pictures of my dick!

QUINTON

haha after he told her his penis was no biggie.

HAWKEN

LOL. Poor Zekey's penis. Never even had a chance.

DEX

Did she accept those pics, Zeke?

ME

What? No! She knew I was drunk and that I would regret it. Thank God!

DEX

cocking my head at you...pun intended Would you really have regretted sending her a dick pic?

QUINTON

Dude, Foster, it would've been a nice old drunk flaccid dick pic sooo let's answer that with a resounding yes!

ME

And not only did I offer her dick pics, I told her about the pictures I saw.

DEX

Ooooh yeah. Forgot about that part.

QUINTON

Did you tell her she looked sexy as fuck?

ME

Uh...not in so many words but also yes.

HAWKEN

Meh. Women like to hear that. I think you'll be okay.

ME

Even women you hire to take care of your kid??? 😬

HAWKEN

Umm...let's go with yes?

COLBY

Zeke, I'm sure if you write her and apologize for being a little under the influence last night she'll think nothing of it. Water under the bridge. Now go eat before you get on that plane.

I call down to room service and order every carb loaded item on the menu begging them to bring me a Sunrise burger with all the drippy egg and the French fries even though burgers aren't on the breakfast menu. Of course, I offered to give a hefty tip to the cook as well as the room attendant. While I wait for my food, I slip into the shower and let the hot water splash over me while trying like hell to come up with something—anything—I can say to Ada this morning to make last night not seem so bad.

Hey Ada, I wasn't really offering you dick pics last night. Dex stole my phone.

Lame.

Hey Ada, just kidding about those photos. I didn't see a thing.

Nope. That's not going to work. I was too specific in my texts.

They weren't as sexy as I originally said. I don't think they're particularly good, actually.

Pfft. Like I could even begin to say something like that to a woman. Especially when it's entirely untrue. Those pictures of her were stunning. So amazing, they're engrained in my head forever and ever and I don't even feel bad about it. New deposits into the spank bank are always welcome.

I'm really sorry about my behavior last night. That wasn't me.

"Ugh, except it WAS me. But it was *drunk* me and it was completely unprofessional and I wouldn't blame you if you walked away. But please, for Elsie's sake, don't do it until I get home."

Yeah. That might work.

Do I send now or later?

Now or later?

If I send now, she may be too distracted by Elsie to give me the time of day.

But then again, maybe distraction is what she needs.

There's a knock on my door just as I'm stepping out of the bathroom from my shower. Delivery of my room service. I gulp down a bottle of Gatorade and half a bottle of water and then dive into my extra thick burger.

Junk food never tasted so good.

The text can wait. This hangover has got to go.

Just as expected, practice today kicked my ass. My body hasn't felt quite right all day thanks to a night of bad decisions. I even thought I pulled a groin muscle when trying to block a shot today but thankfully, a few extra stretches and a muscle massage after practice helped ease the pain.

After my third shower of the day, a long dinner with the team, and another room service delivery because hangovers make me fucking hungry, I'm stuck staring at my phone trying to decide how I'm going to start this conversation with Ada. I avoided my phone all day not wanting to start something I either couldn't finish or didn't want to, but now, I need to check on Elsie and that means I also need to talk about last night.

"Ugh. There's no easy way to do this."

ME

Hey.

ADA

Hi Zeke.

ME

I'm so sorry I missed Elsie's bedtime. Long day. She okay?

ADA

Yeah she's great. We had a fun day of shopping and a lunch date and ended our night with a dance party in the kitchen. *Video of Elsie dancing to Taylor Swift* She woke up an hour ago not feeling well. She was a little fevered, but nothing some Tylenol and a good snuggle can't fix. She fell back asleep pretty easily.

I lean back on my bed with a heavy sigh. I hate not being with her when she's not feeling well.

ME

Her Uncle Dex would be proud of her Swift dancing. Wish I could've been there for her. Thanks for taking care of her for me. I really appreciate it.

ADA

Oh, you're definitely invited to the next dance party.

ME

Deal.

ADA

Flew cross-country today, huh?

ME

Yeah. Toronto last night and Vancouver today and tomorrow. Can't wait to be home.

ADA

It's definitely quieter at night without you here.

ME

Is that a good thing or a bad thing?

ADA

Neither good, nor bad, I suppose. Just a general observation. It's nice having someone to talk to. When you're not here, I have to talk to myself.

ME

You're pretty easy to talk to.

ADA

I like to think so. At least that's what I tell myself. 😊

ME

Soooo about last night.

ADA

Did you drink water and take Advil before going to bed? 😉

ME

What do you think?

ADA

Oh man. 😬 I think you probably woke up with one hell of a hangover.

ME

Bingo. Haven't felt that shitty in a long time.

ADA

As long as you enjoyed celebrating, sometimes it's worth what comes after.

ME

I enjoyed celebrating, but I acted like an immature prick and I owe you an apology.

ADA

For what? Seeing a few pictures of me that were in my room? The room I asked you to walk into?

ME

Among other things, yes.

ADA

It's really okay. You're a fun drunk. You had me laughing a good bit.

ME

I swear I didn't mean to snoop. I have the utmost respect for your privacy. The album really did fall to the floor when I accidentally knocked it off.

ADA

I believe you, Zeke.

ME

Okay. Good. That makes me feel a tiny bit better.

ADA

Can I ask you something?

ME

Of course.

ADA

Did you mean what you said?

ME

About...?

ADA

How I looked in those pictures?

The fact she's even asking me this question causes a

weird feeling to stir in my chest. Does she really think I would lie about something like that? Does she really care what I think?

ME

Just because I was drunk doesn't mean I wasn't being honest, Ada. In fact, if you want raw honesty...

I press send before finishing my sentence because straight up middle school fear has me by the balls right now. If I say what I'm thinking, it could shift things between us a little and I certainly don't want things to be any more uncomfortable than I've already made them. I would've thought she had those pictures taken for her husband, but the album had Kinsley's logo on the front so they had to have been taken relatively recently. Which means she did it after her husband had passed.

But then why?

For another man?

God, I could really be crossing the line if those pictures had anything to do with another man.

But fuck it. I have to be honest with her.

She deserves that.

ME

I didn't want to stop looking at them.

It takes a couple minutes for her reply to come through and I sit here holding my breath wondering if I said the wrong thing. Finally, the three little dots appear and she sends another message.

ADA

💜 That's sweet of you to say.

ME

Can I ask you something now?

ADA

Of course.

ME

You mentioned when we interviewed that you weren't seeing anybody…

ADA

Correct.

ME

I know those pictures weren't meant for me or my eyes obviously, but I saw Kinsley's logo on the front so you must've had them done in the time you've lived in Chicago?

ADA

Yes.

ME

Forgive me. I guess I'm struggling with the idea that you may have had them done for some other man who then didn't appreciate you or show you the kind of love you deserve since whoever that man may have been is no longer in your life.

She doesn't reply for quite some time and I really start to worry once again that I've overstepped.

"Shit."

ME

Ada?

ME

I'm sorry.

ME

Shit. I hope I didn't cross the line.

ME

Sometimes I don't think before I speak. I didn't mean it. I mean...I guess I did mean it, but if I hurt your feelings I apologize. Sincerely.

ADA

You didn't hurt my feelings Zeke.

ME

Thank fuck. I've literally been holding my breath.

ADA

Don't ever apologize for telling me how you feel. What you said was so sweet it made me cry.

ME

Oh shit. I didn't mean to make you cry!

ADA

It was the good kind of cry. Not the bad kind. So, it's okay. And since you're being honest, I'll be honest too.

ME

Okay.

ADA

I didn't have those pictures taken for anyone but myself. After I lost Luke I kind of fell into this hole of self-doubt and depression. Getting back on the horse and putting myself back out there again isn't something I ever thought I would have to do once we got married.

ME

I understand that feeling more than you know.

ADA

Yeah. So, when I met Kinsley and we became friends, she encouraged me to come in and have it done. She knew what it would do for my own self confidence and she was right. She helped me look at myself in the mirror again and realize how desirable I am. And that I have something to offer to a new partner if that's what I want.

Desirable is right.

ME

Is it?

ADA

Is it what?

ME

Is it what you want? A new partner?

I don't know why I'm so goddamn nervous asking her that. It's not like we're together. The asshole part of me doesn't want her to find someone else because that would mean the end of our arrangement. The end of being

Elsie's live-in nanny. It'll be bad enough when she finds someone but to have to see him around, touching her? Loving on her? Especially after I've seen her body in those pictures...

Blech.

No thanks.

A man can only take so much before he cracks.

The non-asshole part of me, though...the single guy who now lives with a hot single nanny...

The single guy who knows he's attracted to her...

Yeah.

Sometimes he wonders what it would feel like if something were to happen between them.

ADA

> I don't know. I've been alone for three years. At this point, I think Luke would be sad to know I haven't even tried to talk to someone else. I also think sharing life with someone you love is always better than being alone.

ME

> Yeah.

ADA

> So, I guess by my own logic I'll need to put myself out there eventually.

ME

> Yeah.

ADA

> But please don't think I'll ever leave Elsie. I love her to pieces so you're stuck with me. 😊

ME

That's not a terrible thing, Ada 😄 We're happy to have you.

And that's not a lie.

For the first time in what feels like an exceedingly long time, life feels relatively happy. Seeing Elsie happy makes me happy. Ada's presence around the house makes me happy. Watching baseball with her late at night makes me happy. Having her around for any kind of conversation makes me happy. Seeing her wildly made-up face that would scare anyone on the street but she encourages it because it makes my kid happy...yeah that makes me happy. Laughing with her makes me happy.

I enjoy coming home from work because I know she'll be there.

I smile when I think about her.

And I haven't smiled thinking about a woman since long before Lori left.

That has to mean something.

Right?

The alarm goes off on my phone but I've already been up for the past two and a half hours. After texting with Ada last night, I had a tough time calming down enough to go to sleep. She had invaded my mind for too long. I couldn't get visions of her out of my head.

Laying across the bed of white.

Her soft hair haloed around her.

Her eyes penetrating me with a wanton stare.

She wanted me.

She desired me.

At least, that's how it appeared in the picture. As if I was her photographer and she was calling me to her. Her yearning stare like a siren's song. I'm not too proud to say it. I didn't fall asleep last night until I was buck naked with jizz coating my stomach and chest. My dick finally getting the release it was begging for.

With nothing but restless energy when I woke up, I braved the hotel gym hoping nobody would recognize me. Luckily at five o'clock in the morning, nobody else was up and I had the place to myself to run through an early morning gameday warmup. A warmup I was able to easily accomplish because I'm riding a high that is Ada Lewis.

By all means, I have no reason to be.

Sure, we texted last night.

Yeah, we both said pleasant things, but that's as far as it went.

Nothing specific was spoken between us. I didn't profess my undying devotion to her or anything. But last night, things felt right.

They felt good.

And then I felt good.

My dick felt good.

Gulping down the rest of my electrolytes, I dry some of the sweat from my face and then open my hotel room door so I can hit the showers before we bus to the arena. I turn on the shower head and peel out of my workout clothes. The heat of the water feels amazing on my screaming muscles. I make quick work of washing my face and my hair and then squirt a generous portion of soap onto my washcloth, working it into a lather for my body. When I finish scrubbing myself I stand under the water and close my eyes. The heat and steam renew my body with energy and anticipation for the day ahead.

I think through the day, tonight's game, and then to our plane ride home.

Will she wait up for me tonight?

Will she be smiling when I walk through the door?

"Ada."

My head falls back at the thought of her.

The sound of her voice when she laughs.

Her genuine smile.

Her cute messy bedhead after she first wakes up and comes downstairs for coffee.

Her enthusiasm for sports.

The love she has for her brother.

The love she has for Elsie.

The comfort she seems to have with me.

I don't have to look down to know my dick is hard and aching for release again. I reach for the soap bottle and squeeze some into my palm. With one hand braced against the tiled shower wall, I wrap my soaped fist around my stiff shaft and let out a long, contented sigh as I slowly begin to stroke myself.

"Ada." Her name is a sweet whisper from my lips as I pump my hand up and down my hardened length, squeezing tighter every time I bring my fist down. As if I'm pushing myself into her tight warm body. Connecting myself to her.

"Fuuuck."

I bow my head and squeeze my eyes closed, capturing as much of a mental picture as I can of a stunningly beautiful Ada sprawled out in front of me, her thighs squeezing me tightly, holding me against her as I push inside her again, and again, and again.

"Mother fucker."

I envision Ada's sweet lips covering my cock, her tongue circling the tip and then taking me in all the way until I'm touching the back of her throat.

"God, yes."

My hands in her hair, woven around my fingers as I fuck her mouth.

She makes me feel so good and she doesn't even know it.

This is the release I've needed.

The release I've looked forward to.

The release I knew she would cause me to seek out.

My balls tighten and my chest heaves and then I'm coming with a long satisfied guttural groan.

"Sweet fucking hell, Ada. What are you doing to me?"

10

ZEKE

We're on the ice for our last night in Vancouver and the energy in the arena is high. My warmup stretches before the game were solid and my body feels good going into tonight. Much better than yesterday. As the team runs through their drills I focus on my own warm-up. Gliding back and forth, shuffling from one foot to another in quick succession and sliding along the ice with one leg outstretched and then the other. I bend at the waist and stretch my hamstrings and then drop to my knees for a groin stretch, putting as much pressure on my inner thighs as I can.

"Lookin' good Sir Humps-a-Lot!" Dex smiles as he skates around me. "Puttin' on a good show for the ladies, I see."

"Yep," I answer with a chuckle I know he can't hear. "Just needed to cool off my nuts before the big game, Foster. They're so large, you see. I wouldn't want to set them on fire with the friction and all."

"I don't know. Swollen nuts sounds a like a problem for a doctor to solve."

"Nah, they're not swollen. Just weighed down by all of my offspring for your mom to suck down later."

Dex cackles at my teasing. "Right. Hey, more power to you, man." He skates off laughing as I finish my stretches and prepare to block a few warmup shots. I feel good.

Loose.

Comfortable.

Ready to win this game and get home to my ladies.

I haven't stopped thinking about Ada since last night. Well, in all honestly, she's all I've thought about since before we left town, but she's been a constant on my mind since we talked last night. She was on my mind when I came all over myself before falling asleep and she was on my mind again when I jizzed in the shower this morning. She's definitely taking over my every thought. Without going too far in depth about our personal lives, I was able to learn why she had those boudoir pictures taken and how she feels about getting back on the horse, so to speak, in terms of her dating life. Hearing her say she didn't have those pictures taken for another man calmed this odd rage-y feeling in my chest and replaced it with curiosity.

Wonder.

Intrigue.

I'm probably crazy for even considering the idea of something happening between Ada and me. She's my kid's nanny for Christ's sake. But I can't help it. She's infiltrated my mind and I have a feeling she's there to stay.

The middle of the second period has us in the lead three to two. The Vancouver Wolves are a strong team this season but I'll be damned if I allow another fucking puck into my net. At the next face off, Landric shoots the puck to Malone who goes wide around the net giving possession to Foster. Dex launches it forward but Vancouver blocks his attempt. He chips the rebound back toward the net but it's blocked again.

"Come on, guys."

Ovchevik steals the puck for Vancouver and it's passed back and forth as the play comes my way. Shay tries to take control but he's checked by Rowling. Cornell snaps the puck narrowly missing the net when it banks off my pads. I shift back and forth from one leg to the next as the fight to get the puck in our net heightens. Rowling is on it again, shooting from my left, but I drop to my knees and butterfly my legs for the block, my groin muscle pulling slightly as I go down.

"Fuck!"

Vancouver is relentless in their pursuit of their next goal. The pressure is all on me to block each and every attempt they make while my guys fight like hell to retake possession. There's a flurry of activity around the net as the guys on both teams are shouting at one another, their sticks slamming together trying to grab the puck. Ovchevik leads the Wolves around the net to my right and I'm fast on my feet shifting sides and extending my right pad to block his shot.

And that's when all hell breaks loose.

I'm pushed back into the net, my leg still in its extended position and something in my upper thigh twists.

"AH! Fuck!"

I fall forward on the ice, the muscle in my right upper thigh spasming on the inside.

"Shit!"

"Whoa, whoa whoa!" I hear Nelson shout. "He's down. Miller's down!"

I hear a whistle blow as my team surrounds me.

"Zeke, you okay?" Nelson asks from his knees in front of me. "Talk to me."

Trying to catch my breath and not panic, I slam my hand down on the ice. "My leg! Fuck! It's my leg."

Milo's hand is on my back and he motions for our team trainers and medical staff. "Groin pull?"

"I don't know." I groan. "Maybe. It fucking hurts."

Jason, my personal team trainer, is next to me in a matter of seconds. "Talk to me, Zeke."

"I overextended Jason. Fuck! I think it's my groin. Inner thigh. I can feel it throbbing. Like it's twisted inside and seizing."

"Alright sounds like a muscle spasm. We need to get you off the ice. Do you think you can move it?"

"If I try, it might be the first time you see me cry, man."

"We've got him," Colby tells Jason. He and Milo reach down together, picking me up and guiding me off the ice on one skate so I can allow my injured leg to be as motionless as possible.

"You've got this, Miller. You're going to be okay, man."

I cringe and say nothing as I'm passed off to the training team.

Fucking fuck.

The medical team gets me undressed and onto the examination table so Jason can quickly diagnose the problem. All the while, a million thoughts are surging through my head.

Are we winning yet?

Was Ray warmed up enough to take my place?

How could I have been so goddamn stupid?

Did I not stretch enough?

How does a fucking muscle twist itself that easily?

What the hell did I do?

Am I out?

How many games?

Shit. Was this it?

Is this an injury I can't come back from?

Did I just end my hockey career with a fucking groin injury?

Am I going to need a cane?

I'm not walking with a fucking cane for the rest of my life.

I do not want a goddamn nurse in my house.

Unless her name is Ada.

Fuck...Elsie.

Did she see me get hurt?

Were they watching?

What time is it in Chicago?

Fuck!

I have to make it back to the ice.

"Jason." I grit my teeth as he palpates my right thigh. "Fuck, that hurts."

"Yeah, I know," he says softly. "I can feel it."

"What's going on?"

"The good news is I think you just over-extended and twisted the muscle. It's definitely kinked a bit and that's what you feel spasming."

"It's never done that before. Why now?"

He shakes his head. "Hard to tell until we do an MRI. Could be a weakening groin muscle that could cause you bigger problems later. Or it could just be a fluke and you went down the wrong way and it's seizing."

"So, I can get back in the game?"

He huffs a laugh. "Can you play on one leg?"

"Fuck you, asshole."

"That's what I thought. You're done for the night."

Not what I wanted to hear.

I squeeze my eyes closed. "And then?"

He's quiet as he gently pulls my leg out to the side. I wince and inhale a sharp breath as he stretches me. "Can you bring your leg back in?" he asks as he adds a bit of resistance. He watches as I follow his instruction and nods. "Good. How much does that hurt?"

"Like a fucking bitch."

"Okay. That's enough." He massages my thigh, trying to knead through the kink in my muscle and add compression to the pained area. "I think we get you into an ice bath and then reassess in the morning assuming the pain goes away. If it's just a kink, and I'm thinking that's what it is, the pain should subside relatively quickly. Like getting a

Charlie horse. But if the pain persists throughout the night, we have bigger fish to fry."

"I hate fish, Jason."

He gives me a sympathetic smile and squeezes my leg. "I know you do, Zeke. I promise I'm going to do all I can to get you back on that ice, but you need to promise me you won't push it too soon. In case nobody has said it lately, you're no spring chicken."

"I love you too, man," I tell him with two middle fingers.

Five and a half hours later, though who knows what time it really is here in Chicago, I'm finally home. I considered getting a hotel room for the night so I wasn't coming home late and scaring Ada or Elsie, but damn, I sure could use a good night's sleep in my own bed tonight. My leg feels better but it's still sore. I hate that I'm babying it as much as I am but I need to get back on that ice. Tomorrow is going to kill me if Coach puts me on the injured list.

"Hey." I hear her before I see her. Dropping my bags by the door I look up to see Ada walking over from the living room, a concerned look on her face.

"What are you doing up?"

She looks at me like I'm crazy. "Are you kidding? I've been worried sick since you were taken off the ice."

"I told Carissa to text you."

"She did. That doesn't mean I'm going to go to bed like

I don't give a shit, Zeke. You're hurt. What can I do to
help?"

By all means I get that I should probably be thankful
she gives a shit about my wellbeing but after the emotions
of the night, the adrenaline spike followed by the energy
drop, the pain and relative fear of the unknown, I'm just
not in the mood to be the nice guy.

"Nothing. I just want to go to bed."

"Okay. I'll get your bags for you." She steps forward but
I hold out my arm to stop her.

"Just leave it."

"No, it's fine. Don't worry. I can—"

"I said leave it, Ada!"

She freezes and stares at me wide-eyed and taken
aback. As if I just hit her. For a moment I feel bad but it's
been a long fucking day and I need time alone in the solace
of my own room so I can process all the shit going on in my
head. Without saying another word, I forget about the
drink I was going to have and cautiously walk up the steps
and into my room. Shutting the door behind me, I exhale a
long breath and rub the tension from my forehead.

Sleep.

I just need sleep.

Tugging off my clothes, I toss them in the hamper and
sit down on the edge of my bed. I turn my body one leg at a
time, my left leg sliding under the covers with no problem,
my right leg reminding me it hasn't had the best night when
I lift it. I take my last waking minutes to replay part of the
night in my head, trying to remember exactly what I did
that caused this stupid injury. It's not like I haven't made
the same move in my pads hundreds of times.

Was I not warmed up enough?

Did I forget a stretch or two?

Whatever it was I can only attribute the fact I'm lying here with an injury that will undoubtedly keep me out of our next game to one thing.

No. Not really one thing.

One person.

Ada Lewis.

Perhaps had I not been so hung up on her these last few days I wouldn't have been distracted. I would've made certain my body was ready for tonight's game and I wouldn't be lying here in bed with an injury I possibly could have avoided.

Yeah, that's right, asshole.

Blame Ada.

This is all her fault.

I know it's not.

But tonight, I'm too defeated to deal with it.

Tonight, I just need someone else to blame.

"Daddyyyyy!" Elsie's piercing scream stirs me from my sleep. "Daaaaddy!" Her cries echo down the hallway. I'm so damn groggy it takes me a hot second to realize Elsie really is crying for me.

"I'm coming!" I try to spring out of bed to run to Elsie's room but am forced to slow down when my leg doesn't move as fast as I want it to. Wondering if she's sick or if she's had a bad dream, I pull my door open, and step out to get to her. Then remember I'm in my underwear.

Ada.

Shit.

Trying to do the gentlemanly thing, I spin back around to grab my pajama pants and that's when it happens.

The same fucking muscle in my leg seizes and starts to spasm and I'm helpless and on the floor, cringing in pain all over again.

"Fuck!"

"Daaaddy!"

Ada's bedroom door swings open and she flies into the hallway.

"Elsie?" She looks toward Elsie's room ready to run there when she hears me cursing on my bedroom floor.

Her brows furrow as she takes in the sight of me on the floor, in my underwear, gasping in pain, and she turns back toward my room. "Oh, my God, Zeke. Are you—"

"I'm good," I pant, holding my leg.

I'm so not good.

"I'll be fine."

Pretty sure that's a lie.

She shakes her head, crouching down near me. "But you're—"

"Elsie." I wave her off in the direction of Elsie's bedroom. "Check on Elsie. Please! She needs you."

Ada nods and all I can do is watch helplessly as she quietly enters my daughter's bedroom. I hear a few mumbles between them but can't hear what they're saying. I hear Ada singing a song I don't recognize and then there are a few quiet moments. I take the time to pull myself back toward my bed, resting against the side of the mattress before Ada is back in the hallway pulling Elsie's door closed.

Her sympathetic eyes meet mine and she sees the pain I'm enduring. She's on her knees beside me in an instant. "What can I do? Should I call nine-one-one?"

"Is she okay?"

"Yeah. She's fine. Bad dream. She's still getting over that little virus she had, so I gave her a little Tylenol to help take the edge off and sang her back to sleep. She's all good. Tell me what I can do."

I shake my head. "No. I'll be okay." I hiss through my teeth. "I can do it."

"BULLSHIT." Her stare pierces me. "You're not yelling at me again. It's okay to ask for help and I'm right here. Tell me what to do, Zeke."

My head falls back against the side of the mattress. "I just need—"

"What? What do you need? Talk to me."

Finally relenting, I gesture to the inside of my right thigh. "Pressure. It's a muscle kink and Jason held it as tightly as he could."

"Pressure," Ada repeats as if she's psyching herself up for the job. She lays her hands on my thigh, gripping the inside as tightly as she can. "Like this?"

"Yeah."

I want to close my eyes and pretend I am not sitting here in the darkness of my goddamn bedroom with the hot nanny's hands dangerously close to my dick, because if I so much as look at her right now, even though I'm in pain...

Fuck.

Do not think about it, Miller.
For the love of Christ think about literally anything else!

11

ADA

My heart is thumping in my chest.

I literally have my hands wrapped around Zeke's thigh, gripping as tightly as I can as he breathes through the pain. Wearing nothing but a pair of black Calvin Klein boxer briefs, his entire body is on display. Even in the darkness, with only the glow of the hallway light illuminating part of his room, I can see the broadness of his chest and the ridges of his abs. Good Lord, even when he's not trying, the guy has the body of a God.

"Is this too much? Am I squeezing too hard?"

"No. It's good. It's fine."

"Okay. Got it. We're good." I hear my pitch changing like I'm trying to calm a child.

Shit.

Why am I nervous all of a sudden?

"Then what? What did he do next?"

Zeke looks at me apprehensively, swallowing before he answers. "H-he massaged the..." He swallows again. "Jason, he uh, massaged the muscle until the spasm stopped."

SUSAN RENEE

Why does he look nervous?

Is he nervous too?

Because I'm touching him?

Oh God, I'm touching him.

Like...touching, touching him.

And he's barely wearing any clothes.

Oh, my God, I'm dangerously close to his penis.

Don't touch the penis, Ada.

Steer clear of the penis.

And stop thinking about it.

We can't both be nervous.

You can do this.

You can take care of him.

He's in pain.

He needs this.

"Yeah. Okay. Massage the penis."

His eyes fling open. "What?"

"What?" I repeat, my eyes bulging, shocked at my slip of tongue. "No! I mean *muscle.* Massage the muscle. Not the penis. Fuck! Who massages a penis? Nobody massages a penis." I stumble over my own words, apparently unable to control what comes out of my mouth. "Oh God. I'm sorry. Sorry. I'm so sorry Zeke." My hands start to shake as I dig into his thigh, applying pressure to his kinked muscle.

God, please don't fire me after this.

"You're doing fine, Ada," he says surprisingly calmly.

Pshh. He thinks I'm doing fine. Me on the other hand? I've somehow become a hot mess of unsettled energy. My stomach is fluttering, my mouth is dry, and I feel like I'm starting to sweat.

Zeke Miller's groin is literally in my hands and if some-

140

thing goes wrong or I move the wrong way, I could be the reason he doesn't get to play and I don't know if I can handle that. Not to mention the fact that—oh, my God! What was that?

Was that his penis?

Did I just touch his penis?

Did I seriously just brush my hand along Zeke Miller's penis?

It was hard.

His penis is hard.

Oh, my God. What do I do?

Do I apologize or just pretend it didn't happen?

He chuckles. "You definitely don't apologize, Ada."

Wait.

"What?"

He huffs a laugh again, watching me with a look of amusement. "You know you've been speaking out loud for several minutes, right?"

"What? I have?" I shake my head, my whole body starting to quiver now. "N-n-no, I haven't."

"Zeke Miller's groin is literally in my hands," he repeats my words right back to me and holy fucking shit I think I could throw up right now. The look of embarrassment and utter dread I give him makes him laugh even harder but this time he reaches up, sliding his hand into my hair, and cups the side of my face. Butterflies flutter through my stomach in a frenzy as he studies me for a moment. An awkward moment, where we're both staring at each other. And then he caresses my cheek with his thumb and I don't know how in the hell he's suddenly so calm. My heart is beating so fast it feels like it could literally fly out of my chest.

God, I'm dying to know what he's thinking .

"You're adorable when you're nervous."

"Me?" I squeak. "Who said anything about being ner —" He stops me with his lips as his mouth covers mine

Oh, my God. Zeke is kissing me!

He's tentative at first, soft, slow. Like he's testing me, wondering if I'll give in to him or push him away. Like he's waiting for me to catch up. I have to admit, he's totally caught me off guard. I'm on my knees beside him, both hands grasping his thigh, and he's kissing me.

And I'm not backing away.

"Ada." He breathes my name against my lips and my breath catches in my throat. The way he says my name, with reverence and lust, sends a spark right through me and warms me in places I should not be thinking about right now. He takes full advantage of my silence, gripping my hair tighter, his fingers grasping. He presses his lips harder against mine but still he's tender.

I moan ever so softly against his mouth and it's like I flipped a switch on him that I didn't know existed. He wraps an arm around my body and lifts me across his lap so that I'm straddling him and oooh shit, when I said he was hard I had no idea he was this hard. An involuntary gasp falls from my lips and when I feel just how aroused he is I whimper in response. He slides his hand down my back to my ass and rocks me hard against him. We're like two teenagers making out fully clothed on his bedroom floor. Well, okay, I'm wearing clothes. Also, I'm pretty damn sure I'm about to get lost in Zeke Miller.

"Zeke, your leg." It's all I can get out with all the

breathing and panting and kissing and moaning going on between us, but I don't want to hurt him.

"Shut up. I know what I'm doing."

"And just what are you doing?"

He rocks me against his hard cock again. "What does it look like?"

At this point I don't give a damn what it looks like because I only care what it feels like.

And. It. Feels. So. Damn. Good.

I need this.

I want this.

If he's going to let me take it, then dammit, I'm here for it.

I rock myself against his cock this time, his hand palming the side of my head as he licks inside my mouth with an urgent but gentle tongue. Every stroke in time with my movement against him pretending his tongue is striking my clit every time I rock forward.

"Yes," I moan into his ear, my arms wrapped around Zeke's neck as my covered tits rub against his heated chest. My pebbled nipples begging to be touched.

"Zeke..." I'm so close. It's been too long since a man has given me this much pleasure and I can't hold back. My legs squeeze his waist as I grind against him trying like hell to reach my desperate release.

"Fuck, Ada." He grabs my ass and pulses me against his hardened shaft and I'm right there. Fully clothed and not a hand anywhere except my ass, this man is about to make me come and it's all that I want. All that I need. It's everything. My orgasm climbs up my body, my legs feeling the burn from my movements.

"Oh, my God, Zeke," I pant, leaning back and riding him as hard and fast as I can. He leans forward and captures my nipple between his teeth and I snap. Something inside me clenches and releases and I'm coming with more force than I ever remember.

"Oh...my...God. Yessss."

He continues to move me over his cock, his entire body quivering, and then he throws his head back against the mattress. "Ahh...fuck." His cock twitches between my legs and I know he's reached his climax. I can feel his cock as it throbs between us. He brings a hand to the back of my head as it rests on his shoulder, his fingers stroking through my hair. Both of us in a state of relaxed satisfaction, my thoughts go directly to Zeke and his pain.

"Are you—"

He doesn't let me finish my sentence. His hands cup my face and his mouth covers mine again in a slow tender kiss.

Like he's claiming me.

Or thanking me?

Shit. Did I misread this entire thing?

What does this mean?

Our lips separate and our foreheads touch but I stay silent, not sure what he wants to have happen next.

"Fuck, I needed that," he whispers against me, brushing his nose with mine.

"Yeah," I mutter. "I guess I did too."

And then it hits me.

This was the first time in three years I sought out an orgasm where I wasn't alone.

The first time in three years I reached an orgasm in front of someone else.

Because the last person to help me get there was Luke. My husband.

And now I've just dry humped Zeke Miller. My boss.

Oh, God.

What have I done?

"Uh, I should...go," I say, backing off of Zeke's lap carefully, praying I haven't added to his injury.

"Wait—"

"I'm sorry, Zeke." I shake my head, backing toward the door.

His brows furrow but his eyes grow large. "Ada, why are you—"

"I shouldn't have...we shouldn't...I didn't..." I continue to shake my head, ashamed, embarrassed. "I'm sorry."

"Ada."

"Good night, Zeke."

And then I'm out of his darkened room, stepping down the hall and into my room where I close my door quietly and sink to the floor as a flood of tears runs down my face.

"I'm sorry, Luke. I'm so sorry."

Elsie's giggles ring out from the kitchen where we are happily enjoying breakfast. She's definitely feeling a little better this morning, which is great. Me on the other hand? I'm not sure how I'm standing upright since I'm fairly sure I've only had about three hours of sleep, but I didn't have a choice to sleep in. Being here for Elsie is my job. Even if her dad kept me up last night doing things I'm certainly regretting now.

Except that it felt good.

So good.

And I miss feeling good.

It's been a long time.

I don't have any right to be upset with Zeke. Last night was as much my fault as it was his. I could have said no and I didn't. I could have stopped it, but I didn't want to.

I wanted him.

And I wanted to feel again.

"Daddy! You're back!" I look up from the eggs I'm making on the stove and Zeke is standing in the doorway. He's dressed in a pair of black pajama pants and a Red Tails t-shirt. I was sure to give Ada a small heads up about her daddy's injury so she wouldn't pummel him in excitement this morning and hurt him even more. On any normal morning, she would run to him and jump into his arms. This time though, she stops short and pets his thigh like she's petting an old dog which makes me chuckle to myself. "Is your leg hurting bad, Daddy?"

He doesn't hesitate to lean over and lift her up into his arms, her little legs dangling around his waist. "First of all, I need a great big monster-sized hug because I missed my baby girl so, so, sooo much."

Elsie giggles when he squeezes her tightly to his chest. "I missed you too, Daddy."

"Ada said you had the sniffles. How are you feeling this morning?"

"Good. Ada gave me medicine last night when I waked up."

"I'm really glad that helped you sleep. I bet you needed it. Were you a super good girl while I was gone?"

"Mmhmm! And guess what?"

"What?"

"Ada taked me to the animal place and we petted all the puppies and the kitties and even Mr. Purrito!"

My brow pinches. "Mr. Purrito?"

"Yeah!"

I finally make eye contact with him and tell him that Mr. Purrito is my favorite cat from the animal shelter.

"Well, I'm really glad you got to make some new furry friends. Did you just eat your breakfast?"

"Yep. Ada made me eggs and toast and bananas and chocolate milk!"

"She did?"

Usually, breakfast is a bowl of cereal and maybe a piece of fruit but I needed something to keep my hands busy this morning so she got a special breakfast.

"Mhmm! Can I color my picture now, Daddy?"

Zeke spies the open coloring book and crayons on the table where Elsie was sitting earlier. "Of course. But I need a kiss first." He points to his cheek. "Right here."

She places a big sloppy kiss on his cheek and then he lowers her back to the ground and watches her scurry away to her coloring. On the other side of the table, he spies the contents of his gym bag.

The bag he told me to leave by the front door last night.

Everything from inside the bag has been washed and is now neatly folded and piled on the table because, again, I needed something to distract me this morning while Elsie snuggled on the couch and watched a television show.

I see the guilt that washes over him when he catches my eye. He gestures to his bag with his head and whispers, "Thank you."

I give him a kind nod and a coy smile because I am so out of my element right now and have no idea how I'm supposed to act or what I'm supposed to say.

Am I supposed to acknowledge what happened between us last night or pretend it didn't happen?

"Ada." Zeke steps forward shaking his head. "I'm so—"

"It's fine, Zeke. Really. Everything's...fine."

He was going to say sorry.

He regrets it too.

I knew it.

I grab a rag and begin to obsessively clean the counters, trying my best to mask my disappointment. "It was late and you had a rough night. Would you like some eggs?"

God, why does he have to look so...confused? Hurt? Worried?

Please don't make this weird.

"Uh, yeah. Sure. Thanks."

I gesture to the stools in front of the kitchen island. "Have a seat."

"Wow, he's out for the whole week?"

"At least," I report to Kinsley. "He said they told him it's not a muscle tear which is good news. It's just a slightly pulled muscle and they want him out for the week before they reassess."

"Damn, how's he taking it?"

"Uh..."

How can I put this?

"Do you have a minute?"

"Of course, Silly. We're both sitting here, aren't we?"

I told Zeke I needed to run errands today and he told me he would spend the day with Elsie since he now has a few days off. I didn't mention that one of my errands was coffee with Kinsley. What he doesn't know won't kill him, I suppose.

"I need to tell you something."

"Uh oh. Is this a good something or a bad something?"

I shrug and bob my head. "Uh...I guess maybe both?"

A sly grin spreads across her face. "Oooh this ought to be good. Spill the tea, my friend."

"Okay, so, last night when Zeke came home, I waited up because I wanted to know about his injury."

"Okay."

"He came in the door and of course was grumpy. I mean, rightfully so. He kind of scolded me when I offered to help him."

Her face contorts. "What the fuck? Did you put him in his place?"

"Noooope. Buuuut umm...I may or may not have dry humped him." I cringe and cover my face haphazardly with my hand.

Kinsley nearly spits her drink all over the table. "Girl! What? You did WHAT? Oh, my God!" She laughs. "You tell me every fucking detail right now."

"Okay so long story, short, Elsie had a bad dream last night and Zeke and I were both trying to get to her but—"

"But then your bodies collided in the hallway so you dry-humped before you got to her?"

I snicker. "No!"

"Oh okay. 'Cause that would've been hilarious to witness. Just saying. Please continue."

"His groin muscle spasmed again and he fell in his bedroom. So, I got Elsie back to sleep and then ran to help Zeke and he asked me to do what his medical staff did which was apply pressure and then massage the muscle until it stopped spasming."

Kinsley sits back in her chair, admiring me as she takes another slow sip of her coffee. "So, you had your hands on his groin? Way to go, friend. Score one for Ada."

"Yeah. Only I got really nervous because come on. It wasn't just any groin muscle in my hand. It was Zeke Miller's, you know? Star goalie for the Red Tails and that came with all sorts of pressure in and of itself. And then before I knew it he was chuckling and then laughing at me because I was nervous and then he kissed me."

"Aaaand then you dry-humped him? Sounds like it escalated pretty quickly." She laughs.

I bob my head. "Well, it's not like that was my plan all along! He kept kissing me and when I didn't stop him he shifted me over his lap and holy shit, Kinsley, he was...you know..."

"Hard as stone? Erect-a-mungo? Achingly bulbous?"

"Ew, don't say bulbous. But also, yes. All of those things."

"Sounds like he enjoyed the groin massage. How did he

sit there and hump you with a pulled groin muscle though?"

"Wellll..." I cringe embarrassed to have to admit, "I may have done most of the humping." I palm my forehead. "I tried to make sure I wasn't hurting him, but he told me to shut up and that he knew what he was doing and then there we were making out like teenagers."

"Oh, my God. That's fantastic!"

"No! Not fantastic, Kins."

"What? Why?"

"Because!"

"Because why?" She stares me down and when I don't answer, she adds, "Give me a reason."

"Because I...I..."

She goads, twirling her finger. "Use your words here, Babe. Because you...what?"

"Because the last man to give me an orgasm was my husband. So last night came with a shit ton of regret."

Kinsley's shoulders deflate as she watches me from across the table. She slides her hand over mine and squeezes. "Ada, it's been three years."

"I know."

"You've grieved. You've moved on with your life. You've started over, Sweetie. And I don't say those things like I don't think you should ever think of him again. Certainly, you're always going to love Luke. What you had together...he was your first love."

"He was." I nod, feeling the tears build up in my eyes.

"But Ada." She leans forward and squeezes my hand even harder "Look at me."

When I finally allow myself to make eye contact she says matter-of-factly, "But he does not have to be your last."

I don't respond with words. Only a head nod that I understand what she's saying.

"Can I ask you something?"

"Yeah," I tell her.

"Did it feel good? Last night?"

I don't even have to think about my answer. "Yes."

"Did you enjoy it?"

"So much."

"Did he?"

"I thought so, but then this morning I think he tried to apologize which means he regretted it and—"

"Whoa, whoa, whoa. Not necessarily. Did he say he regretted it?"

"No."

"Then don't put words in his mouth. It sounds like you're trying to make yourself feel guilty about having a moment with him. Stop beating yourself up about it. Nothing you did last night was wrong and you certainly don't need to regret it or feel guilty about it. In fact, if any two people on this earth deserve to feel good, it's the two of you. You've both endured the loss of a loved one, just in two vastly different ways. So, if that means you work-out a little pent-up frustration together from time to time, then so be it."

"Why do you make it sound so easy?"

"Because it is." She chuckles. "Ada it's just sex. It's pleasure. It doesn't have to be super meaningful, but it can be if you want it to be. You two are adults. Live your lives however you want to. He's a great guy, Ada. A good man and a good father. Who knows? You could have the perfect life with him. And if you don't mind my saying so, I'm pretty damn sure Luke would want that for you."

Finally, a few tears spill over and run down my cheeks. "Do you really think so?"

"I know so. No way is Luke up there in Heaven looking down on you and wishing you were dried up and alone for the rest of your life. That's preposterous. Do you like Zeke?"

"He's my boss."

"That's not what I'm asking. I know he's your boss. I asked if you like him?"

I shrug, feeling the corner of my mouth lift. "I don't not like him."

She pats my hand with every word. "Then. Stop. Denying. Your. Own. Happiness."

I nod listening to her words and repeating them back to myself as silent affirmations.

"Thank you, Kinsley."

"You're welcome. Now get your ass home and get you some big D." She leans forward again and whispers, "It is big, right?"

I huff out a laugh. "Oh, my God. You have nooo idea."

12

ZEKE

It's been three days and we haven't talked about it.

Three long fucking days.

I can't stop thinking about Ada and what we did the other night. And because I'm off the ice for the week, I've been spending more time at home, which means we're around each other a lot. But even then we're not talking. What happened that night on my bedroom floor wasn't something I planned. It wasn't something I had ever thought about doing. But it happened. Thinking back on it, I find it hard to believe she even went along with it after how I treated her when I got home earlier that night.

I was a complete dick to her and she still came to my aid.

I was practically naked and she was still willing to touch me, to rid me of my pain.

I was an asshole yet she still let me kiss her.

She let me take her in my arms.

She made out with me like we were two horny teenagers because I encouraged it.

I wanted her.

I still want her.

But the longer these days go by and she doesn't acknowledge what's going on between us, the more discouraged I become.

Maybe she's just not that into me.

I guess I'm just as much at fault for us not talking as she is. Whenever there's down time in the house, when Elsie is napping or when she's gone to bed, I've made myself scarce. I've spent time watching hockey plays for the team. I've communicated back and forth via phone and email with my agent and the couple of charities I work with. I've been reading a romance book that Milo and Charlee recommended because Milo's right. Those books can tell guys exactly what women want if we're paying attention. And now? Now I'm about to fold laundry because I'm that desperate to hide from the one person I wish I could know better.

I know I should be a man and strut downstairs and refuse to leave her alone until she talks to me. But what if after finally growing my balls, she turns me down? What if she tells me she regrets what we did? What if she didn't like it? What if she was underwhelmed and disappointed? Or my biggest fear, what if she decides she doesn't want to be Elsie's nanny anymore because of me?

I don't want to be the guy who drives her away.

I don't like being the guy who crossed a line he had no business crossing, but I got caught up in the moment and went for it anyway. She was beautiful...and kind and...fuck, she was adorably nervous and now I think I'm attracted to everything about her.

So why am I upstairs holding a laundry basket in my hands instead of holding her?

Because I'm a scared dumbass, that's why.

I empty the dryer of the clean laundry inside it and carry the basket to my room to fold. Several of Elsie's outfits are in here along with a few of my gym pants and t-shirts. It's the rest of the contents of the basket that catches me off guard.

Panties.

Several pairs of panties.

They're soft. Like satin or silk.

Purple ones.

Red ones.

Black ones.

Pink ones.

Then there's red lace, white lace, black lace, and pale blue.

"Fuck, I picked the wrong load of laundry," I murmur to myself, admiring the pile of Ada's panties I just folded.

I'm trying to hide from Ada, not be reminded of her over and over again, so what the fuck am I doing?

Does she always wear panties like this?

Fuck me, now I'll always be imagining her in these panties.

I'd die to see her in any one of them.

And then I'd die again to rip any one of them off of her.

Picking up a few of the folded panties, I bring them to my nose and inhale deeply. They don't smell like her, obviously. They smell like laundry detergent and dryer sheets.

What did you expect perv?

Shit. I need to get out of here.

I need to talk to someone before this boils over.

She's making me crazy.

I need my family.

Leaving the rest of the laundry unfolded in the basket, I grab my keys and phone from my dresser and head downstairs where Ada and Elsie are hanging out. Or so I thought. When I turn the corner into the living room I see Ada sitting on the couch running her fingers through Elsie's hair as she sleeps on her lap. The sight of the two of them together like this is like a sucker punch to my gut all over again. Elsie loves Ada so much and I'm pretty damn sure, from the sight in front of me, that Ada would do just about anything for my kid. Ada brings a finger to her lips letting me know Elsie is asleep and I nod. I whisper to her that I've got to run into the arena quickly for a meeting and then I high-tail it out of there before the sweetness overload makes me do something I might regret.

Less than twenty minutes later and I'm pulling open the door to the gym where I know the rest of the guys will be.

"Miller?" Milo asks with a furrowed brow from his treadmill. "Didn't think we'd be seeing you here this morning."

"Yeah man, are you cleared?" Quinton asks.

"Not yet, but shit happened and I need to talk about it."

"Uh oh." Dex smirks from his treadmill sprints, sweat beading on his face. "Is this good shit or bad shit?"

I plop down on one of the nearby workout benches and sigh heavily. "Both."

"Girl problems," Hawken says. "Am I right?"

"How did you guess?"

He shrugs with a laugh. "Because it seems like anytime any one of us is stressed about a girl and needs to talk it out, we're in this gym."

"Of course we are." Colby nods. "This room is how we work through our frustrations. And it's a safe place to talk because we're the only ones in here." He turns to me. "The floor is yours, Zeke. What's on your mind?"

"Ada. Ada is on my mind."

"Iiii KNEW IT!" Dex beams. "We're fucking the nanny!"

The rest of the guys are about to tell Dex to shut the hell up but when I don't fight him on the subject they all turn to look at me.

Colby's brow lifts. "You're not saying anything, Zeke."

"Nope."

Silently he takes in my meaning and wipes a hand down his face. "So that's what happened? You and Ada?"

"We didn't fuck. Not exactly."

"Not exactly?" Dex chuckles, wiping his face with his towel. "Dude, I hate to tell you this but there is no not-exactly when it comes to fucking. You either did or you didn't."

"So dry humping on my bedroom floor in nothing but my underwear doesn't count?"

Dex cocks his head. "Dude, I'm sure it goes without saying if any part of either of you was dry, then no it doesn't count, but please explain. Inquiring minds want to know all the juicy...er...non juicy bits."

Milo backhands Dex in the chest. "Speak for yourself hornball." He looks back at me. "We don't need to know all the juicy bits, but you clearly came here to talk about it. So, tell us what's bothering you."

Quinton swings his leg over the bench I'm sitting on and joins me. "Yeah, did the uh, the dry hump not go well or something?"

"Just the opposite. Or so I thought," I tell them. "Long story short, Elsie had a bad dream and when I got up to run to her, my groin muscle kinked up again and I couldn't move so Ada got to her and took care of it and then came back to check on me."

"Were you naked, Miller?" Dex smirks. "This story would be fantastic if you were naked."

"No asshat. I wasn't naked."

"Damn."

"I said I was in my underwear."

Dex perks back up. "Okay! There's potential here. Continue."

Milo cringes because he's a half decent human who understands my pain. "And Ada?"

"Shorts and a t-shirt. Anyway, I had her do exactly what Jason did for me when I was off the ice. She put pressure on the muscle and then massaged it until it relaxed."

"Oh no." Milo chuckles. "Let me guess."

I bow my head, shaking it in disbelief. "Believe me I tried everything to not think about her hands being that close to my junk, but I couldn't stop thinking about it and before too long I was...you know."

Hawken claps my shoulder. "Bro, did you pop a boner in front of the nanny."

I nod. "I sure did and there was no stopping it. And then she accidentally brushed it with her hand when she was massaging and…" I start to chuckle. "It was adorable the way she completely freaked out and I suddenly had the urge to kiss her so I did. Then one thing led to another and I couldn't stop myself. I wanted her."

"And she didn't say no? She didn't deny you?"

"No."

Dex narrows his eyes. "I fail to see the problem here."

Standing from the bench, I start pacing across the floor. "Well, for starters when we…you know, finished, she didn't have much to say and then she got all apologetic and left and we haven't talked about it since."

"When was this?" Colby asks.

"Three fucking days ago."

"You guys made out in the middle of the night three days ago and you haven't so much as mentioned it?"

I shake my head. "Negative. I tried to bring it up the next morning but she skirted around the subject and we haven't talked since. What the fuck is that supposed to mean? Is she not into me? Did I do something wrong? I mean I know it wasn't full blown sex but—"

"You didn't do anything wrong Zeke," Quinton tells me.

"How do you know?"

He cringes. "Uh, well, because I live with Ada's best friend."

My head snaps to where Quinton is still sitting. "Wait, what? What does that mean? Have Ada and Kinsley been talking? About me? About us?"

He shrugs. "I mean, you were definitely the topic of conversation a few days ago according to Kinsley. They met for coffee the other day."

I flail my arms out to my sides. "And you didn't think you should tell me this?"

"Whoa, whoa, whoa." He lifts his hands in defense. "Listen, Kinsley is my person, but I don't tell her everything that is discussed in this room or between us as brothers, so I try to show her the same respect. Ada told Kinsley things that she mentioned to me, but this is between you and Ada. It's none of my business."

"Come on man, you have to tell me something. Don't keep me hanging here, Shay. What did she say? Wait, no." I squeeze my eyes closed. "You know what? Maybe I don't want to know. Do I want to know? Because if it's bad, then maybe it's better if I you don't tell me, but if it's good I want to—"

"Zeke?" he interrupts.

"Yeah?"

"Shut your pie hole." Quinton rolls his eyes and then releases a long sigh. "From the sounds of it she enjoyed things just as much as you did."

My shoulders relax and I release a huge sigh. "Thank you, Jesus."

"But she's feeling very guilty because of her husband."

Hawken's eyes practically pop out of his head. "Husband?"

"Late husband," I reassure him. "He passed away several years ago in the service."

"Oh." Hawk swipes his hand over his forehead. "Phew. You had me worried there for a minute."

"Yeah well that's the other problem I have."

"*You're* still married," Dex remembers, pointing at me. "See? I told you, you needed to get that shit taken care of."

"Yeah, I know. And trust me, the very next morning I fired off an email to my lawyer asking him what I could do about serving Lori with divorce papers when I haven't heard from her in years. I don't know how I'm supposed to find her when she clearly doesn't want to be found. I don't know enough about the law in Illinois to know whether three years away from each other means we're no longer married or not, but I've never signed anything so to me that means we're still legally together and if that's true, then I can't be a cheater. I won't."

Dex scowls. "Uh, why the fuck not? Lori left you and never looked back. It's possible she's slept with hundreds of men since then. Ada, on the other hand, is right fucking here and you two are clearly attracted to each other."

"You may be right about all those things, but I cannot and will not give Lori any fuel whatsoever to come after me for adultery. I won't allow her to take Elsie from me. I'll be damned if she ever lays eyes on her again. When Elsie is old enough and can decide for herself, I'll support whatever she wants to do but right now? No fucking way is Lori running in and out of her life whenever it conveniences her."

Colby folds his arms over his chest. "So, all the legal issues aside, do you feel like this thing with Ada is something you want to pursue?"

"I don't know. Yes? Maybe?" Rubbing my hands over my face, I inhale a deep breath and release it in one heavy sigh. "It's like she's taken over my mind, you know? I can't stop thinking about her. I want to be wherever she is. I want to spend time with her and get to know her more, but it's been so long since I've tried to pursue a girl. I'm a fucking shy teenager all over again."

Dex's brow lifts. "You weren't shy the other night."

"Right. But I've been literally hiding from her ever since."

"Then cut that shit out. Be a man and talk to her."

Hawken laughs and throws his towel at Dex. "Says the guy who found out the girl he couldn't stop thinking about all summer was carrying his child and then literally ran away from her."

"Fuck you Malone." Dex gives his best friend the middle finger. "I came around eventually."

"Dex is right," Quinton adds. "You don't want to keep hearing how Ada is feeling by talking to me or Kinsley. Ada needs the chance to explain her feelings to you and she needs to feel safe talking about it. I'm sure three years ago she never in a million years pictured her life being as it is now, life changes people."

"Three years ago, I didn't picture my life as a single dad, either.

Milo nods. "True. The good thing is, you two are both adults. And neither of you have done anything wrong, so take a deep breath and remind yourself it's okay to be attracted to each other. It's okay to have feelings for each other if that's what's happening. You're allowed to explore those feelings and decide for yourselves what you want."

"I guess you're right. I just need to bite the bullet and find some time to talk to her."

The door to the gym opens and Coach Denovah steps in with his clipboard in hand. He spots me with the guys and double checks his papers.

"Miller? You haven't been cleared yet have you? Did I miss something?"

"No, Sir. I uh...just needed to...uh...see Jason," I lie.

"Good. He's in the exam room now."

"Great. Thanks." I turn to my brothers and give them a half-hearted shrug and a quick roll of the eyes. "I'll see you guys later."

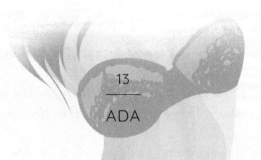

There's nothing better than picking up germs from a kid and then feeling ten times worse than she ever did...said no nanny ever.

Ugh. I should've known Elsie's fever would somehow morph itself into some nasty virus that I would end up with. I woke up feeling pretty great, but it's been downhill all day. The body aches and chills are the worst, and it sucks that no amount of clothing is keeping me warm enough. Zeke has been at the arena most of the day hoping to get cleared for play, but Elsie has been an absolute trooper helping to take care of me as much as a cute four-year-old can. Really that means snuggles on the couch, covering me with a blanket, and kisses on my arm telling me everything is going to be okay very soon.

And I believe it because Doctor Elsie said so.

The front door opens as I'm cleaning up the kitchen after dinner. Elsie runs to greet her dad, but I keep my distance. The last thing Zeke needs after recovering from an injury is to get sick.

"Daddy!"

"Elsie!" Zeke swings her up into his arms and she giggles. "How's my big girl?"

"Daddy, I'm Doctor Elsie and I'm making Ada all better."

"Why?" I hear him ask. "What's wrong with Ada? Where is she?" The genuine concern in his voice is heartwarming.

"I'm in the kitchen," I call out. "And I'm fine."

Elsie doesn't get the chance to answer Zeke before he makes it into the kitchen. Cocking his head he takes me in from head to toe as I stand in my sweatpants, heavy socks, long sleeved shirt, and a cardigan sweater. "Are you okay?"

"Yeah. I wave him off. I think I just caught whatever virus Elsie had. No big deal. I'm probably getting a cold."

I mean I kind of feel like absolute shit but I'm not going to tell you that.

"But you know..." I grab another Lysol wipe for the counter. "You should stay away from me just to be sure. I don't want to be the reason you don't get to play."

His brow furrows but then I ask, "Speaking of which, did you get cleared?"

"Monday. I'm back on Monday," he answers quietly, still watching me like he can't understand why I'm still upright.

I sniffle and then give him as much of a smile as I can muster. "That's great."

"Daddy?"

"Yes, babe?"

"We need to fix Ada."

"Oh, we do?"

"Mhmm."

"I think that would be a nice idea. What does Doctor Elsie think we should do?"

"Umm..." Elsie taps her cheek as she thinks. "She needs Mr. Rainbow-Bunny-Bunny-Rainbow."

Zeke's eyes grow and he gasps. "You know what? I think you're right. She does need Mr. Rainbow-Bunny-Bunny-Rainbow. Do you know where he is?"

Elsie nods excitedly as Zeke lowers her back to the floor. "Yes! He's on my bed. I'll be right back, Daddy!"

He watches her run from the room and then turns back to me. "Okay. She's out of ear shot. How are you really?"

"Who is Rainbow-Bunny-Bunny-Rainbow?"

"A stuffed animal. Please answer my question because no offense but you don't look so hot."

"Thanks for the compliment," I try to tease, but he doesn't laugh. "I'll be fine, Zeke. Really. It's probably just a cold."

"I highly doubt that."

"Why?"

"Because you are physically shivering right in front of my eyes. Do you not feel that?"

"I..." I sigh. "Yeah. I know. I'm just struggling to get warm."

He lowers his bag from his shoulder and unzips it. From inside he pulls out a red Chicago Red Tails hoodie and walks over to me. "Here, put this on."

I take a step back. "Zeke, no, you shouldn't get too—"

"Bullshit. You're sick and you're freezing, Ada. I'm not

going to just ignore that. Besides, I'm amped on all kinds of vitamins during the season. I'll be fine. Put this on." Something in my stomach flutters when he steps up to me and pulls the hoodie over my head and then holds it out for me to push my arms through. "I'm sorry I wore it earlier but just to get to the arena this morning. I promise it's clean."

It's ridiculously too big on me but it fits well over my other layers so that's a plus.

It smells just like him. A little laundry detergent, a little shower soap. That's a mega plus.

"Thank you, Zeke."

"Of course." He brings a hand to my forehead, his brows drawing together. "You're burning up, Ada. What else can I get you? Would you like some tea?"

I shake my head. "No. I had some earlier when I took some Tylenol."

"Did you eat something?"

"Elsie and I had chicken soup for dinner. I had a few bites."

Knowing that I've had something to eat and drink today seems to appease him at least a little bit.

He holds my face tenderly in his hands. "You should be resting."

"And who was supposed to explain that to the four-year old bundle of energy?"

He cocks his head again. The very edge of his lips turning up momentarily. "You could've called me."

"Not necessary. I promise I'm fine."

He stares at me for a few seconds before changing the subject. "Look, I know this is terrible timing given you don't feel well but I'd really like to talk about the other night."

"Here he is, Daddy!" Elsie exclaims, running back to the kitchen with a multi-colored stuffed rabbit in her arms.

Phew.

Saved by the child.

Zeke's shoulders fall, but he hides his frustration from Elsie and turns his attention to her. "Okay, well you'll have to introduce him to Ada and tell her all about him."

As Elsie brings me the bunny I crouch down so I'm on her level. "Who is this?"

"This is Mr. Rainbow-Bunny-Bunny-Rainbow," she says proudly. "I made him at the mall and he keeps me company when I feel yucky like you."

My eyes meet Zekes and he mouths, "Build-A-Bear."

Aaahhh.

"Wow Elsie! You made him all by yourself?"

"Mhmm! I put a heart in him and then I helped give him all the stuffings and look!" She squeezes the bunny's paw and Zeke's voice says, "I love you."

"Aww, that's so sweet, Elsie."

"Yeah and Mr. Rainbow-Bunny-umm, Bunny-Rainbow will help you get better!"

"I bet he's going to make me feel so much better really fast. Thank you for sharing him with me."

"Yeah! And Daddy will give you medicine and juice and he can snuggle you so you feel better too!"

"Oh. Uhh..." I'm not exactly sure what to say, but before I can politely bow out, Elsie grabs my hand.

"Come on!"

With me in one of her hands and her dad in the other, she leads us to the living room couch. She tells Zeke to sit down in the middle and then climbs up beside him on his left. Then she points to the empty seat on his right. "Now you sit there and Daddy will snuggle you so you feel better."

"That's really not necessa—"

"Doctor Elsie's orders, Ada," Zeke murmurs. He opens his arm over the top of the couch and then gestures with his head for me to sit next to him.

I have no idea what Zeke wanted to say to me about what happened the other night, but if he was going to tell me it should never have happened, to which I would agree, and now he's opening his arms to me, this could be all sorts of awkward.

His eyes never leave mine as I glance between him and Elsie.

"Come on, Sunshine. I promise not to bite."

Elsie giggles and nudges him. "Daddy, you're funny. You don't bite."

Okay, I'll do this for her.

And maybe a little for me because cuddling with Zeke does sound nice.

And because I really am freezing.

I take the seat next to Zeke, bringing my knees up to my chest and wrapping my arms around them. Zeke's strong arm reaches around me and pulls me against his warm body and if I didn't know any better I would think I was in Heaven right now.

"Comfortable?"

"Yeah," I whisper.

"Warm enough?"

"Not yet. But I'm sure I will be."

Zeke tugs the throw blanket from the back of the couch. "Hey Else, will you help me put this over Ada so she can be warm?" She hops down from the couch and helps as her dad places the throw over me one-handed. His other hand never leaves my side.

"Better?" he murmurs.

"Yes. Thank you. And Thank you Elsie."

I am physically wrapped up in Zeke's comforting scent and for the first time today I feel like it would be okay if I let go a little and tried to relax. It's been a long time since I've been held by a man in a way that made me feel safe. He's not trying to put a move on me. He's not trying to sneak inappropriate or flirty touches. He's simply being a good man and I can appreciate that more than he'll ever know. The shivering still hasn't stopped but as he rubs his hand up and down my shoulder and arm, my eyes begin to feel very heavy.

Somewhere in and out of sleep, I feel Zeke place a kiss on the top of my head and whisper, "Just relax. I've got you."

Like they were the words I needed to hear, I burrow into him tightly, leaning my head in the crook of his chest, and drift off to sleep, allowing myself to trust in his care for the rest of the night.

Floating.

I'm floating.

SUSAN RENEE

And I'm so fucking cold.

I try to move my body but the vise I seem to be in is stronger than me.

I try to speak but my words are nothing more than a mumble. "Wha-what's—"

"Shhh. I've got you, Ada. Don't worry."

His voice is soft and tender. Comforting. Opening my weighty eyes a smidge, I finally realize Zeke is carrying me in his arms.

"Zeke?"

"Hey Sunshine. You're still fevered. I'm taking you to bed."

"But Elsie..."

I have a job to do.

He chuckles, looking down at me as we climb the stairs. "Ada, Elsie is fine. She's taken care of. You've been out for hours. You conked out pretty hard."

"Oh, I'm so sor—"

"Don't worry. She's perfectly fine. You on the other hand haven't stopped shivering. I have more medicine up here for you to take and then you're going to sleep this off and see if this fever can break."

I don't notice at first that he passes my bedroom, but when he lays me down on a bed in a room I know isn't mine, my brows furrow.

"Zeke, this isn't my room."

"I know. You're staying with me tonight."

I open my eyes a little further because hell, if I don't want to see his face right now to figure out what he's thinking.

"Zeke..." I shake my head. "We can't."

"Yes we can." He hands me a glass of water from his nightstand along with a few Tylenol. "Drink. Take these." He watches me swallow them down and then he covers me up with his duvet and an extra blanket before climbing into bed behind me.

"Zeke..."

"Ada, I'm not leaving you tonight. Not when you're like this. You're freezing cold and you're shivering." He cocoons me against his chest, wrapping his warmth around me. "You helped me when I needed it. Now let me help you."

"But you could get sick."

"It's a chance I'm more than willing to take." He lifts a hand and smooths it over my hair. "Sleep. Just relax and sleep. I won't let go. I promise."

His hand shifts over my stomach and he pulls me snug against his body. He kisses the back of my head before nestling in and releasing a long and deep sigh. I'd be lying if I said I didn't love the feeling of being in someone's arms again, but I also realize this is not how a typical nanny and boss are supposed to act toward one another.

"Zeke?"

"Yeah?" he whispers.

"We should talk."

He huffs an amused chuckle behind me. "About what?"

"You know what."

"Tomorrow." He breathes, squeezing me to him a little tighter. "You should rest. It can wait until tomorrow."

As much as I want to fight him on the issue, especially knowing that we're alone at the moment and it would be a suitable time to talk with Elsie not around, my body feels heavy and my eyes are begging to close. I give up. He's right. We can talk tomorrow.

"Okay," I mumble. "Good night."

"Good night, Ada. I'll be right here if you need me."

I startle awake several hours later knowing full well Elsie has to be up and therefore I need to be up. I feel surprisingly better but insanely gross at the same time. I'm sweating profusely which tells me my fever clearly broke overnight, but also feel like I got hit by a truck. My body is heavy and slow to move but realizing I'm now fever free fuels me. I cautiously scoot my body into a sitting position and notice the small pile of clothes neatly folded on Zeke's side of the bed with a note scribbled on top.

> *"Take your time or sleep all day.*
> *I took the day off and I've got Elsie.*
> *There's water and Tylenol on the bedstand*
> *if you need it.*
> *Use my shower. I'll check on you in a bit."*

Zeke's bedroom door is closed and he's nowhere to be found, but from downstairs I can hear Elsie's squealing giggles. I can't believe he took the day off after being off the ice all week. I would've expected him to be itching to get back out there, so knowing he's doing all this, for me, and for Elsie, it means a lot. The two of them clearly have fun when they're together. I smile, listening to them for a minute, and then take a closer look at the clothes waiting for me on the bed. My black sweatpants, a pair of my red lace panties and matching bra, and a sweatshirt I don't recognize. I pick up the red crewneck and unfold it. On the back, in large white letters, is the last name MILLER and the number 1. The front says PROPERTY OF CHICAGO RED TAILS.

He wants me to wear his sweatshirt.

Again?

Should I be reading into this?

He did have me sleeping in his bed.

Is this his way of communicating with me?

I lift the sweatshirt to my nose and inhale a deep breath, smiling at Zeke's recognizable scent. There's just something about wearing a shirt that smells like the man it belongs to that gives me all the smiley feels. Standing up from the bed I immediately strip the mattress of the damp sheets and blankets. I feel terrible enough that I made his bed a sweaty mess. I'm certainly not going to leave it here for him to deal with. The least I can do is toss his sheets in the wash.

But first? Shower time.

I grab the pile of clothes and step into Zeke's master bathroom, noting the similarities and differences between his bathroom and mine. His is definitely bigger. The walk-in shower is huge with all sorts of nozzles and dual shower-heads. There's even a button for music and special shower-only lighting.

Wow!

Once I figure out how to turn on the water, I strip out

of my sweaty clothes and step into the hot, welcoming downpour.

A shower never felt so good in my life.

I turn to reach for my shampoo and surprisingly find the raspberry scented brand I use every day. I look to the right of my shampoo and find my conditioner, shower gel, and face wash as well.

How sweet of him.

I lather my body in more soap than I usually use. Fever sweats are no joke and I am ready to wash it all away. I rub my hands over and around my neck and down my arms and then slide them up and over my breasts, reveling in the feel of the warm water, the soap, and the sensitivity of my nipples. For just a moment I close my eyes and imagine Zeke standing in this shower with me.

His strong body towering over me.

His hands caressing my body.

Holding my breasts.

His thumbs flicking over my nipples.

The nice guy I've come to know taking care of me in every sense.

Touching me.

Washing me.

Pleasuring me.

Loving me.

Whoa. Let's not go too far, Lewis.

Snapping back to reality, I remember Zeke telling me last night that we could talk tomorrow...which is now today. An uncomfortable wave of nerves washes over me at the thought of how this conversation is going to go between us. How we've managed to go this long without talking about our middle of the night make-out session several nights ago is beyond me. We're clearly both professionals when it comes to ignoring the elephant in the room.

But it's time.

Today is the day.

We need to talk.

14

ZEKE

There's no denying it now. I'm falling for Ada.

Somewhere along the line I gave up caring what anyone thinks about the fact she's my nanny. She loves my kid, and my kid loves her. What more can I ask for?

Holding Ada in my arms last night, even as sick as she was, felt like a little slice of Heaven. It felt good knowing in some small way, I was helping her. She was comfortable in my arms. Both on the couch and in my bed. She let go and let me take care of her. I listened to her sleep for at least a solid hour before I finally allowed myself to crash and when I opened my eyes this morning, I knew exactly what I needed to do.

ME

Grady, where are we on those divorce papers?

178

GRADY

Searching for Lori. Got a lead on a friend
from her parents but she hasn't checked
in with them over the past year either. Last
known home was Iowa.

ME

Fuck.

GRADY

Don't worry. I'll find her. I promise you
that.

ME

Can I ask you kind of an awkward
question?

GRADY

I'm your lawyer, Zeke. You can ask me
anything.

ME

If I uh...let's say I kiss someone. And that
someone isn't Lori...

GRADY

Are you asking me if it's considered
cheating on your wife?

ME

Well, yeah. I mean Lori hasn't said one
word to me since the day she left three
years ago and I haven't as much as even
thought about another woman since then.
But say I meet someone now and we...
kiss.

GRADY

Did you sleep with her?

ME

No.

Well, technically yes, but not in the sense that he's asking.

GRADY

It would be okay if you did. It's not adultery. Nobody is going to say you're cheating on your wife.

ME

Are you certain?

GRADY

One hundred percent. She abandoned you. She abandoned Elsie. She might think she has rights if she ever comes back but if or when she does, I promise you I'll take care of it. In the meantime, you enjoy your life. Don't stress over the one part of it that you have no control over right now. I'll find her and we'll end this. We'll make sure she gets served.

ME

Thanks Grady.

GRADY

Sure thing.

"God, I love that kid," I say with a chuckle as I enter the kitchen after putting Elsie down for a nap.

Ada smiles at the sink as she washes some of the dishes.

"She is definitely an amazing little girl. And with a heart of gold. She must get that from you."

"You think so?"

"Mhmm. And so smart too. Dr. Elsie knew just how to take care of me."

I shrug with a grin and lean on the counter opposite Ada. "I mean let's not give all the credit to the four-year-old. She'd be nowhere without Nurse Daddy."

"I guess you have a point." She laughs. "So, it's really you I should thank then. For taking such good care of me."

"It was my pleasure, Ada. I'm glad you're feeling better."

"I am. Much better. Thank you."

"The sweatshirt looks good on you, by the way," I tell her, raking my eyes over her body. There's nothing better than the woman you're attracted to wearing your name and hockey number on her back. Well, except when that woman is underneath you with her pussy clenched around your cock and she's screaming your name as she comes...but I digress. I wish like hell I was Superman right now, with x-ray vision so I could see what she looks like in the red lace bra and panty set I know she's wearing under my sweatshirt. It's almost like the one from the boudoir picture I saw, which is what made me choose it.

And red happens to be my favorite color.

There's an awkward silence that falls between us and it makes me anxious. I know this would be a safe time to finally talk things out about the other night, but how the hell do I bring this up?

"Hey how about that dry hump, huh?"

"You touched my penis and it made me happy."

"The sound of you coming is music to my ears."

"I'm really attracted to you but this is all sorts of weird because you know, you're the nanny."

"Can I kiss you again and still pay you to watch my kid? Is that weird?"

Hell.

I can't say any of those things to her. And on top of all this, I still have Lori to worry about. I shouldn't have to worry about her as she hasn't been in my life for years, but technically I have to assume we're still legally married. And until I can track her own and manage this situation I'm trapped in a marriage that isn't a marriage at all.

I'm glad I have the best lawyer money can buy. Grady's a good guy. He understands my situation. If anyone can help resolve this, he can. My teammates are right. I need to put an end to all things Lori and get her out of my life for good.

"Zeke?"

"Yeah?"

"About the other night. Would this be a good time to... you know, talk?"

I knew this was coming.

I take a deep breath to calm my nerves and nod my head. "Yeah. Sure."

She turns off the water from the sink and places the last washed dish in the drying rack and then turns to face me. Our eyes meet and whatever awkward tension is going on between us is now palpable. My mouth is dry and I can't think of what to say or how to say it so I blurt out the first thing that comes to my mind at exactly the same time she starts talking.

"You left—"

"—feel like I owe you an apology."

"Did you not—"

"—touched your penis and—"

"—your hands were on me and I couldn't help—"

"—you kissed me and—"

"—you left. And I heard you crying."

Her eyes grow huge at that last part and then they glisten with tears she's trying way too hard to hold back.

Fuck.

"I over-stepped, Ada. You were so...flustered and it was kind of adorable. I lost control and fuck. I'm so sorry. I didn't mean to hurt you, scare you, or make you do something you didn't want to do. God, I was a douche and I'm so sorry."

"No, no, no." She shakes her head adamantly and grabs my forearm. "Zeke, you didn't hurt me."

"You were crying, Ada. I made you cry."

"It wasn't you, Zeke." Her tears cascade one by one down her soft pink cheeks. "Shit. I'm so sorry. It was me."

"Really?" I challenge with an anxious laugh. "You're giving me the it's-not-you-it's-me line?"

"Okay." She shrugs. "So, it wasn't you and it wasn't really me." Her hazel eyes pierce mine. "It was Luke."

My brows furrow. "Luke..." I think for a minute and then remember. "Your husband."

More tears stream her face and she silently nods.

Way to fucking go, Miller. Your horny dry hump drove the girl to tears.

"Ada." My shoulders sag and I sigh and give her my

most sincerely sympathetic expression. "I am...Christ. I'm so sorry. I never even thought—"

"I didn't either," she tells me. "I promise I wasn't thinking it in the moment. What we did, it..." She closes her eyes and I see the corner of her mouth turn up even if for only a moment. "It was unexpected, yes, but not unenjoyable. Not unwanted. And not disliked in any way whatsoever."

Time for some raw honest truth.

"Ada, I haven't been able to get you out of my mind for weeks. I tried to deny my initial attraction to you and then I saw those pictures of you in your bedroom. And I know that makes me sound like some kind of creepy perv of a guy and I am so fucking sorry for that. I just have to be honest with you. You deserve that much. I see you with Elsie and I watch her interact with you and you with her and it is so perfect. You two are perfect together." I give her a desperate smile. "Fuck, I'm attracted to you, Ada." I run a hand through my hair. "I didn't mean for it to happen. I really tried like hell to deny it, but I can't anymore. But I don't want to make it weird for you and I understand if—"

"I'm attracted to you too, Zeke."

"Wait." I lift my brow. "You are?"

"I am. Is that okay? Because I don't want to make it weird either."

I nod several times trying to take in her confession, my voice a shaky kind of nervous. "Yeah. Okay. Yeah. That's good then."

"But if I'm being honest with myself, I should admit that I'm struggling with my emotions right now," she adds.

Wait.

She likes me but she doesn't like me?

"Okay. What does that mean?"

She swallows and peers up at me. "You're the first man I've ever...been with, since Luke."

I reach out and wipe some of her tears away with my thumb as she continues. "It hit me like a ton of bricks when we, you know, finished the other night. He hadn't entered my mind once the whole night until this split second that he popped into my brain and then I couldn't stop the emotions. The feelings of guilt. Like I had just done something very wrong. Like I was hurting him." She sniffles as more tears fall and my heart melts for her.

God, when she puts it that way I feel like a fucking monster.

"Ada, I'm—"

"And I don't want you to ever think I'm trying to take advantage of you," she tells me.

My brows spike. "Take advantage of...Ada, if anyone was taking advantage of someone, it was me taking advantage of you. You didn't ask to sit on my lap. You didn't ask to rock your body against mine. I did that. I took advantage of you. God, I was like a fucking horny teenager."

"Zeke, you didn't do anything to me that I didn't want you to do."

I bring my hand to my heart. "That's a relief to hear. And since we're admitting things, Ada, you should know you're the first person I've been with since Lori."

She cocks her head and gives me a look that says there's no way she believes that. Her disbelief makes me chuckle. "You don't believe me?"

"Well, I mean..." She shakes her head. "I just assumed you...you know."

"Fucked around with any woman who would have me?"

"No. I don't mean that. But, yeah, you know. You're a famous hockey player. You're wildly attractive. Your body is..." She shakes her head in amazement as she pats her hands down my torso and I try not to laugh. "Solid. And I know what my brother has gone through with women who simply want bragging rights with athletes and—"

"And you think I play those games?"

She bows her head. "I'm sorry, Zeke. I shouldn't have assumed."

I lift her chin with my finger so I can look into her beautiful eyes. "I promise I'm telling the truth. You can ask any one of the guys. They know when the puck bunnies come out to play, I leave. And now they all do too. Up until three years ago most of the guys were single. I was married to Lori at that time so I never needed to go out and meet women. Now, Lori is gone and I have Elsie to think about. I'd rather be here snuggling with her any night of the week. What kind of father would I be to her if I was out sleeping around every night?"

"That's fair. And I believe you," she says.

"I haven't as much as looked at another woman until you walked into my life, Ada. And now, I think about you all the damn time. I wonder what you and Elsie are doing during any given day, and I wonder what you're thinking, and I want to be here with you at night when Elsie goes to sleep. I miss you when we're on the road. I miss your smile and your laugh and your sunshiny attitude. I want to know you. More of you. All of you."

"And you're not put off by the fact you hired me to be your nanny?"

I cringe. "Well, when you put it that way it sounds like we're walking the line of forbidden relationships."

"Yeah."

Remembering what the guys have said to me more than once, I explain, "But then I remind myself we're both adults. We get to be in control of whatever happens here."

"I suppose you're right."

"Hey." I tenderly cup her face in my palm so she'll look at me. "I'm sorry for pushing you too far the other night. And I promise I'm not pushing you into anything more, okay? I can appreciate your feelings and your grief. I get it. It's different for me because Lori left me. She didn't love me anymore. She didn't love the life of a hockey wife. But you loved Luke and he loved you. You shared an unwavering bond, so I understand the need to work through those feelings when they arise."

"But what if...what if I want to try?" Her voice quivers and her eyes flit between my eyes and my mouth. "I've worked my way through my feelings. I did the therapies. I grieved. For years. I didn't want the ending of that night to go the way it did. Trust me. I thought it was...it felt...good. Really good. It felt right. And I wanted so much more until I scared myself. So, what if I want to try?"

"Then I'll be here. I'm not going anywhere and hopefully neither are you. I'll be here okay? For you. Whenever you want. I've waited three years to even think about another woman. I can certainly wait a little longer."

"But what if I don't want to wait?"

My breath hitches as nervous excitement blooms in my stomach. "What are you saying, Ada?"

"I'm saying I think I'd really like you to kiss me, Zeke."

She wants me to kiss her.

Inside I'm reeling like a teenage boy who just got permission to suck face with the hot girl. Outside, though, I take a slow steady breath and try to be the man I want to be for her.

The caring compassionate man she needs.

"I think I can do that."

I slide one hand around her waist and the other around the back of her head. With my thumb, I lift her chin so it's angled toward me and then I lower my mouth to hers.

Hell, her lips are soft. Supple. Sweet.

She opens her mouth and my tongue sneaks past her lips.

Jesus, she's delicious.

She tastes like the mint of her toothpaste, the strawberry of her Chapstick, and the promise of compassion and loyalty. I slowly swipe my tongue once, twice, three times, against hers, desperate to make up for all the moments I didn't kiss her before. Determined to fill my senses of her now.

I slide my hand up her back and step into her, pulling her tighter against me, not a care in the world that she's undoubtedly feeling my obvious arousal between us. She drags her hand lazily from my chest to my waistline where she hooks her fingers into my pants and I am once again keenly aware of how close she is to touching my dick. Her tongue peeks out to glide against mine and when they touch the sound that comes out of me is the perfect blend of a satisfied sigh and a pleasured moan. Ada Lewis has a perfect pair of lips and stepping away from them any time soon would be a fucking tragedy.

I want to carry her to the kitchen table and lay her out in front of me so I can see all of her. I want to strip her down and taste every inch of her. I want to gaze into her sunset-colored eyes as I make her come in every way imaginable.

"I'm all done with my nap!" a little voice calls from the top of the stairs. Ada startles and pulls her lips away, but I don't let go of her just yet.

"Did you go potty?" I ask from the kitchen.

"Oops! I need to go right now!"

"Okay."

I bring my forehead to Ada's and take a deep steadying breath. Her lashes sweep over the very top of her cheeks and then her eyes are on me.

"Has anyone ever told you that you're an amazing kisser?" she whispers to me.

Her question brings a smile to my face. "If anyone here is amazing, Ada, it's you. Fuck, I didn't want to stop."

"Me either." She bites her bottom lip and squeezes my bicep. "But for what it's worth, thank you for talking this all out with me. And for not skirting around it anymore."

"You're welcome. And listen, the ball's in your court, okay? Obviously, I want to explore things with you, but I don't ever want to put you in a situation you're not comfortable with. I won't push you. Take all the time you need. I promise I'm not going anywhere."

"Daddy can we play mermaids?" Elsie asks as she skips

into the kitchen. I scoop her into my arms and give her a playful cringe.

"Are you sure you don't want to play something like... hockey?"

She shakes her head, adamant. "No. I want to play mermaids. You be the daddy mermaid and Ada is the mommy mermaid and I am the baby mermaid."

Resigning with a sigh, I nod and wink at her. "Then you better get your magic wand so you can help me grow my fins."

15

ADA

CARISSA

Hey ladies! Are y'all coming to Saturday's game?

TATE

Yep. My sister's coming into town to hang with the kids. I'll be there.

RORY

Seeing my man in his uniform makes me horny. Of course I'll be there!

CHARLEE

LOL @ Rory! Yeah I'll be there. I got a sitter.

KINSLEY

Planning on it! Is Ada in this chat? We should invite them too.

ME

I'm here! And Saturday is Zeke's birthday 😊 I'm planning to bring Elsie but shhhhh. It's a secret surprise for Zeke.

CARISSA

Mum's the word! I won't tell a soul!

RORY

Awww did you get Zeke a present Ada?

KINSLEY

I'm pretty sure she is all the present he needs if you know what I'm saying.

CHARLEE

Oooooh tell us more! Spill all the tea!! 🙏

ME

It's nothing.

KINSLEY

Pretty sure a dry-hump session isn't nothing.

ME

KINSLEY!

RORY

😲 WHAAAAAT? OMG!

CARISSA

Ummmm I feel like we missed something MEGA HUGE! ADA! Are you and Zeke like, together-together now??

ME

No. Long story.

KINSLEY

Don't let her fool you. They might not be official but there's definitely something there.

CHARLEE

Eeeeeeek! I'm so excited for you! Zeke deserves to find someone who makes him happy!

RORY

Tate? You're being awfully quiet.

TATE

😬 Full disclosure: Dex came home the other day ecstatic that he was right.

RORY

About what?

TATE

About...and I quote "Zeke fucking the nanny."

ME

OMG 🙊 I swear it wasn't exactly like that.

RORY

I feel like there's really no in between here. You're either fucking or you're not.

TATE

LOL exactly what Dex said!

RORY

Well, we are siblings sooo. 🤷

ME

Okay then we're not. It was a dry hump in the middle of the night and nothing more.

KINSLEY

Bet it wasn't all dry. 😏

RORY

BAAAHAHAHA! This is so much fun and
now I can't WAIT for Saturday! You better
be ready to spill Ada!

ME

Yeah, yeah, yeah.

"Hey Elsie." I smile, stepping into her room where I find her reading to her stuffed animals inside her teepee. And by reading, I mean making up whatever story she wants to tell because she doesn't read quite yet. "I've got something for you."

Her eyes light up and she gasps in excitement. "A present?"

"Kind of, yeah. Do you remember how today is your daddy's birthday?"

"Yeah."

"Well, he has to play hockey tonight and I thought it would be a fun idea to surprise him and go watch and cheer him on. Do you think he would like that?"

"Yeah! He would really like that! And I could shout GO DADDY!"

I give her a high five. "That's right. So, I got him a surprise and it's kind of a surprise for you too and then after I show it to you, maybe you can help me show him tonight at his hockey game. Do you think you can do that?"

"What is it?"

I hand her a pink gift bag with pink and white tissue paper. "Here. Open it."

She takes the bag and drops it to the floor so she can see what's inside. She reaches her arms inside and pulls out the contents, letting the tissue paper fall away. She's holding a Chicago Red Tails hockey jersey. But not just any jersey. This one was specially ordered just for Elsie and has been bedazzled all over so that it shimmers at every movement.

"It's sparkly!" Elsie squeals. "Can you help me?"

She holds the garment up to me and I unfold it for her so she can see all of it. She marvels at all the shimmering beads decorating several parts of the jersey and then I point to where Zeke's last name is usually written across the back.

"Can you read what this says, Else?"

She touches every letter with her finger as she says it. "It says D-A-D-D-Y."

"That's right. It does! Excellent job. Do you know what D-A-D-D-Y spells?"

"Nope."

"It spells Daddy. And this number right here, what number is that?"

"One."

"That's right!" I beam. "So, this shirt is a super special shirt just for you. Nobody else can wear it because Zeke is your daddy and he's number one so when you wear this shirt everybody will know that he is your daddy and nobody else's."

"Yeah and you can have one too."

"I do have one," I tell her.

"Is it sparkly too?"

"Of course, it is. But mine doesn't say Daddy on the back like yours does. It says MILLER on the back because that's your last name and that's your daddy's last name too."

"Are we going to match?"

I nod excitedly. "Yes! We get to be twins tonight. How does that sound?"

Elsie jumps up and down. "Yes! Yes! Yes! Can we make our hair look the same too?"

"We sure can. Whatever you want."

"Ada! Elsie! Over here!"

Kinsley waves to us as we carefully maneuver down the stairs to where the wives and girlfriends are sitting. "Oh, my goodness look at you two beautiful ladies!"

Elsie smiles and jumps up and down. "Yeah and look! We match!" She gestures to our matching bedazzled hockey jerseys. We did a pretty fantastic job of matching everything else too. Black leggings, red converse sneakers, and because it's what Elsie asked for, we both have braided pigtails and the number one painted on our cheeks.

Kinsley winks at me and then holds her hand up for Elsie to give her a high five. "Of course, you do! You both look amazing! Did you make that shirt all by yourself?"

Elsie shakes her head. "Nooo. Ada made it for me."

"No, no, no. I didn't make them," I correct her. "I just had someone else make them."

Rory leans over, smiling at us. "Elsie, you look amazing! I love the sparkle. Has your daddy seen this shirt yet?"

I pipe in, standing over Elsie. "Daddy doesn't even know we're here tonight."

The ladies all gasp and smile and Charlee holds her arms out to Elsie for a hug. "So, you're surprising your daddy for his birthday?"

"Uh huh!" she says with a huge smile while jumping into Charlee's arms. "And Ada said I can get ice cream!"

Charlee gives her a tight squeeze. "Well, everyone deserves ice cream when it's someone's birthday!"

The ladies spend time doting on Elsie before the team comes on the ice for warm-up and I make myself comfortable next to Kinsley.

"Sooo." She leans over and looks at me with a hint of mischief in her eyes. "How are things?"

"Good." I nod reassuringly. "They're good."

She pats my knee. "Did you ever find the opportunity to talk things out? You know...with Zeke?"

I nod. "Yeah. We talked the other day."

"Aaaand?" She raises her brows in expectation.

I try not to smile in response but I fail. Miserably. "And it ended with us kissing until the little squirt down there," I gesture to Elsie, "woke up from her nap."

Charlee leans over our way too, whispering, "Did I just hear you say you and Zeke kissed? Again?"

Kinsley squeals. "Yes! They kissed again!"

"Oh my God!" She claps her hands excitedly. "So, are you two official now?"

"I..." I trail off not knowing how best to answer her question. "You know, I guess I'm not sure. He said he was attracted to me and I said the same. We talked about Luke and Lori and how our pasts have affected us in moving on with our lives and he kind of put the ball in my court. He said he didn't want to push me into doing anything I wasn't comfortable with but I told him I kind of wanted to...you know, try."

"Yeah, you do!" Kinsley grins.

Charlee takes my hand and gives it a squeeze. "Well, I, for one, am extremely happy for you both. Zeke has been a great guy since I've met him and you certainly seem to be catching his eye."

"Thank you, Charlee."

"Trust me. He hasn't been the least bit interested in giving attention to anyone but Elsie since the day Lori left. He was a sad sap when Milo and I got married but he's a different guy now. You guys just keep on writing your own little romance book and we'll cheer on your happily ever after."

Kinsley sighs dreamily and touches Charlee's knee. "Oh my God, it's like a second chance romance for each of them!"

"Right?" Charlee wags her brows. "And a kinky little single dad slash nanny trope on the side."

Kinsley laughs. "Eeeeek! There's no way this doesn't end well for them. It's fate. I just know it."

Our own little romance book.

A second chance at love?

With Zeke Miller?

Could this really happen?

Could I be that blessed?

The music in the arena changes and announcer calls over the loudspeaker, "Let's hear it for our very own CHICAGOOOOO RED TAAAAAAILS!"

The crowd cheers as our home team comes onto the ice for their pregame warmup. Zeke is the last one to hit the ice and when he does, my stomach flutters with nervous excitement. He skates around the net several times and then immediately starts his warm-up routine. I watch with apprehension, praying to all the possible gods that his groin muscle is healed enough to be back and that he can get through tonight's game without further injury.

He starts with his side-to-side shuffles, turning his leg out and coming to an abrupt halt in each direction. He does the same sort of exercise again but goes down on his knee with each shuffle. I cringle slightly each time thinking any minute now his muscle is going to seize and he'll be in pain all over again. Then he lowers himself down to his knees on the ice and spreads his legs.

"Hey Ada," Rory says, gesturing to the ice with her head. "Remember when I showed you the stretch?" She wags her brows.

Knowing exactly what she's talking about without talking about Zeke in front of his four-year-old kid, I nod with a smirk. "Yeah?"

"Feast your eyes, girlfriend. Feast your eyes."

Just as she showed me weeks ago, Zeke is now in the so called "hump" position, pushing back and then thrusting his hips forward on the ice.

Holy mother of...

Yep. I know these are stretches he has to do to keep his muscles warm and loose but holy hell, it's hot no matter how I look at it. We might be sitting close to the ice for this game, but when I watch Zeke stretch his body, even covered in pads, I am anything but cold.

16

ZEKE

"**F**uck, it feels good to be back!" I inhale a deep breath, filling myself with the sights and sounds of the arena on game night. There's nothing like the energy around here when we're about to take the ice. It's a feeling I'll never tire of and I am so fucking grateful to be well enough to play tonight.

Colby chuckles beside me as we stand inside the tunnel ready to take the ice. He claps me on the shoulder. "We're glad to have you back, man. Makes for a nice birthday, huh?"

"Sure, as hell does."

"Cheers to that. We're celebrating tonight, right?"

"Uhh...probably not. I told Ada I would be home."

"Because tonight, gentlemen," Dex starts. "Tonight, our man Zeke is absolutely going to fuck the nanny."

My head snaps his way. "What?"

"Dude, it's your fuckin' birthday." He shrugs. "And you want to. You know you do."

"Doesn't matter what I want to do, Foster. Until those divorce papers have been delivered…"

"Yeah, yeah, I hear you. All I'm saying is it's your birthday and from what you were telling us earlier, things are going well between the two of you. So just go for it. Nobody has to know. Well, except me, of course. I need to know. I always need to know." He winks and then finds his place in our team huddle.

Do I want to get Ada alone sooner rather than later? Hell yeah, I do. I just don't want anything to go wrong with this divorce. Grady has to find Lori. It's the only way I'll be able to let go and allow myself to blow off a little steam and have some fun. And Ada Lewis is definitely the fun I want to have.

"Clean game tonight, brothers," Colby says. "Let's go kick some ass for Zeke's birthday. What do you say?"

We all chant, "HUSTLE, HIT, AND NEVER QUIT!" and then we line up at the gate to the ice just as the announcer says, "Let's hear it for our very own CHICAGOOOOO RED TAAAAAAILS!"

The crowd goes wild as we skate onto the ice. I take a few laps around the net before starting my stretches paying close attention to my groin muscles. I feel great going into this game. I can only pray it stays that way because if this injury happens again I could very well be out for the season and fuck if I can live an entire season without being on the ice with my team.

I start my pregame warmup with a burst of quick side to side shuffles, stretching my legs and feeling the ice under my feet. I circle back to the net and then drop to my knees, spread my legs wide and then reach forward until my gloved hands are on the ice. Listening to the music playing overhead, I pull my hips back and pulse against the ice. I'm well aware of the females in the arena that start screaming the moment any of us go down to this position. But I can't think about any of that right now. I have to pay close attention to the muscles I'm stretching so I can be sure my trainers were right and I'm in tip top shape to do my job tonight.

Some of the guys are stretching around me while others are practicing a few skating maneuvers when the music changes and the arena's organ player starts to play a familiar tune. I look up from my stretches and am shocked when I see the whole arena up on their feet. But it's not just them. My entire team has circled around me as everyone sings, "Happy Birthday dear Miller...happy birthday to you!"

Shit.

A boisterous smile grows across my face and my cheeks redden as the arena cheers for me. I shake my head and lift my hand acknowledging their applause and then continue stretching.

The guys skate over to me and give me a helmet tap, or in Dex's case, a slap on my ass.

"Happy birthday Sir Humps-a-lot. Way to put on a show for your girls."

My brows pinch together. "Huh?"

He gestures to where the WAGS usually sit. "Your girls. You didn't tell us they were coming tonight."

What?

I rise to my feet and turn in the direction Dex was gesturing and my jaw drops. My stomach summersaults, my chest warms, and my eyes damn near start to leak. "Holy shit. They're here."

Standing with Carissa, Charlee, Tate, Rory, and Kinsley, is Ada, holding my daughter on her hip. The two of them are sporting matching Red Tails jerseys, their hair braided into pigtails with my number written on their cheeks.

My girls.

God that feels so good to hear.

My girls.

It's perfect.

They're perfect.

And they came for me.

Ada brought my daughter to the game all on her own. To surprise me.

Elsie and Ada wave to me and blow me kisses and all I can do is wave back. When they're behind the glass, there's no way for me to talk to them, not to mention Coach would have my ass if I wasn't focused on tonight's game. But holy shit if my energy level didn't just skyrocket.

"Dex?"

"Yeah, man?"

"We're going to kick some Boston ass and win this game tonight."

He grins. "Yeah. And?"

Finally, I say what I know he's been longing to hear me say for months. "And then I'm going to fuck the nanny."

His smile widens and he throws his head back in laughter. "Fuckin' right you are." He pats my helmet and looks me straight in the eye and says, "You've got this Zeke. You've never let us down."

I know that's not true. I've let them down numerous times, but I'll take all the pep talk I can get. No fucking way is a puck getting into my net tonight. Not if the two good luck charms I've got on my side have anything to say about it.

We get through the typical pregame ceremony and then the puck is dropped and I'm focused on one thing and one thing only. Blocking every single goddamn shot.

I track the puck down the ice as possession banks from us to Boston and back to us. Shay takes his first shot of the game when he has the chance but it's blocked and rebounded by Boston. The play comes my direction and I have an eagle's eye on that tiny piece of black rubber. It's almost laughable how their right wing comes barreling down on me. I can tell by his stance, and the way he's holding his stick, that he's going to shoot to my right. Without fail, he taps the puck with the end of his stick and it flies to me, but my glove is already in the air waiting for it.

Be less predictable next time, dumbfuck.

I tap the puck to Landric who races back down the ice. He swings around the net and passes to Nelson who pivots and shoots but just misses the score. Boston brings the play back to me, O'Brian on the far side passes to Lebank. My eyes are on the puck as I hunker my stance, trying my best to predict his next move. He swings back his stick and I know he's going for it. At the moment his stick hits the puck, Scoval pivots around the net to assist but knocks me over in the process.

"Fuck!"

My fall draws a reaction from both the crowd and the

rest of my teammates. Foster drops his gloves and goes after Scoval with Malone right by his side.

"Touch my goalie again and I'll rip you to shreds, you stupid ass fuck," I hear Dex shout as he throws his first punch. I'm not sure what has Dex so fired up but I could almost kiss the guy for looking out for me. If there's one thing our team does well, it's that no matter what, we always have each other's backs. Malone tries to pull the guys apart but he's ganged up on by two other rival players who think he's trying to get in on the action. That sets off Nelson and Shay and now we have a brawl on the ice and all hell is breaking loose.

Aww, my team loves me.

Thanks for making me feel all warm and fuzzy inside, gentlemen.

I'm pissed that Scoval got in the way and shoved me, but watching the guys fight for my honor is just a little heartwarming and a lot of fucking fun. All I want to do as I stand myself back up is laugh, but I keep my game face on for their sake. These guys will look for any way to distract us from our gameplay. They're a tough team to beat, I won't lie, but I'll be damned if they're getting the win tonight.

After a minute or two, or ten from what it feels like, the refs finally get involved and break up the fight. A snippet from Taylor Swift's "Shake It Off" plays overhead which makes me chuckle. If Dex is hearing this, it wouldn't surprise me even a little bit if he were to break out into some sort of ice dance just for the hell of it.

Fuck, I would almost be willing to pay him to do it.

While I'm waiting for the refs to clear the fights and hand out their penalties, I steal a glance at the jumbotron and I'll be damned. Remi is with my girls. The ladies are all dancing but Remi has Elsie on the stairs dressed adorably in her bedazzled jersey and he's holding her hand as they dance to Taylor Swift.

I should've known she'd be dancing to this.

He turns Elsie around and that's when I see it. The back of her bedazzled shirt—except where it would usually say MILLER, it says DADDY instead. My heart melts and just for a moment I forget about the game play and watch my kid living her best life with Remi by her side. Fuck, it truly takes a village to raise a kid and knowing the entire Chicago Red Tails family is willing to spread some love and attention to my little girl makes me so fucking happy.

By the time we get the game back into play we only have about thirty seconds before the buzzer sounds for the end of the first period. We head off the ice and down through the tunnel to the dressing room. Though the score might be tied at zero at the moment, the guys seem anything but angry about it. Their energy is high, and they're all smiles when I'm the last one to walk in the room.

"You alright, Miller?" Coach asks.

"Hell yeah. I'm perfect. Why?"

He gestures to the rest of the team. "Because for some reason these asshats decided to go to bat for you tonight. What the fuck was that?"

Dex shrugs. "I call it fun."

The guys laugh and even Coach smirks a bit, but he tries to keep his composure. "Maybe next period we focus on scoring and not throwing our fists at the other team, huh?"

"Sorry, Coach," Dex tells him. "But after Miller's

injury the last time he was on the ice, I didn't want him getting hurt tonight. There's too much on the line."

"On the line? What's that supposed to mean?"

"It means he's got a hot date tonight, Coach!" Quinton adds.

"Yeah. His nanny is here watching so we can't have him getting hurt in front of her." Dex wags his brows. "Gotta protect that groin if you know what I mean."

"The nanny? Miller, you're fucking the nanny?"

"No, Sir." I laugh at his shocked expression.

"Not yet, anyway," Dex quips.

Coach rolls his eyes and swipes a hand down his face. "For Christ's sake. Do you know what? I think the less I know, the better, alright? Let's not get into this now. We've got a game to win." He goes over his thoughts on the next period and then gives us a few minutes to rest and relax. Jason takes me into the therapy room to massage and stretch my legs again. He doesn't want me taking any chances out there if I can help it.

He palpates the inside of my right thigh checking my groin muscle for any sign of weakness. "You feeling good? No pain?" he asks, bringing my leg up to my chest and then out to the side.

I shake my head. "No pain. I feel great."

He nods approvingly. "Good. Are you being cautious out there?"

Cringing slightly, I huff a sigh of frustration. "Maybe a little, but I don't want to be."

"I get it. That's normal. Everything feels good though, so I wouldn't worry too much. Maybe just try not to butterfly with every block you make and you should be fine.

We'll check you again at the end of the game. Just be careful and if you feel even the slightest pull, get yourself off that fucking ice and let the second string take care of it."

"Will do."

Second period is even better than the first. So far it's been a shutout for me and the guys have scored three times. They're playing an amazing game tonight. Hawken has done a spectacular job leading the offensive line in keeping the puck inside Boston territory. And in those few moments when the puck does come my way I've had no problem protecting my net from unwanted predators.

Just before the start of the third period Milo catches Elsie, Ada, and Remi on the jumbotron again and points it out to me. Remi has a fudge popsicle in his hand and gives it to Elsie. He gives her a big high five as the crowd around them cheers for the little cutie now enjoying one of her very favorite frozen treats. I'll have to thank Carissa for that one because I'm certain she had a hand in it. Remi offers his hand to Ada and pulls her out to the steps.

Oh God, what is he doing now?

She's all smiles as the music switches to "Lover" by Taylor Swift. And the only reason I know this song is because Taylor is one hundred percent Dex's hall pass and he has a massive crush on her, so we listen to every album she's ever created throughout the season. Numerous times.

Remi wraps his arm around Ada and slow dances with her, even dipping her and pretending to kiss her cheek. Fuck, I've never wanted to be a huge red fluffy bird more than I do right this very moment. Ada takes it all in stride and even gives Remi a sweet kiss on the cheek in return.

I've never been happier to know that Remi has a crush

on Gianna, our Zamboni driver because I'm hella-fucking-jealous watching him dance with my girl.

I know, I know. She's not mine yet.

But she will be.

I want to dance with Ada like that.

I want to hold her in my arms and feel her body against mine.

I want to sing to her while we sway.

And then I want to kiss her so fucking sweetly that she's desperate for more.

"Looks like your girls are having a great night, Zeke," Milo says, watching as the fans cheer them on.

I shake my head in disbelief that they're even here. That the woman I'm falling for is wearing my name and my number tonight. That she's adorably matching my daughter and helping her have a fun night amongst an arena full of adults.

"Milo, I don't think I've ever wanted a game to be over faster in my life."

He laughs. "I don't doubt that at all, my friend. You leave that to us. We've got your back." He skates off to get into position for the puck drop and we are on our way to bringing home another win.

17
ADA

At the end of the final buzzer, instead of flying off the ice, Zeke turns toward us and motions for me to bring Elsie down to the gate where he can reach her.

"Daddy!"

"Elsie! Come here, baby!" I help lift her over the gate into Zeke's arms, grinning at how tiny she looks against his padding, and then pull out my phone for a quick picture.

"You want to skate with Daddy?" Zeke asks her.

Her little face lights up. "Yeah!"

Carissa, Tate, Rory, and Kinsley join us coming up behind me. "We'll take Ada with us and meet you downstairs," Carissa tells Zeke.

"Alright."

I wave and we turn to head up the stairs but Zeke stops us.

"Ada."

I pivot and look back over my shoulder. "Yeah?"

"Thank you," he tells me with a beaming smile. "Thank you for this." His eyes slide down my body and I'm not sure if he's thanking me for bringing his kid to the game or if he's thanking me for the view of my ass I'm giving him as I climb the stairs."

"You're welcome. It was a great game. We had a blast."

"And my girls looked fuckin' adorable."

"Daddy!" Elsie takes Zeke's cheeks in her hands so he has to look at her. "You said the bad fuck word."

My jaw drops dumbfounded but Zeke just laughs and takes it all in stride. "No, you said the bad fuck word."

She giggles. "You just did it again."

He scrunches his face. "I know. I'm sorry. I promise I'll watch my mouth, okay?"

"Okay Daddy. Spin me!"

"Okay let's go."

We watch as Zeke spins Elsie around a couple times and then skates across the ice to the exit gate carrying his baby girl with him down through the tunnel and out of sight.

Carissa whistles once we reach the top of the stairs and we're all together. "He's got it bad."

"Yeah he does," Rory snickers. "It's super cute."

"What's cute?" I ask, feeling like I'm missing something.

"Zeke's crush on you."

My cheeks blush at the mention of Zeke's feelings for me because the feeling is mutual. "You think so?"

"Think so?" Kinsley scoffs. "Did you not see the way he was checking you out back there?"

I may have noticed, but I keep my comments to myself and simply smile at my friends.

When we finally make it down through the tunnels to the hallway outside the locker room I spot Zeke's parents standing along the way.

"Mr. and Mrs. Miller, how great to see you both."

Zeke's mom recognizes me but her brow is furrowed and a look of worry is evident on her face. "Elsie isn't with you?"

"Oh, no." I tell them, shaking my head. "Zeke took her onto the ice after the game. He's got her."

"Oh, thank Heavens." She clutches her chest. "I got worried for a moment."

"Well, no need to worry. She's in good hands."

She laughs and gestures to the locker room door. "With the guys in there? We shall see."

As we're laughing over a toddler commanding a bunch of professional hockey players in their locker room, Zeke steps out with Elsie on his shoulders.

"Pappy! Nana!" Elsie exclaims. Zeke stops short, surprised to see his parents lingering in the hallway, his brows pinching together, he cocks his head.

"Mom? Dad? Is everything alright?"

"Of course. Why wouldn't it be?"

"Uh, because you guys rarely ever come to a game let alone down here to see me."

"Well, we didn't have Elsie with us like we used to so we had the time and wanted to watch you play," his dad says.

"Plus, it's your birthday and parents should want to see

their kids on their birthday, right?" his mom asks. "It was a great game, Son. You should be immensely proud of yourself." She kisses Zeke's cheek and whispers, "Happy Birthday."

"Thanks, Mom. Yeah. And after being off a week I was glad to get back on the ice."

"Well, you two kids should definitely go celebrate with your friends," she explains. "So, we thought we would take Elsie back to our house for the night."

I'm about to shake my head and tell them that's not necessary since I can take her home but then it hits me. If they take Elsie for the night, that means I could have Zeke all to myself.

Hell yes!

Thank you, Jesus.

Please say yes, Zeke.

Please say yes.

"Uh, yeah. That's fine. Elsie is that okay with you?"

"I'll make you pancakes in the morning," his dad tells her. "And you can help add the chocolate chips."

"Yeah! Let's go! Bye, Daddy!"

Elsie's enthusiasm for her grandparents, or rather chocolate chips, makes me laugh. Zeke leans over and gives her a big kiss on her cheek. "Goodnight sweetheart. Be a good girl and sleep well, okay? I'll pick you up tomorrow."

"Okay Daddy. Bye Ada."

I too give her a quick peck on the cheek. "Night night sweetheart. I'll see you tomorrow."

Zeke says another thank you to his parents and watches them walk away with Elsie. For the first time since I got here, I'm grateful, if not even a little excited, to be spending the evening with Zeke. Or at least, I assume that's what's happening.

But maybe he has other plans.

"Soooo that means you two are coming with us to Pringle's, right?" Tate asks with a smirk.

I catch Zeke's gaze and bite my bottom lip. I don't know what he's thinking exactly, but something inside me boldens enough to speak up.

"Yeah. Zeke deserves a night out on his birthday."

His eyes pierce mine and something in my chest flutters. "Only if you're coming with me."

I would love to come with you.

Or before you.

Or after you.

Whatever you prefer.

"Of course, I'll come with you."

He nods and I can tell he's trying to hold back his smile. "Yeah. Okay. I guess we'll be there. I just have to umm..." He gestures behind him with his thumb. "Jason wants to stretch me and then I just need to shower." He holds his hand out to me. "Come with me?"

"For your stretch?"

"Yeah."

Is he serious?

I raise my brows. "Uh...is that...okay?"

"I wouldn't ask you if it wasn't." He chuckles. "Come on."

He slides his warm strong hand over mine, entwining our fingers, and leads me down the hallway. And I'm just here wishing I won't ever have to let go. The girls wave at me, a few of them winking as Zeke directs me toward the physical therapy room. When we reach the third room on the left we find the room empty.

"Good," I hear him mumble before he rounds on me, his hands grasping the sides of my face, and crashes his lips to mine, literally taking my breath away. His lips aren't soft and supple as they were the last time we kissed. This time he seems hungry. Needy. Like my lips are his lifeline.

"I've been wanting this since I saw you up there in the stands," he says, his tongue swiping through my mouth. "You're wearing my name, Ada. My name and my number. Do you know what that does to me?"

My hands climb up his chest as his smooths down my back and sneaks under the hem of my jersey, his warm fingers tickling my bare skin. God it feels good to have his hands on me. He's suddenly all possessive and protective all in one and I allow myself to get lost in him for however long he'll have me. I have no idea how many minutes we stand here, tongues dancing, bodies shifting, tasting each other before there's a clearing of a throat at the door behind us.

I jump away from Zeke but he just smiles lazily and starts taking off his pads.

"You know puck bunnies aren't allowed down here, Miller," a man says.

Oh shit.

We're in trouble.

Something he said must piss Zeke off though, because he steps up against the man, his eyes steely and cold. "She's not a fucking puck bunny and if you ever refer to her in that way again, you'll be walking out of here with a box of your fucking belongings. She's with me and that's all you need to know. Do I make myself clear?"

The man nods and now I'm the uncomfortable elephant in the room. "I can," I gesture out the door and step back, "wait outside or...maybe meet you—"

"No, it's fine," the man in the polo shirt says to me, shaking his head in amusement. "I apologize. We haven't met yet." He offers me his hand. "I'm Jason. The physical therapist."

I offer him a kind yet nervous smile. "Pleasure to meet you. I'm Ada. The uh...well, I'm Elsie's...his daughter's uh...nanny." I mumble that last word because now that I'm saying it out loud I realize how inappropriate I must sound, confirming to a stranger that Zeke Miller was, indeed, making out with his nanny. I don't miss the look Jason gives Zeke. The one that says "Really? You're fucking the nanny?" Maybe that's not what he's really asking, but they're clearly having an unspoken conversation because they both smirk at each other and break out into a laugh.

"Alright man let's do this," Jason says, patting the exam table. "Everything still feeling good? No pain?"

"Nope. All good. Scout's honor."

Jason palpates Zeke's inner thigh, poking, prodding, I assume looking for any sign of a weak muscle.

"OUCH! FUCK! SON OF A BITCH!" Zeke shouts, grabbing his leg as Jason lifts his hands, his eyes bulging.

My heart sinks.

Ooh no.

"What? Where does it hurt?" Jason asks, his brows pinching together. "Is it tight? Did it snap? What?"

Zeke winks at me and then grins at Jason. "Nah, I'm good. I'm just kidding."

Jason huffs. "Are you fucking serious right now?"

"That's what you get for interrupting our kiss."

He laughs. "Yeah well if I hadn't interrupted I'd still be standing in the doorway waiting."

Even I can't hold back my giggle, but I cover my mouth with my hand anyway.

"God, I ought to punch you in the nuts for that stunt, asshole."

Zeke laughs. "Oh, fuck. Don't do that. I might need them later."

No, I *might need them later.*

Jason shakes his head in complete disbelief of Zeke's little prank and then gets back to work. He pulls his leg out to the side and adds resistance as Zeke brings his legs together. It may seem like nothing is going on here with these stretches but I can already see the change to Zeke's expression. He takes his job very seriously. As does Jason.

"That okay?"

"Yeah. It's good."

"Alright, how about this?" He bends Zeke's knee up to his chest and then unfolds it out to the side, stretching his thigh muscle completely.

"Good," Zeke tells him. "Zero pain."

"Alright. That's what I want to hear. Keep stretching every day, even tomorrow when you're off, and we'll see you back here early Sunday morning."

"Thanks Jason."

Zeke picks up the pieces of his uniform and leads us out of the therapy room down the hall to the locker room.

"I'll wait out here for you."

"Like hell you will," he tells me with a smirk. "Everyone's gone by now. I'm almost always the last one out. Get in here."

"Zeke, what if—"

"We won't." He answers my unasked question and holds the door open for me, grabbing my wrist and pulling me close to him. "Look, Elsie's gone for the night. This opportunity doesn't happen often. If that means I only have eighteen hours with you, then so be it, but you better believe I sure as hell am going to take advantage of every one of those eighteen hours. So, get in here. I'm not letting you out of my sight."

I want to scoff and tell him he's being ridiculous.

I want to shake my head and stand my ground.

But I can't.

Because I would be lying if I didn't spend many moments watching him tonight fantasizing about what could or would happen between us if we were to have time alone together.

My heart rate picks up and a devilish smile spreads across my face. "Alright."

I watch as Zeke puts away his gear and takes off his skates. Then he tears off his sweaty t-shirt leaving him standing in nothing but a pair of black compression pants, his taut abs and rippling muscles on perfect display.

Hooooly hell.

"Come here," he says, curling his finger at me.

I step up to him as he pulls up a song on his phone and then sets it down on the bench. He gently lifts my purse from around my head and body and deposits it in his locker and then turns back to me. His one hand grips my waist, the other curling up and around my back as he pulls my body against his and then he starts to sway to the sounds of Taylor Swift.

We dance for several long seconds right here in the middle of the deserted locker room.

My heart pounds inside my chest as I twine my arms around his neck, breathing him in. He's this perfect mix of earthy woods, sweat, and something distinctly Zeke. Honestly, it makes me weak in the knees. Thankfully, his hard body is here to support mine—and I do mean hard. The compression pants he's wearing tell me he's every bit as into this as I am.

Anticipation thrums through me as I imagine all of the unusual ways our night could end.

"There's something I never knew about myself until tonight, Ada," he murmurs in my ear as he pulls me in even closer, our bodies moving together in sensuous harmony.

"Oh yeah? What's that?"

"I'm apparently a very jealous man."

I tip my head back so I can see his face. He's not smiling but he doesn't look angry either. I feel him inhale a slow deep breath and release it in a contented sigh.

"And what do you have to be jealous of?"

"I've never wanted to be a big feathery red bird more than I did watching you dance on that jumbotron with Remi tonight."

His confession makes me chuckle lightly. "Aww, if I had known you were jealous, I would've told him no."

"I'm glad you didn't."

"Why?"

"Because I liked watching you." His seemingly innocent reply sends a bolt of lust straight through me.

"You did?" I ask, silently wondering what else he'd like to watch me do.

He nods and places a soft kiss on my temple. "You were so carefree. Happy. Genuinely smiling. And I stood there watching you but picturing us and that's when I knew."

My brows furrow. "Knew what?"

"Knew I would unequivocally break my own rules for you."

"Rules? What does that mean?"

"You were the nanny," he says. "You were only ever supposed to be the nanny. But I knew at that moment that I wanted you. I want that kind of happiness and I want it with you."

"Zeke...I..." My words trail off, because while I'm over here thinking about sex, he's thinking about...happiness.

"I want you, Ada." He ghosts his lips over mine, a whisper of a kiss. "And if you'll let me, I'll spend the rest of the night showing you just how much I want you." He groans, as if holding himself back pains him. "I crave you. Desire you. I need you." He gives in, punctuating his declaration with a searing kiss and then brings his forehead to mine.

"Say yes, Ada," he murmurs, dragging his lips from mine to whisper in my ear. The pure want in his voice makes my insides flutter. "Please for the love of Christ say yes because I don't think I can keep myself away from you for one more night. I'm aching to touch you. I'm dying to taste you. I'm desperate to make you mine."

He leans in, brushing his lips over mine, his kiss all

consuming. Our tongues tangle together as I tunnel my fingers into his hair, tugging it softly before pulling away. "Who would I be to deny an aching, dying, desperate man his biggest wishes?"

"Thank fuck," he mutters and spins me around. Kissing me as his hand slides under my ass so he can lift me up and wrap my legs around his waist. My heart is beating faster than any puck to ever fly down the ice as anticipation of what's to come courses through my veins. We're all tongues and teeth and lips, and moans and groans. It's hot and I feel my desire for him, for this, for us, pool between my legs.

Thoughts of Luke invade my mind, but I try my damnedest to ignore them.

This is fine.

We're fine.

I'm fine.

I don't need to feel bad about this.

I'm allowed to feel good.

Zeke lowers himself down to the bench, his hands kneading into the soft flesh of my ass through my leggings as he slides my center down over his straining erection and groans into my ear in response.

"Fucking hell, Ada. You're so goddamn beautiful. How did I get so lucky?"

Yeah, he knows just what to do and just what to say to make me quiver with need. There's no way in hell anything can be wrong between us when it feels this right.

"I'm the lucky one, Zeke."

He rocks me against him like he did that night in his bedroom, his cock hitting me in just the right place to make me want to take the reins and ride forth to my happy ending. He lets me go, free to chase what I want. What I so desperately need. And I don't hold back. I buck against him as he drags his tongue through my mouth. I imagine what that tongue would feel like swiping across my breasts, teasing my nipples, circling my clit.

"Oh God, yes." I'm so close. Almost there. I lean my head back, my mouth open in anticipation of the end I know is coming.

But it never comes.

Zeke grabs my hips and slides me off of his lap so he can stand up.

I don't know what's happening.

Why did he stop?

Did I do something wrong?

Isn't this what he wanted?

"Zeke?"

He doesn't say a word. Only leans into his locker and pulls out a white towel.

"What... why'd you stop?"

"Need a shower," he rumbles, his voice deeper than usual. My brows lower in confusion. How did we go from dry humping to talking about showers? Plus, I'm the one who's dripping wet.

"Are you taking me to the showers?"

He wipes his towel down his face. "God, I fucking wish. But not this time sweetheart."

Unexpected disappointment waves through me. "Why not? We're alone, aren't we?"

"We are, yes. But no fucking way am I allowing our first time to be during a five-minute shower." He shakes his head, pinning me with a hard stare. "You deserve so much more than a quick fuck, Ada. I want to be able to lay you down and marvel at this beautiful body of yours that I've been dreaming about since your first days in my house." He brushes his knuckles over my cheek and down my jaw. "I want to take my slow sweet time pleasuring you, watching as you come apart beneath me, over and over again."

"That sounds...nice."

"Nice?" His brows shoot up and he chuckles.

"Yeah. What's wrong with nice?"

"Sweetheart, there's nothing nice about the things I want to do to you." He tugs me closer, rubbing me over his erection. "I want you writhing in pleasure and screaming my name until you're hoarse."

His comment catches me off guard, a light gasp sneaking from my mouth that makes him smirk.

"Yeah. I think we can come up with a better word than nice." He sets me down on my feet and gives my ass a light spank. It feels like a promise of what's to come. "And I'll give you time to think about it, to make sure you really want this, while you sit right here on this bench and wait while I grab a quick shower." His lips curl into a devious smirk. "That is, unless you want to watch."

"I thought watching was your thing," I say, licking my lips and playing coy. Because hell yes, I want to watch this god of a man shower, but I rein in my raging hormones and sit down like he asked.

"Seeing *the* Zeke Miller taking a shower is the newest addition to my bucket list," I tell him. "But I like anticipation, so I'll wait right here."

"That's my good girl," he murmurs before kissing my forehead and walking toward the showers, leaving me staring after him, utterly dumbstruck, like those four little words didn't just upend everything I thought I knew about myself. Seriously, who knew that something as simple as *that's my good girl*, would have me ready to offer myself up like a buffet. Because as I watch him walk away, all I can think is, I'll do damn near anything to hear him say those words to me again.

W e walk into Pringle's about thirty minutes after everyone else, the party having already started. The bar is packed as usual after a winning home game, but I lead Ada to the private section in the back that is always reserved for the team. It's hard to go anywhere in public when so many people know who we are as hockey players. I'm grateful Pringle's has always been good to us. I suppose it's a symbiotic relationship of sorts since having us here brings in customers for them as well. Either way, we love it here and have for years.

"Chug! Chug! Chug! Chug! Chug!" The guys and their girls chant as Carissa and Dex each chug their glass of beer. Watching her glass empty in seconds, Carissa will be the clear winner again as she is every single time.

"Dammit!" Dex shouts slamming his glass down on the table. "Every fucking time!"

"What's going on?" Ada asks in my ear.

"Oh, Dex challenged Carissa one time in a beer chugging competition and she whipped his ass big time. He can't let it go so he's always asking for a rematch."

"And he never wins?"

I laugh shaking my head. "He never fucking wins. It's amazing."

"Hey!" Dex points to me from his seat. "Don't talk about me like I'm not right fucking here. You're not doing my self-esteem any favors."

I tip my head back and cackle at his weak scolding. "Right because if there's one thing I think about when your name is mentioned, it's low self-esteem."

Carissa wipes the back of her hand across her mouth and then parts her lips and gives Dex an exaggerated "Ahhhh. Better luck next time, Foster."

Colby shakes his head in amazement from the other side of the table. "My wife, ladies and gentlemen. Isn't she fucking hot?"

Dex shrugs and opens his mouth but Colby quickly covers it much to Tate's amusement. "Don't answer that."

"Took you long enough bro." Dex smirks turning his eyes on me. "Did you uh..." His eyes shift to Ada and then back to me. "Succeed?"

"Wouldn't you like to know?" I grin.

"Yes. Yes I very much would. Give me something good to be happy about right now. I just suffered another humiliating loss."

"Then perhaps you should quit playing, Dex," Hawken suggests.

"Fuck you, Malone. That is not how we set the example for our kids! If at first you don't succeed, try, try, again."

Hawken laughs. "Dude, for one, I'm pretty sure that saying wasn't meant to apply to chugging beer as fast as you can and two, Rory and I don't have kids yet sooo..." He shrugs and then gives Dex the double bird.

"You're no longer the fun uncle," Dex tells him.

Quinton rises from the table and gestures to Ada and me. "You guys want a drink? This round is on me."

"Nah. I'm not drinking tonight but thank you."

"What the fuck, Miller? You had a damn shut-out tonight and you don't want to celebrate?"

"Yeah I do want to celebrate." I clear my throat and squeeze Ada's hand in mine because even she is giving me a questioning look. "Just not with you asshats."

Her cheeks pinken and she tries not to smile when I lean over and whisper in her ear, "I want a clear head so I can enjoy what happens later."

She doesn't have time to react to what I just said to her before Kinsley is up and out of her seat. "Hey Ada, you want a shot?" She pulls Ada from my grasp. "Let's do a shot and then dance."

"Yes! Dancing! Okay." She yanks her purse from around her neck and hands it to me. "I'll be back."

"Oh, that sounds fun!" Rory squeals. "I'll come too!"

"Wait for us!" Charlee, Tate, and Carissa join them as well.

I watch her walk with Kinsley to the bar where she orders a shot for all the ladies. Once they all have a shot glass in front of them, they lick their hands, tap their shot glasses on the bar, and lift them to their mouths, shooting back what is obviously tequila. Then they each grab a lime and suck it between their lips.

Hell.

Now my dick is at half-mast and I have to adjust myself. I never thought I would be jealous of a lime. The ladies head to the small corner of the bar where several people are dancing and work their way into the moving crowd. Ada raises her arms over her head and swivels her hips to the pulsating beat of the music. Just for a moment our eyes meet and now she knows I'm watching her. Not that I'm being shy about it.

She runs her hands over her body.

Her waist.

Her hips.

Her breasts.

All while keeping eye contact with me. She licks her lips and drops it low and I know she's baiting me into joining her. How can I not watch her when she is putting on a show like this? She's dancing with her friends, yeah, but the way she's moving her body? Yeah, that's one hundred percent for me. And I don't mind the visual fore-play one bit.

Though it's not doing a thing to help the flag status in my pants right now.

There's nothing better than a woman confident in her own skin. Her laugh and her smiles and the way she moves her body is having a strong effect on my dick, but I can't look away from her.

"Dude, you've got it bad," Milo says from the table, watching me.

Colby chuckles while taking a slow sip of his beer. "He so does."

"What?" Their talking distracts me enough to turn my head away from Ada for just a moment.

"Ada." Milo gestures with his head. "You're totally into her."

A contented smile forms on my lips. "What if I am?"

"Not a bad thing at all, my man. You deserve to be happy. It's fun to see you pining after someone."

I scrunch my face. "I don't think I'm pining."

"Dude, you're a fucking sucker for her," Dex adds. "Everyone sees it. You're pining with a capital P."

"Do you even know what pining means, Dexter?"

"Yeah. It means you want to stick your dick in her so badly you can't see straight."

I guess he has a point.

But it's more than wanting to stick my dick in her. I want to be the one who makes her feel good. I want to be the one she begs for. I want her to be desperate for me, for my touch, begging for the pleasure only I can give her. I want her crying out my name, over and over, as she comes undone right in front of me. I want to be the one who makes her happy in every way possible.

"I fucked up with Lori," I confess to them as I turn my head back to watch Ada. "I won't make the same mistake twice."

"And what mistake is that, pray tell?"

"I didn't...I don't know, love on her enough."

Quinton scowls. "No fucking way. I don't buy it."

I shrug. "I can't possibly have given her enough attention when I was home. She never said it but in the grand scheme there has to be a reason she left, right? And I'm not saying that because I want her back. Fuck that. If she didn't love me, then far be it for me to keep her trapped in a relationship she didn't want to be in, but still. That has to be the reason. I didn't give her enough."

Which is why I'm going to give Ada fucking everything.

Quinton sits back in his chair. "I'll politely agree to disagree. You gave one hundred and twenty percent when it came to Elsie and Lori and keeping up with the rigors of the job."

I shake my head. "Nah. When I think back on how things were at home I think that was my downfall. I spent my free time with Elsie. I didn't try to make Lori feel loved and cared for and appreciated."

"Do you feel those similarities with Ada?" Milo asks me.

"No. Ada is completely different from Lori. She has this..." I watch her swing her hips with her friends still laughing and smiling without a care in the world. "This confidence about her. She's comfortable in who she is. She has a story, you know? She's kindhearted and whimsical, funny, and compassionate. She knows where she's been and she knows who she is and she's creating her own new path." I breathe in and release a deep sigh. "And I find myself wanting to be part of it."

My phone buzzes in my pocket alerting me to an incoming text message so I pull it from my jeans to see who it's from.

GRADY

Found her. Paperwork delivered! You're free.

ME

Grady I could fucking kiss you right now. This news could not have come at a better time! Thank you!

GRADY

My pleasure! Talk soon.

"Fucking hell, this might just be the best day of my life."

"Good news?" Colby asks, watching my smile widen.

"Yeah. Grady found Lori. Said divorce papers were served and I'm free. Thank fucking Christ."

Dex pats me on the back excitedly. "Thank God. Now can we *please* fuck the nanny?"

I laugh. "You cannot fuck the nanny, Dexter. But I...I can finally fuck the nanny."

"Damn right you can. Time to go get your...whoa, what's happening over there?"

Dex gestures to where the girls are dancing. And my smile begins to fade when I see a group of men step into the circle to try to dance with them. My heart rate accelerates and my nostrils flare as I watch one of them put his hands on Ada's hips. I see when her sincere smile morphs into a completely fake one. I notice her body posture stiffens and the laughter in the group subsides as several ladies are approached. They're not scared at all. They know we're close by, but that doesn't mean they want the attention they're getting from men they don't know.

"No fucking way," Colby says, standing from his chair, his eyes glued to Carissa.

"Yep, that's our cue." Milo stands as well and I'm right behind him stalking towards Ada. Not in a predatory way. Unlike Colby, I'm not looking for a fight tonight, but no way in hell am I going to let another man put his hands on my girl while I'm standing mere feet away. If anyone touches her, it'll be me.

"The lady's with me." It's all I have to say to the man before his hands are up in defense and he's backing away having recognized who I am.

That's right, dickwad. I'm Zeke fucking Miller, now back the fuck off.

Ada watches me with an ornery smirk on her face, but she doesn't say anything.

Thank God, she's not pissed with me.

I place my hand on her hips as the music changes to something with more of a slow, sultry beat. She brings her hands to my biceps and stares up at me, her eyes telling me everything I know she can't, or won't, say aloud.

"You alright?"

"Mhmm," she says. "Just been waiting on you to come join me."

"I don't like seeing some other guy put his hands on you."

"Good. Because I didn't like some other guy putting his hands on me." She lays her cheek against my chest, inhaling deeply, as if my scent alone calms her. The thought kicks m into action and I pull her tighter against me, sliding my leg between hers, so she's straddling my thigh.

"I want to be the only one who touches you."

"I want that too." Her voice is quiet, but somehow I hear her loud and clear, and her words go straight to my crotch. My dick is hard enough to pound nails, and I'm positive she feels what she's doing to me. This woman is intoxicating. It's easy to block out everybody else in this bar when I'm dancing with her. As if everyone simply disappears.

It's just us.

Dancing.

Feeling.

Wanting.

Anticipating.

The song comes to an end but I don't want to take my hands off her. The mere thought of adding space between us is unbearable. I need her hands on me, her body pressed into mine, like I need my next breath.

I stare down into her eyes looking for that sign of needy desperation that I feel when I'm with her and wholeheartedly believe I see it gazing back at me. Our eyes stay locked and I continue to move us slowly even though the tempo of the song is faster now. The rest of the bar fades away, leaving us in our own little bubble of lust.

Our own personal space.

She tilts her chin, her eyes flitting between mine and my lips, and I know she wants me to kiss her. I lean my head down so I'm mere centimeters away from her. Enough that I can smell a hint of citrus and tequila in her breath.

"Zeke," she murmurs against my lips.

"You want me to kiss you." It's not a question but a fact.

"More than you know." Her eyes fall closed and she nods only the slightest bit. "I'm dying for it." Her earlier words about not denying a dying man his wish tumble through my brain as I slide my fingers through her long locks, gathering her hair in my fist, as I would if I were going to press my lips against hers. Her tongue darts out, wetting her lips, and my god, every cell in my body wants to suck that plump pink lip into my mouth.

Fuck, I want to ravage her.

But I can't do that, not here. Which means, it's time go. "Pick a number sweetheart." I bring my mouth to her ear and murmur. "Any number, between one and five."

She opens her eyes and studies me, her brows pinched.

"Trust me. Pick a number."

Her lips turn down in the cutest pout. "Three," she finally answers.

"Three it is." I nod, more than ready to rise to the challenge. "You ready to get out of here?"

"Not until you tell me what three means." She bites her bottom lip anxiously but I smile and pull it from her teeth with the pad of my thumb and then bring my lips once again to her ear.

"It means when I get you home you're not sleeping tonight until you've had three very satisfying orgasms."

She gasps beside me, but I don't move and neither does she.

"It means I get to strip you naked and feast my eyes on your beautifully sexy body, and when I've had my fill I'm going to lick your pretty pussy until you're dripping wet and screaming my name."

"Zeke," she sighs breathily.

"Then, I'm going to use my fingers... make sure you're really ready to take me."

"Yessss...please."

"And when I think you're ready, I'm going to slide my cock into your tight pussy and fuck you so hard the only words you'll remember will be more, please, and Zeke."

"Take me home, Zeke," she pleads. "I'm ready now. Right now."

19
ADA

We rush out of the bar, tossing a goodbye to our friends over our shoulders, ignoring Dex's teasing jabs on our way out, and make a mad dash for Zeke's car. Like a gentleman, he opens the passenger side door for me and even helps secure my seatbelt, brushing his arm against my chest in the process.

"You did that on purpose." I gasp with a smirk.

His hungry eyes meet mine and I can feel the tension in them. "Did I?"

He closes my door and walks around to the front, sliding in next to me, not saying much at all. This may very well be the quietest twenty-minute drive we've ever had. If he's anything like me, he's thinking about every detail of what might happen the minute we walk through his front door.

Because that's what's running through my head.

What his tongue is going to feel like on me.

What it will feel like when he's pulsing inside me.

Does he have condoms?

Should I tell him I'm on the pill?
Why can't he literally live next door?
This drive is almost painful.
How could I turn the table and tease him a little?
Give him a little taste of his own medicine...
Make him feel all hot and bothered before we even get in the door.

Turning my gaze toward him, I study his face. Clenched jaw, steely focused eyes, hands gripping the steering wheel. A glance at the speedometer tells me he's pushing the speed limit and that makes me smile to myself.

He wants to get home.

He's tense.

Turned on.

He wants this as much as I do.

I reach over and slide my left hand across his thigh, squeezing ever so slightly. The light hiss of a gasp telling me I've caught him off guard.

"You okay over there?" I ask knowing full well he's anything but okay.

To my surprise though, he moves my hand from his thigh to his stiff bulge allowing me to feel how turned on he is for me. "Does this tell you anything?"

"That must be uncomfortable," I tease him.

He lets out a little scoff and gives me a sideways smile. "Totally worth it."

I trace my thumb over his erection and hear him mumble "Christ."

A number of dirty thoughts run through my mind. "I could help you with this you know."

"Not necessary," he answers softly.

"I don't believe I said anything about it being necessary."

Maybe I'm crazy.

Maybe I'm stupid.

Or maybe I'm just a woman extremely turned on by the man she's going home with, because I want this man right now. I want to see what he does when the tides are turned and I'm the one in charge. And more than that, I'm desperate to please him.

I give his jeans one strong tug and smile when the button pops open. Zeke glances down to my hand before his eyes are back on the road. "Ada, what are—"

"Shhh," I tell him as I gently pull the zipper down, sneak my hand into his boxer briefs, and free his hardened cock from the confines of the tight fabric.

"Fuuuuck, Ada."

A proud smile spreads across my face as I grip his straining shaft in my hand, massaging his velvety soft skin between my fingers. He closes his eyes for just a second before I take control of what I've started.

"Eyes on the road Mr. Miller."

"What are you doing?"

Marveling at your impressive cock.

Praising the penis Gods on your behalf.

Fantasizing about what you taste like.

"Exploring."

I can tell I'm affecting him. His breathing has picked up and he moans with every movement of my hand, but he also shifts in his seat, settling in and spreading his legs. Allowing me the opportunity to play. "I know I should be stopping you, but I'm not going to lie. Your hand feels fucking good around my cock."

I lift a brow. "Your cock?"

He looks at me questioningly.

"No Sir," I correct him, squeezing his shaft a little tighter in my hand, making his mouth open as he draws in a tight breath. I lean over the small console and swirl my tongue around the head, licking the precum from the tip.

"Ada. Fuuuuck."

Licking my lips, I state matter-of-factly, "This cock is no longer yours. You see, I've licked it. And now that I've licked it, it's mine."

He laughs. "Fucking hell."

But he's not laughing anymore when I lean over and take his entire swollen cock into my mouth as far back as I can possibly go.

"Motherrrr fuuuuck, Ada."

He slides a hand into the tendrils of my hair as if he's going to guide me, but he lets me have complete control.

"This okay?" I ask, taking just the tip into my mouth this time, swirling my tongue over the sensitive skin.

"More than okay," he groans. "It's fucking phenomenal."

His praise emboldens me. I live for every moan and groan he shares with me. I want every one of them. Opening my mouth wider, I suck him in until I feel him at the back of my throat.

"Jesus fuck," he moans. "You're going to make me lose control."

"Then you better get us home quickly," I tease before I

squeeze the base of his shaft with my hand and suck the rest of him into my mouth hard and fast. He can't let his head roll back. He can't move from where he's seated, and he can't close his eyes. I glance up enough to see him biting his lip and trying to steady his labored breathing, but it's a losing battle.

Smiling to myself, I suck harder. Faster. Squeezing him as he hits the back of my throat over and over and over again.

"Ada...fuck," he gasps, tapping my head. "I'm going to come, Ada."

I refuse to relent. I want this orgasm more than I've ever wanted anything. I won't edge him. I'll get him to the finish line because I'm hungry for him. Keeping my pace, I lick and suck and squeeze and lick and suck and squeeze until I feel his body tense beneath me.

He tightens his hand in my hair. "Ada!"

His cock swells between my lips and then pulses as he comes violently in my mouth.

"Fuuuuck me."

I swallow every drop of him I can get, reveling in the sound of his voice when he comes, desperate to hear that sound again. When I finally pull him from my lips there are a few drops of cum that I happily swipe off the tip with my fingers. He's sitting back in his seat, watching me with complete fascination as I lick my fingers, devouring his last few drops from my skin.

"I..." he starts, shaking his head in disbelief. "Nobody's ever done that for me before." He draws his knuckles down my cheek with a tenderness I did not expect.

"You've never had a blow job?"

He chuckles. "Honestly, I'll be damned if I can

remember even one after that little stunt you just pulled. But what I meant was nobody has ever given me a blow job while I was driving."

Turning my head, I realize we're sitting in his driveway and smile because it never dawned on me that we had stopped.

"You are incredible, Ada." He rubs his thumb over my glistening lips. "Now stay put while I put myself back together and get your door for you, because once we're in that house, you belong to me." He eyes me with a heated stare that either says he's going to reward me for the phenomenal blow job or punish me for it. Either way, I'll take whatever he has in store.

Not bothering to park his car in the garage, he climbs out and makes his way to my side opening the door for me. He offers me his hand and helps pull me from my seat and then leads me up the walkway to the front door. Since I've done it way more times than I can count by now, I punch in the code and unlock the door, pushing it open and stepping inside.

But I don't get three feet in the door before his hand wraps around my wrist and he tugs me against him, my back to his chest. He kicks the door shut with his foot and kisses the side of my neck just under my ear.

"I meant what I said in the car. Every fucking word," he growls against my skin, causing goosebumps to pop up on my arms and a wave of warmth between my legs. "Take your clothes off. Now."

"Right here?"

"Right fucking now, Ada." His voice is a dark command I can't help but obey. I turn so I can see his face as I strip down in front of him. He watches my every move as I pull my jersey up over my head and let it drop to the floor. I kick off my shoes and then shimmy out of my black leggings so I'm standing before him in nothing but a pair of red lace panties and a matching bra. His eyes dilate as they rake over my body but he doesn't say a word and that's how I know when he said he wanted my clothes off, he meant all of them.

Holding his gaze, I reach back and unclasp my bra, letting the straps fall down my arms, and then pull it from my body. I toss it onto my pile of clothes and then push two fingers down my hips hooking them into my panties until they're also at my feet leaving me naked for Zeke's viewing pleasure.

He stares at me for what feels like many long minutes and I wonder what is going on inside his head.

He's not smiling.

He's not saying anything.

Does he like what he's seeing?

Is he not as impressed as he thought he would be?

Is he having second thoughts?

Oh God, what if he's having second thoughts?

This is bad.

Unbelievably bad.

Maybe we shouldn't do this.

Maybe he's not ready.

I can tell him it's okay.

We're both adults.

Standing here now a bit uncomfortable I move to cover my body, slightly turning to grab my clothes but his hand grips my waist to stop me.

"Don't."

"But—"

"Don't cover what's mine."

"Yours?"

He turns me so my chest is against the front door and then drops to his knees. "Yeah." He breathes out harshly. "All mine."

Without warning he pushes my legs open from behind me, grabbing my hips and pulling them out to give himself room. He palms the flesh of my ass, rubbing me, kneading me, spreading me with his thumbs, and then he plunges forward and laps at my pussy with his tongue.

All at once every single thought I had in my brain melts away and is replaced by one frenzied sensation after another. My hands fly to the front door to steady myself and the room spins as my jaw flies open and I gasp so hard I nearly lose my breath.

"Hooooly shit." I can't keep my body still because his tongue flicking at my clit has my body in a tailspin of immediate need to feel more of him. His whole tongue. His whole face. His whole hand. Whatever he's doing, whatever he's going to do to me, I already need more of it.

Zeke spanks my flesh, making me cry out, and then rubs the pain away with his hand. He turns on his knees and dives underneath me so he's kneeling against the front door. He lifts my legs one at a time and places them over his shoulders so I'm practically sitting on his face.

"Zeke, I'm going to fall!"

"No, you're not. I've got you. Right where I fucking want you." He inhales a deep breath, his nose parallel to my clit. "Fuck, you smell amazing. And you taste like

Heaven." His hands holding my ass, he pulls my body against his face, flattens his tongue, and licks me from pussy to clit, flicking my clit three or four time in a row when he reaches the sensitive nub.

"Ooooh my God!" I gasp and release a visceral groan louder than humanly necessary, but I can't help myself. Every one of my nerve endings is on fire. My heart is racing and my clit is pulsing with desire and I'm starting to sweat. "Zeeeeke."

He chuckles against my clit, the vibrations fueling the fire inside me. "You like that, Sweetheart?"

"For the love of God, Zeke, do not stop."

"Oh, there's no plan to stop. This caveman eats until he gets his fill and right now, Ada, he is so far from full. I plan to eat you as if you're my first meal..."

He swipes his tongue through me.

"My last meal..."

He sucks my arousal into his mouth.

"And every goddamn meal in between. Hang on. We're moving."

Zeke stands up with me sitting on his shoulders and I wrap my arms around his head just to hang on. His hands on my ass, he slides them up my back and then down again, flicking my clit with every step he takes. I don't know how he knows when to stop when he can't see where he's going but he lowers me down perfectly on the carpeted steps leading to our bedrooms. He leaves my legs over his shoulders, spreads me once again with his thumbs, and plunges his tongue into my pussy, licking me, eating me, feasting on me as I shiver beneath him.

"Oh fuck, yes." I squeeze my eyes closed. "It's so good. So, fucking good."

"Don't close your eyes, Ada," he demands, pulling his face away and piercing me with his hungry stare. "You're going to watch me eat you. Watch me devour you." He tenderly presses two fingers inside me and I whimper at the full feeling. "You're going to watch me take every last drop this sweet pussy can give me."

He curls his fingers and rubs them against my inner wall. "You're deliciously wet, Ada. Eating you is my new favorite thing." He pulls his fingers out, much to my disappointment, and sucks them into his mouth. "Mmmm. Fucking delicious."

"Zeke," I plead, desperate for him to deliver the release I so badly need. "Please don't stop. I need you."

"Need me where, Sweetheart? Tell me what you want and I'll give it to you."

He could've brought me in here, spread my legs, and fucked me to chase his own orgasm, but he did no such thing. His sole focus since we got home has been me and my pleasure. I swallow back any fear of rejection because this man makes me feel so goddamn wanted and so fucking sexy.

"I need you to eat me like you're a goddamn animal until I come all over your face."

His lips turn up in a proud smile. "Yes ma'am."

He doesn't wait for further instruction. He plunges his two fingers back inside me and curls them up, flicking my inner wall with a torturous pulse as he leans forward and laps at my clit like a ravenous creature.

Licking, sucking, circling.

Licking, sucking, circling.

"Oooh my fucking...yes!"

My mouth falls open and I'm panting as I buck my hips against his mouth, fucking his face with wild abandon, not a care in the world as I reach for my climax.

"Yes...yes...yes...yes! Zeke, oh, my God, yes!"

He doesn't stop. He quickens his pace flicking my clit and then sucking it as hard as he can as I ride his face. "Oh God, Zeke, I'm going to come. Oh, God! Oh God! Yes!"

With his free hand he reaches up and tweaks my nipple and my body tenses as I fly wildly over the edge screaming his name.

"ZEKE! Fuck! UNNNNGH"

Holding me still as I come down from my high, he lazily laps at my dripping pussy, causing smaller little after-shocks when he touches my sensitive skin, and then pulls himself away.

"That's one, Ada," he tells me as he wipes his mouth with the back of his hand. "Now get your sweet ass in my bed, head on the pillow, legs spread, and your hands on the headboard, and then wait for me."

20

ZEKE

She is so fucking beautiful.

Maybe equal parts shocked and turned on at how demanding I am with her tonight, but she's taking it in stride and so far, I've heard no complaints.

Thank God I heard from Grady tonight so I could indulge in pleasuring Ada without a worry in the world. I'm finally free from the chains that have been holding me back for the last several years. Free to rebuild a life with someone I genuinely care about. Someone I know cares about me and even more, loves my kid the way I do.

I watch Ada as she climbs the stairs one at a time, a little weak in the knees, and turns down the hall toward my room, although after tonight I have every intention of calling it ours. When she's out of eyesight, I collect her clothes, stuffing her red lace panties in the pocket of my jeans for safe keeping. I punch in the number for the alarm at the front door and turn off the lamp in the foyer we had left on.

And then I head upstairs for round two.

When I finally strut into the darkened bedroom illuminated only by the moonlight, I find Ada right where I instructed her to be. Her head on my pillow, legs spread so I can see her swollen pink pussy, and her hands holding onto the headboard. She doesn't say a word as I step over to my dresser and pull out a few condoms, tossing them onto the bed.

"Do you trust me, Zeke?"

Her question catches me off guard. "Do I trust you?"

"Yeah."

I climb onto the bed hovering over her and place a soft lick and kiss over each of her nipples, her back arching in response. "You're literally laying on my bed, spread eagle and bared for me and you think I wouldn't trust you?" I chuckle. "Sweetheart, it's probably me who should be asking you that question."

"You don't need the condoms," she says softly.

I pull back and gaze into her eyes. Not questioning her in the slightest but wondering what she's thinking. I'm about to ask when she adds, "I've been on the pill since Luke died. And I haven't been with anyone since."

"Neither have I," I confess to her. "I can tell you I'm clean but I can understand if you don't—"

"I trust you," she murmurs, and I see the sincerity in her eyes. "When you're inside of me, I don't want to have anything between us. I want to feel you, Zeke. All of you. Only you."

Be still my fucking lonely heart.

"You're sure?" I need her to tell me this is what she wants because I'll be damned if we end this night with any regrets whatsoever.

"One hundred percent."

I climb off the bed and toss the condoms into the trash and then slowly strip off my clothes for her. I pull my belt from my belt loops and unbutton my jeans. She licks her lips when I shove my pants and boxer briefs down, freeing my stiff cock, and step out of them.

"Fuuuck me," she breathes, marveling at my naked body standing before her.

"Oh, I plan to, Sweetheart." I crawl back up the bed holding myself over her once again, my cock brushing against her wet pussy.

Fucking hell she feels amazing.

Cupping her face in my hand, I lean down and kiss her gently, our tongues weaving together before I pull back. "I want this, you, us, so fucking much, Ada, but I need you to know, you're in control here. If at any point it's too much, just say so."

Her smile makes me weak in the knees. "It's not too much, Zeke. It's never too much. As far as I'm concerned, it's not enough."

"Good," I tell her as I roll to her side and spoon her from behind, my hands palming her soft round breasts. I squeeze her nipples between my fingers and catch her earlobe between my teeth. "Because you're going to be a good girl and ride my cock until you scream a second time."

"God yes," she whimpers. I slide my hand over her thigh and in between her legs until I'm gripping her pussy in my hands. And then I roll to my back with her body lying on top of mine, her back to my chest. My cock teasing her entrance. I murmur in her ear, "You're going to feel me stretch you, Ada. Fill you, claim you, and then we're going to fuck. Hard and fast until you come apart on my cock."

She's already panting and when I slip a finger through her pussy she's so slick I could eat her all over again. "So, fucking wet for me already."

"Yessss," she hisses when I pull my finger out and wipe her arousal around her nipples.

"Can't wait to suck that off. Are you ready for me?"

"Like this?"

"Just like this, Sweetheart." I grip my cock, stroking myself once, twice, three times and then line myself up with her entrance knowing she can't really see, but she can absolutely feel me. I have her scoot down just a bit and then with one slow thrust, I'm sinking inside her and we're both sighing in tandem.

"Jesus fucking Christ," I murmur. Her pussy is even better than I imagined.

Soft.

Warm.

Tight as hell.

"You feel as amazing as you taste."

"Zeke." My name is a twisted half sigh, half moan from her lips as she adjusts to the fullness of me.

I grip her hips and hold her still, thrusting myself into her slowly several times over, my eyes nearly rolling back as I indulge in the warmth and tightness of her sweet pussy. "I love how well you take my cock, Ada. You've got me so fucking hard."

"More," she pants against me. "Need more. Want more."

"I'm all yours, Sweetheart." I spread her legs wide, to

the outside of my own, placing her feet flat on the mattress on either side of me. "Ride me. Fuck me. Use me for your pleasure. Take me as deep as you want. I want to feel you come apart on my cock."

Ada pushes up with her feet and sinks back down on my cock. "Just like that, Baby," I groan. "Fuck, that's incredible."

She repeats her movement as I slide my hands up her soft body to her breasts, squeezing them in my hands.

"Oh my God, Zeke," she cries. "It's too good."

"You like that?" I murmur.

She moans, picking up her pace. "Yessss."

"Your pussy was made for me, Ada." I slide a hand down and rub her clit and she gasps loudly.

"Oh Fuck! Zeke!"

"You do it, Ada," I breathe against her ear. "Touch yourself. Feel how fucking wet you are. Play with that pretty pink clit while you take my cock and don't you dare stop."

"Yessss, Zeke."

I help her out a little by lifting my hips every time she slams down on me, heightening the sensation for both of us. If I'm not careful I'm going to blow my load all over the damn place, and I can't have that happening too soon so I focus all my energy on Ada. Her pleasure. Her happiness. Her orgasm.

We're in the throes of passion now, both of us working up a sweat, our bodies working in tandem. I bite down on her earlobe and then suck it into my mouth. "Such a fucking good girl, Ada. Give me more. I want everything. Everything you can give me."

Her mouth falls open, the sounds she's making with every thrust has me wanting to give her everything in return. I could listen to her all night long.

"Zeeeeeeeke."

"I know, Baby. You're almost there. Come on. You can do this. Keep your hand on that clit and ride this cock. Take it all. Fucking milk me."

I bring a hand to her breast and move the other to her neck, holding her tightly against my throbbing body. "Yeah, yeah, yeah, yeah, yeah," I growl into her ear. "You're fucking perfect, Ada. Let me hear you. Fucking scream for me."

She rubs at her clit harder and faster, her jaw wide open and her eyes squeezed closed. Her voice rising in pitch with every sound she makes. "Yes, yes, yes, ooooh..." And then suddenly her body is stiffening, she lifts her legs in the air and she's screaming, "Oh, MY FUUUUUU-UCKING GOD!"

So proud of her accomplishment, I loosen my grasp on her body and rub gently down her torso to her legs. "That was incredible, Ada." My dick is still painfully hard and I'm in need of my own release so I kiss the side of her head tenderly and then roll us both until she's on her stomach. "That's two. But you've got one more in you."

I tug her hips up in the air and grab one of the pillows to push underneath her so she's comfortable. Then I warm the globes of her ass with the swift spank of my palm. "This won't take long, Sweetheart. You've got me hard as fuck and I need to come inside you."

"Yes," she moans, shimmying her ass and making me smile. "Please, Zeke."

I don't even have to touch her to know she's glistening wet for me so I inch myself inside her, taking my slow sweet time, until I'm in balls deep.

"Ooooh fuck, that feels good," she moans.

"Yeah? You like having my cock inside you?"

"Yessss."

"You want more?"

"Sooo much more," she whimpers.

"Grab the edge of the bed, Baby."

Her arms fly out to grip the edge of the mattress as I pull her hips up even higher and pound into her.

"Yes, Zeke! Feels so good. Oh, God, yes!" she cries out, panting with my every thrust as I quicken my pace watching her slick pussy suck me in over and over and over again. Her confidence knows no bounds and hell if she isn't a remarkable sight. Fucking Ada isn't like anything I thought it would be.

It is one hundred billion times better.

It's indulgent.

It's intense.

It's enthralling.

It's all consuming.

"Perfect, Baby. God, you're milking me. Do you feel that?"

"Zeeeeeke, I'm going to cooooome" she cries, her voice wavering to the pulse of our rhythm.

"Me too, Ada. I'm right there. Fuck!" Our bodies slick with sweat, I relentlessly thrust inside her chasing the end that I can feel nearing. "Shit. Ada, I'm there. Christ. Come with me. I want to feel this pussy clamp down on my cock and take me one more time. Take it all. Empty me."

At first I hear her gasp and then she doesn't make another sound. Fearing she's holding her breath, I spank her to get her to breathe and that's when she comes hard on my cock, squeezing it like a vise and not letting go until I'm exploding inside her.

"Ah, fuck. Fuck! Fuck! Ada, Jesus Christ."

As my body slows and with my cock still pulsing inside her I lean forward and pepper tender kisses across Ada's back while we both catch our breath. Once we've both come down from our high, I pull myself out of her and gently lower Ada's body to the mattress, rolling to her side and pulling her into my arms.

"Are you okay?"

"Mhmm." I can't tell if she's smiling or not but the tone of her voice sounds like she's more than satisfied. I grin lazily behind her and kiss the back of her head.

"Good. I'll clean you up, I promise. I just need to hold you for a minute."

I inhale a deep breath behind her, catching the scent of our sweat mixed with her raspberry shampoo. It's a scent I could wrap myself in and live in for the rest of my days. Though we lay here in the silence of my bedroom, I can still hear her voice in my mind. Every moan, every groan, every cry she let out for me in the throes of passion.

"That was pretty incredible, you know?" I murmur, squeezing her tighter against me. "You were absolutely breathtaking."

She doesn't respond right away and I wonder for a moment if maybe she's fallen asleep, but then I hear the faintest sniffle.

"You okay?"

Sniffle.

"Mhmm."

Oh no.

Is she crying?

"Ada?"

Sniffle.

"Yeah?"

"What's wrong?"

Sniffle.

"Nothing's wrong, Zeke."

Fuck.

Something is wrong.

My heart drops into my stomach and I immediately feel nauseous, but I sit up to try to get her to look at me.

"Shit, Ada. You feel bad don't you? You're regretting this."

Dammit! Exactly what I didn't want to have happen.

"Did I hurt you? Fuck. Ada, I'm so sorry. I didn't mean it, but if you're regretting this, I..." I push my hand through my hair. "God, fuck, we shouldn't have—"

"No." She turns so I'm hovering over her and stops me, shaking her head, her tears still streaming down her face. She brings a hand to my cheek.

"No, Zeke. Nothing is wrong. I'm three hundred billion percent perfectly fine." But she's still sniffling and tears are still streaming down her face.

"But you're crying." I shake my head completely baffled and quite frankly, scared of what she's going to say.

"I've never felt anything like that before in my entire life, Zeke. What we just did. All three times, it was...exhilarating and fun and hot as hell. You made me feel things I haven't felt in I don't know how long. Physically and emotionally," she cries, each tear shattering my heart for her. "And I'm sorry I'm an emotional mess, I promise it's just the drop in adrenaline because none of these stupid tears have anything to do with me regretting anything we've done. I think I just..." She shakes her head and shrugs her shoulder. "I needed this. I needed to feel again. And I needed to be able to explore those feelings with someone I trust. Someone I care about. I needed this with you."

I bow my head and press my lips to hers, slowly drying her tears with my thumb.

"Thank God, you're not upset with anything we just did because having the pleasure of watching you fall apart not once, not twice, but three times, was earth shattering for me. Thank you for trusting me."

She sniffles again but her mouth morphs into a smile. "It was pretty earth shattering for me too."

"I want so much more of this with you, Ada," I murmur, wiping more of her tears with the pads of my thumb. "I want to spend more time with you. Clothes off and clothes on. I want to date you and spoil you and laugh with you. I want to fight with you and have all the hot makeup sex with you. I want a life with you."

"I want those things too, Zeke."

"Good." I smile softly and nudge her nose with mine. "Then it's settled. You are officially mine and I am officially yours. Just you and me."

"And Elsie," she adds with a sweet smirk.

"Oh yeah. And Elsie of course but thinking about her when I'm naked after having just fucked her nanny three magnificent times, just feels a little inappropriate to me."

256

She crinkles her face and snorts. "It totally does."

"Also, I don't want to think of you as Elsie's nanny anymore."

Her eyes grow huge. "What do you mean? Are you firing me?"

I huff out a soft laugh. "No Babe. Not firing you. How about...promoting you?"

"Promoting me?"

"You're my girlfriend. My lover. My partner. But you just happen to spend your days living in my house with my kid."

She twists her mouth thinking. "Should we discuss the new terms of payment?"

Weird that she wants to have a business discussion when we're both naked in bed, but alright. "Uh, sure."

"Great. Anything you're paying me now will go into a savings account except for what I need to pay my bills."

"Done."

"And if the day comes where we make this umm, partnership, even more official, that money will either be donated to a charity or be given to Elsie."

"Perfect."

"All other forms of payment for my childcare services will come in the form of orgasms."

"I like the way you think."

"Okay then." She beams up at me and I don't think I've ever seen anything more breathtaking. "Kiss me so we can seal this deal and then we should shower."

"Yes ma'am."

ADA

"**H**ow's it coming?" Zeke rubs my shoulders as I push the last bit of tulle through my sewing machine.

"Perfect. Just a few more stitches and this one is done. Did you get the decorations hung up?"

"Yep. The birthday girl showed me exactly where she wanted her streamers and helped me with the tape. Then she insisted each chair have a balloon tied to the back."

"Perfect. Kinsley said she would pick up the cake for us and ooh, what about the food? Does Rory need me in the kitchen?"

"No! I don't need you in the kitchen!" Rory's voice rings out from the other side of the wall. "Hawk and I have everything under control."

"And by control," Hawken shouts with a stuffed mouth, "she means she's got cooking and plating under control and I've got quality tasting under control."

"Uncle Hawk!" Elsie giggles. "You can't eat all the food before the tea party!"

"Ooooh, I can't?"

"Nooooo!"

"Oh. Alright, Squish. I promise I'll stop but I really think you should try one of these cookies because they are delightful."

"He's totally feeding her cookies isn't he?"

Zeke laughs. "Without a doubt, yes, but it's her birthday. As long as she's happy, I'm happy."

I lift up the purple tutu I just finished making. "And as long as the guys are wearing these tutus like Elsie asked them too, I'm ecstatic."

"I don't know what's happened to us over the years." Zeke shakes his head, amused. "Having kids has made us all soft. I think the guys are more excited about this birthday party than Elsie is."

"That's because in her world, grown ass men wear tutus all the time. This is not out of her ordinary."

"I suppose you're right. And in case I've forgotten to say it or fail to say it later..." Zeke leans down and kisses the side of my neck. First near my collar bone and then behind my ear, pushing my hair out of the way to pepper my skin with soft, lingering kisses. "Thank you for going the extra mile for Elsie. All your planning has paid off. I think she's in for one hell of a fun afternoon and that's all because of you."

"It's my pleasure, you know that."

He leans into my ear, his lips so close I can feel his warm breath on my skin. "It will absolutely be your pleasure. I can promise you that. My thanks for being an amazing woman."

"Alright, you two. Get a room already," Hawken teases

as he passes by with food trays in his hands. For a moment, my cheeks redden and I look around praying Elsie isn't near us. Thankfully, she ran off to her playroom. She doesn't know about Zeke and me just yet and I kind of want to keep it that way for a little while. If it were up to Zeke, I'm sure the world would know, but I asked him to keep us on the downlow for Elsie's sake. He might not agree but he understood my request and respects my feelings so he's going along with it, albeit begrudgingly.

Zeke stands straight and smiles at Hawken. "I've got several rooms upstairs. Do you mind watching the kid while we put one to good use? It should only take a few minutes."

Hawken and I both drop our jaws at the same time, laughing at Zeke's audacity, but Hawken recovers and says to me, "I'm really sorry your man can't last for you, Ada. That's a crying shame."

Zeke flips Hawken the bird and winks at me, but I do him one better. Shrugging my shoulders I turn with the last tutu in my hand and explain, "Hey when the beaver's busy she doesn't wait. She goes after that wood with reckless abandon. I can appreciate a quickie."

Hawken places the food trays on the table, shaking his head and grinning. "Whoa. Okay. Who has two thumbs and wouldn't dream of denying the busy beaver her wood in a timely manner?" He gestures to himself with both his thumbs. "This guy."

Zeke pats Hawken's shoulder. "Damn right."

Six guys seated around a table in the sunroom, each one of them dressed in a different colored tutu and donning a tiara on the top of their heads might be the best thing I have personally ever laid eyes on.

"Oh yes, Darling," I hear Dex titter in his best rich-old-British-woman voice. "These cookies are to die for. You simply must have another." He gives a small bite of cookie to Summer sitting next to him, and then holds the plate out for Elsie.

"Oh, thank you, Uncle Dex." Elsie picks another cookie from the plate and takes a dainty bite, her pinky in the air and everything. She plays the princess role quite well if I do say so myself.

"You're welcome, Miss Squish."

Zeke didn't even have to pay his friends to show up for Elsie today. He told them what she wanted and they all willingly said yes and arrived ready to party with the five-year-old. Today I can feel the love through this house. The love for a little girl on her birthday. The love of friendship. The love of families coming together to support one another complete with a living room full of pack-n-plays and sleeping babies. The bond of a special brotherhood. It's kind of like what Luke had in the military. I appreciated it then and I appreciate it now. We girls are always quick to bond and form friendships and sisterhoods with small circles of friends. That select group of women we would bare our souls to, but to also see it among Zeke and his friends is something I hope he never takes for granted.

The guys love him, anybody can see that. And to hear it from Carissa, they've adored Elsie since the day she was born. Not that they don't love all the other babies that have been brought into this world via the couples in this house today, but Elsie was the first. Elsie is who made them all honorary uncles and second fathers. I think it's so sweet and melts my heart to see them play with her. She has them all wrapped around her dainty little finger and it's not only adorable, but incredibly swoon worthy.

"I don't know how on Earth, you pulled this off, Ada," Carissa says next to me as we watch the guys seated around the table with Elsie from the kitchen. "But seeing those six burly men wearing tutus and tiaras and having a tea party with Elsie is next level orgasmic." She sighs. "I'm pretty sure my ovaries are exploding as we speak."

"Right?" Tatum sighs. "Gah! Dex and I were just having an argument earlier over something stupid like dishes in the sink but now watching him in there, playing to that sweet girl's every whim...and with his own daughter next to him too..." She turns to me with a desperate expression on her face, tugging at her shirt like she's trying to fan herself.

"Do you have like, a closet or something we could use quickly because watching my man in there is making me all kinds of hot and bothered."

Charlee, Rory, Carissa, and Kinsley all laugh and then mutter, "Saaaame," before falling into a fit of giggles again.

"I mean, let's face it," Carissa sighs leaning back against the counter with wine in hand, "hot hockey guys in tutus and tiaras are hot as fuck. Well done, Ada."

I take a slow sip of my wine making eye contact with Zeke who gives me a quick wink. "When the five-year-old-to-be asks for a springtime tea party in the middle of winter with all her uncles complete with tutus and tiaras, Zeke agreed she gets what she asks for," I explain to them. An amused chuckle builds up inside me. "Plus, I was not about to pass up the opportunity to see these guys in their tea party glory so Elsie and I sat down and planned the whole thing. Right down to the color tutu each of them would get."

"Well, you did a remarkable job," Charlee states. "Really, this has been amazing to watch. Elsie looks so happy."

"Right?" Rory adds. "Dare I say, Lori would have never put this much thought and detail into a birthday for anyone let alone her own kid."

A feeling of unease washes over me at Rory's words. I turn slightly so Zeke can't see my face and so I'm a little closer to the ladies. "What can you tell me about her?"

"Lori?" Rory asks.

I nod. "Yeah."

"What do you want to know?"

"I guess I don't know." I shrug. "Zeke doesn't talk a whole lot about her. Just that they were married and she left him."

"Yep." Carissa nods. "That's pretty much what happened from what we all understand. They were happy together for a while and excited about Elsie coming along. I remember Colby telling me how ecstatic he was to show her ultrasound picture to the guys when they were in New Orleans for our wedding."

Narrowing my eyes, I shake my head dumbfounded. "So, then what happened?"

"Honestly, I think she just didn't love the life of a hockey player's wife, you know?" Charlee suggests. "It's no secret that their schedule is grueling and they're gone a lot. Sometimes we travel with the team but it's not very often. And now that most of us have kids at home, it's harder and more stressful to travel. So, we stay home."

"Was she close with you guys?"

Carissa, Charlee, and Rory look at each other and shake their heads before Carissa explains, "Well it would've just been Charlee, Rory, and me at that time. Right around the time Dex and Tatum met at Charlee and Milo's wedding we had all found out that Lori left Zeke and Elsie and nobody has seen her since."

"Seriously? She and Zeke don't talk? Doesn't that seem weird?"

Rory shakes her head, her lips pursed. "Not when she wanted nothing to do with either of them. The bitch couldn't handle the privileged lifestyle, and I use that word only because let's be honest, we're very privileged to be living these lives where if we didn't want to work, we wouldn't have to. Zeke commented once that she said she had more life she wanted to live and didn't want to be bogged down having to stay at home with a kid and no husband to be with her."

"Wow." My heart breaks all over again for Zeke even though I know he doesn't grieve that hurt anymore.

"Yeah. It was rough for a while," Carissa tells me. "But Zeke's parents stepped in and helped out with Elsie and the guys rallied around Zeke whenever they needed him."

"And then you came along," Kinsley says, nudging my shoulder.

"And then you came along," Carissa repeats. "And Zeke was never the same again."

"Uh oh. I hope that's a good thing." I cringe at her comment before taking another sip of wine.

She laughs. "An exceptionally good thing. He clearly loves you very much."

Hearing her say she thinks Zeke loves me causes my wine to go down the wrong way and I fall into a coughing fit. Kinsley pats me on the back several times and then I hear, "Everything okay in there, Darlings?"

"Uh, yes." I cough and clear my throat so I too can use my fancy old lady British accent. "Yes, my dear Colby. I do apologize most sincerely. My beverage seems to have caused me a wee bit of stress but not to worry. My faculties are in tip top shape."

"Oh, incredibly good to hear it. Cheerio Darling."

"Yes, Cheerio."

"Uncle Colby," Elsie giggles. "We don't have Cheerios."

"Well, that's particularly good then because everyone knows Lucky Charms are far superior, don't you think? I mean just look at all these marshmallows."

"Oh yes," she says. "The marshmallows are my favorite but Daddy says I have to eat the cereal parts too."

"Very wise man, your dad. He's an incredibly wise man, indeed."

"You alright?" Tate asks me.

"Yeah, I'm good."

Kinsley rubs my arm. "She just gets so choked up when it comes to her favorite goalie having feelings for her."

She's not wrong about that.

Several months ago, I was just a widowed woman playing with cats for a living.

Now I'm living with a professional hockey player, looking after his little girl full time, and easily falling in love with him.

"I know he has feelings me. We've both said as much, but love?" I shake my head. "I don't know if I would go that far."

The ladies all look at one another and clearly there's something between them I'm missing.

"What? You're all thinking something and not saying it, so what is it?"

Charlee cocks her head to the side and smiles. "Ada, the man is crazy about you. There is no question."

"But—"

"But what?" Rory asks. "Do you not feel the same?"

"No, that's not it at all. I just..." I sigh, my shoulders falling. "How do you know?"

"Because I edit romance books for a living and I read about the signs all the time. I saw them for Rory and Hawken and I saw them for Quinton and Kinsley."

"What signs?"

She shrugs. "You know, the little things. The way he looks at you like you're his lifeline. The way he's talked about you. At least hearing second hand from Milo who is rooting for you too, by the way. The way he watches you when you're in his presence. The way his eyes light up when you enter a room. I bet you anything if you walked into the sunroom right now, his heart would melt for you."

My cheeks heat at Charlee's explanation. It's one thing to have these thoughts on my own but to know the girls all see it too, that this isn't a thing just between Zeke and me.

It's a little bit weird for me. Not because we have feelings for each other but because I was hired to be Elsie's nanny.

"Can I ask you guys something and trust you'll give me an honest answer?"

"Of course," they say in tandem.

"Do you guys think it's weird at all that, you know, I was hired to be Elsie's nanny and now we're..."

"Fucking?" Kinsley smirks.

A nervous laugh escapes my lips. "For lack of a better word, yes. I know it took a while for us to get there, but now that we've finally crossed that bridge..."

"The sex bridge?" Kinsley asks, amused.

"Yes. The sex bridge." I nudge her playfully. "I'm not going to lie. It's been the best month of my life, but still...are people looking at us and talking about Zeke sleeping with his employee or anything like that because I would hate for it to be weird for him. Or for the press to say something completely off balance."

"Okay first of all, don't you worry about the press. That's what you have me for. If something ever comes out you two aren't happy with, I'll absolutely spin the narrative in your favor. Seriously," Carissa says with a hand on my shoulder. "Secondly..." She shakes her head. "I don't think it's weird at all. At least no weirder than Colby hating me at first only to find out he was falling in love with me."

"Or me," Charlee adds. "I showed up at Milo's door with a black eye and a couple suitcases in need of a place to stay for a while."

Wait. What?

"You did? Why have I never known this?"

She smiles at me. "Sorry. I assumed you knew."

It dawns on me that I've never asked any of the ladies how they got together with the guys. "I guess now that you mention it, the only one I knew about already was Kinsley." I turn to Tatum. "What about you and Dex? How did you get together?"

An ornery smile spreads across her face.

This ought to be good.

"I stuck my finger in his butthole one night in Key West and he couldn't stop thinking about me from that day on."

Rory cackles but then covers her ears. "TMI, Tate! TMI! I do NOT need to hear about my brother's butthole."

Tate giggles. "I mean...I'm just being honest. But in all seriousness he knocked me up that night and fate brought us back together just before Summer was born."

"Holy shit! That's amazing."

"It really is. But see? When the universe wants to put two people together, somehow or another it works out."

"What about you Rory? I imagine you've known Hawken a long time being Dex's sister."

"Yeah, we're probably the most non-unusual ones of the bunch." She cringes slightly. "Like you said we've known each other for a long time and it just sort of...happened."

"Happened." Tate snorts. "Sure." She winks at me and nudges Rory's shoulder. "You should definitely ask her about the yellow chair in her bedroom sometime."

"Ooh yeah and you should definitely ask her what nickname she's given to her favorite toy." Charlee giggles. "The whole story is just too good."

"Listen bitches," Rory laughs. "That's enough out of all you. We're supposed to be talking about how much Zeke loves Ada and Ada loves Zeke."

"Is that what we're talking about?" I squeal as my eyes grow huge and my cheeks redden. I tip back my entire wine glass, emptying the contents into my mouth.

"Mhmm," Kinsley says, pouring more wine into my glass. "I mean come on. It's okay to admit it. Has he said it yet?"

"What? I love you?"

"Yeah."

"No." I shake my head slowly.

"Well, do *you*?"

"I..." My thoughts jumble, my mouth dries, and my heartrate rises, but I take a deep calming breath and can't help the smile that unfolds across my face. "I think I do, yeah." I swallow back my nerves. "But do you honestly think he—"

"Yes. We do." Carissa nods for all of them. "And if he hasn't said it yet, I have no doubt he will. And soon. Does Elsie know what's going on between you?"

I shake my head adamantly. "Absolutely not. We've tried hard to keep her in the dark because if things go badly..." I swallow down one of my biggest fears. "I'm an adult, I can grieve through any potential heartache but to put a child through that? Again? I could never do that to her. She might not remember her mother being around but she still had a mom and her mom still left her. I could never forgive myself if she had all these hopes and dreams of a family and they were crushed by a breakup."

Kinsley grabs my hand, squeezing it in comfort. "Which is why you two aren't ever going to break up. You're only going to get stronger. And you have all of us to support you both along the way. Positive affirmations here.

No negative thoughts. Do you need me to bring you a positive potato?"

I smile, squeezing her hand back. "I've got two of them already."

"Positive pickle then? Positive pineapple? I can make whatever you need to keep the yucky thoughts out of that head of yours. Oooh how about a penis of positivity?"

"You have one of those?"

She laughs. "I mean...Quinton's never says no sooo..." She shrugs with a grin and I laugh with the ladies.

"Kinsley, your positive mindset knows no bounds and I am so very glad you're my friend."

22

ZEKE

"Daddy where are we going?"

"It's a surprise, Sweetpea. Daddy has one more surprise for your birthday."

"Ada, do you know where we're going?" Elsie asks from the back seat.

"Nope." She shakes her head. "I'm just as clueless as you are."

I want so badly to reach my hand across the console of the car and rest it on Ada's thigh. Or grab her hand and thread our fingers together just to feel her attached to me in some way. To feel close to her. And because I like touching her. I like feeling someone with me.

But I can't.

Ada isn't ready for Elsie to know about us just yet, and even though she's my kid and I'm fairly sure she can handle it, I also want to respect Ada's feelings. Her biggest fear is that something could happen between us that would cause us to break up and she's afraid of putting Elsie through that kind of pain. As if my pain from that happening wouldn't be one hundred times worse. I get it though. I'm an adult. Elsie's a kid who wouldn't understand the complexity of adult relationships and the difference between Ada being her nanny and Ada being a potential future stepmother.

So, for now, Elsie is in the dark and it sucks at times like this when we're all riding together. Ada gives me these little flirty smiles sitting in the passenger seat and I'm forced to clench my jaw and not react the way I want to. I glance over at her just in time to see her lick her lips and then bite down on the side of her bottom lip in that seductive way that makes me want to part her lips with my thumb and pull her mouth to mine.

Fuck, she knows what she's doing.

And it's driving me crazy.

But two can play at this game sweetheart.

With Elsie in the backseat on my side of the car, she can't see me adjust my crotch and then grab myself in front of Ada. From the corner of my eye, I can see Ada's smirk just before she turns her head to look out her window.

"You okay over there?" I ask her softly.

She turns her head, her eyes scanning me and then answers, "Yeah. I'm great." Her brows furrow momentarily as she looks at me and then she reaches over the console. "You've just got something right...here," she says, brushing a hand over my dick that is now getting uncomfortably hard in my pants. My gut reaction is to look into the rearview mirror to see if Elsie can see what's going on upfront but she's busy looking out her window and can't see a thing.

"What is it?"

"Hmm," she thinks aloud, practically groping me. Not

that I'm complaining one bit. "I can't really tell. Maybe a fuzz? Sorry it's hard to get off."

"Keep trying, will you?" I beg, wanting desperately to close my eyes and focus on the feel of her hand on my dick.

"Of course." She squeezes my stiffening shaft and looks up at me with those sensual eyes of hers. "Are we almost there?"

Understanding her double entendre, I nod my head. "Actually yeah. Closer than you think."

"Is that so?" She moans. "I'm super excited for the outcome of this ride," she says, emphasizing the word *come*. "What about you, Elsie? Are you excited?"

"Oh yes!"

Inhaling a deep calming breath and realizing we are in fact almost there, I tell Ada, "I think you got it. Thanks so much." She takes that as her cue and retracts her hand.

"Anytime." I turn onto the last road for our drive and Ada finally notices where we're going. Her eyes grow and she murmurs, "Are we going where I think we're going?"

"Mhmm." I nod with a smirk.

Suddenly I hear a squeal from the backseat when I turn into the driveway of the Paw Palace Animal Shelter. "Mr. Purrito! Ada! We're visiting Mr. Purrito!"

Ada squeals almost as loudly as Elsie did. "It looks like you're right, Elsie! We'll definitely have to introduce him to your daddy!"

"Yeah!" she exclaims, tugging at her car seat straps. "Let's go! I need to get out of my seat, Daddy! Hurry!"

"Alright sweetpea, give me two seconds to get out of the car."

And make sure I no longer show evidence of Ada's hand feeling up my crotch.

Ada comes around the car to help get Elsie from her seat but no way am I allowing her to step into the frosty chill of a winter day in Chicago to do something I am fully capable of doing. Nothing like a freezing cold chill whipping through your bones to shrink your balls and relieve you of a hard-on. No need to be thinking about groin pulls and pucks to the face that would have me out of commission and unable to play. Once we get Elsie out of the car, making sure her hood is up and coat is zipped, I walk with my two ladies into the warmth of Paw Palace, where Ada introduces us to some of the front office staff.

"Oh, Mr. Miller, we spoke on the phone yesterday," one of the women says to me as she offers me her hand. "It's a pleasure to finally meet you. I'm a huge fan of the Red Tails. I watch every game!"

I shake her hand and give her my kindest smile. "The pleasure is all mine and thank you so much for the support. We really appreciate all our fans. And yes we spoke yesterday about this little one picking out a kitten for her birthday."

Ada glances at me, her eyes lit with excitement. Elsie gasps. "Really Daddy? I get to pick a kitten? Just for me? For my birthday?"

"That's the plan, sweetpea." I crouch down to her level. "Do you think that would be okay?"

She jumps up and down in excitement. "Yes! Oh yes! I want Mr. Purrito! Can we, Daddy?" She brings her hands up and places them on my cheeks, which means I'm about to become a sucker for pretty much anything she could ask for. With her big brown eyes staring into mine, she asks, "Can you meet him and then love him and then I can take him home and me and Ada can love him every day? Mr. Purrito is Ada's favorite and I met him and I love him too and he should live at our house."

I glance up at Ada who has stepped away from us and is cringing slightly. She whispers, "I'm sorry, Zeke. I introduced them a few months ago. It's the only one she really knows but don't worry. There are plenty of kittens to choose from."

I look back at my daughter who is still jumping up and down enough that I almost ask her if she has to use the potty. "Well, Elsie, it just so happens that I didn't tell Ada we were coming here today because I wanted to surprise both of you."

"You did?" she asks.

"Mhmm."

"You did?" Ada repeats, her brows pinching in confusion. Both of their expressions are so cute it makes me laugh as I stand up and lift Elsie into my arms so the three of us are at the same level.

"I did. I kind of thought maybe we could let you look for a kitten friend," I say to Elsie, tickling her tummy. "And also see if Mr. Purrito would like to come live at our house as well."

I catch a quick glance at Ada whose eyes are glassy, but her smile tells me she is anything but sad. Elsie on the other hand, is nothing but a ball of excitement in my arms. She claps her hands and lays her hands on my cheeks again and kisses my forehead. "This is fucking awesome!" she shouts, much to our utter shock.

Everyone around us laughs at her unexpected outburst. "Elsie Miller! You said the fuck word."

"I'm sorry, Daddy! I couldn't stop myself! It just," she gestures with her hands, "flew out of my lips like a birdie!"

Ada, laughing, mumbles beside me, "She's so your kid, Zeke. But, I mean, she used it in the right context sooo..."

"I suppose she did." I hold Elsie's hand and whisper to her, "But maybe we should watch our language while we're here, okay? I don't think the kitties or the puppies like inappropriate words."

"Yeah, they might get scared." Elsie nods. "Can we go see the kitties now?"

"Yes, let's do it," I tell her.

Ada grabs my arm. "Zeke, you know you don't have to do this, right? Mr. Purrito has been a long time resident here, but I was never going to ask about—"

"I want to," I tell her, taking her hand and giving it a gentle squeeze. "Would it make you happy?"

She shakes her head, confused. "Of course, but I don't need a cat to make me happy. I can come visit them whenever."

"Not good enough, Ada. You deserve a special gift too. Let me do this for you."

"Yeah, Ada. You need a kitty too then we can have kitty time together."

"Are you sure?"

"I'm positive."

Her shoulders fall as her worry starts to fade and I feel lighter just knowing the smile growing on her face is there because of me. And fuck, do I love making her happy.

"Okay then. Let's do this." Ada gets the all-clear from

the woman in the front office and gives Elsie a high five and then we're soon standing in a room surrounded by a group of kittens.

Two and a half hours later, we're finally back home with a Mr. Purrito, a Miss Kitty Pants, and all the toys, food, treats, and comfortable kitty beds two cats could ever need. The joy I've gotten to see in Elsie and Ada's faces as they snuggled with their respective kitties all evening was better than anything I could have imagined. And the huge hug and kiss I got from Elsie along with a sincere thank you for her kitty gift makes me want to continue to give her the world.

I would do anything to keep my girls happy.

Because that's how much I love them.

Both of them.

And that's when the realization hits me.

I said I loved both of them.

Which includes Ada.

I love Ada.

Somewhere in the last several weeks I've fallen in love with her and I've never told her.

Would she want to hear it?

Is she ready to hear it?

Would it scare her away if I told her?

My phone dings on the kitchen counter as I'm wiping it down, about to close up the house for the night. When I see its Ada, I lean over to read it knowing she may need something and doesn't want to shout down the stairs when Elsie is sleeping.

ADA

Hey. Can you help me with something up
here?

ME

Yep. Be up in a minute.

I turn out the lights downstairs and make sure the
alarm is set and then make my way upstairs. I open Ada's
bedroom door but don't find her in there so I turn towards
my room and step into the darkened room.

"Hoooly shit," I murmur, knowing I need to keep
quiet so I don't wake Elsie. "You are a fucking sight for sore
eyes, Ada Lewis."

Laying on my bed, now covered in a white duvet and
matching white pillowcases, is my beautiful woman
dressed in the very same red lacey piece of lingerie she's
wearing in my favorite boudoir picture I saw several
months ago. Her long dark hair is feathered around her as
she's posed on my bed. Her back arched exposing her
luscious tits, her head tilted back elongating the smooth
column of her neck, her feet expertly pointed. One hand
positioned in her hair and the other reaching between her
legs.

"Fuuucking gorgeous, Ada. Shit, you're making me
hard already."

"Shut the door, Miller," she tells me. "It's time for me to
say thank you for my unexpected gift."

"You know I could say the very same to you right now,"
I tell her as I close the bedroom door. "I feel like I should be
thanking you for *this* gift." I lean on the closed door, my
arms folded over my chest. All the blood in my body

currently flowing toward my dick. "Seriously, I could stand here and stare at you like this all night long."

"You'd never make it that long," she teases.

"Oh no?"

"Huh uh."

"And why is that?"

"Because then you wouldn't get to feel me suck you off."

Jesus Christ, this woman will be the absolute death of me.

"Perhaps, but you know what I can do from over here?"

"What?"

I grab the neck of my shirt and pull it over my head and then unzip my pants. She watches me with intense curiosity as I tug down the flaps of my unzipped pants just enough to free my painfully hard dick and grip it in my hand. "I can watch."

"Watch?" She breathes, licking her lips in anticipation. She's so fucking cute it makes me chuckle. "Watch what?"

"Watch you as you get yourself off for me."

"Zeke...I—"

"Touch yourself Ada," I demand. "Slide a finger through that soft pretty pussy and then tell me how wet you are."

My eyes focus in on her right hand as she opens her legs a little wider on the bed and pushes the hem of her lingerie aside, dragging a finger through her slick warmth. Her gasp alone tells me everything I need to know but hearing it from her mouth is most appreciated. Her back arches even more and fuck, she is a thing of beauty.

"Oh, God...Zeke. I'm wetter than I thought."

"Good girl. That's what I like to hear." I stroke myself a few times, my hand gripping the base of my shaft and then sliding it up and over my head. I'm itching to stalk over there and slide my cock through her arousal so I can feel for myself just how warm and wet and soft she is. Instead, I take a few slow steps toward her around the front of the bed so I can have a perfect view of what she's doing. "Spread those legs a little more for me, Sweetheart. I want to see how soaked you are."

She draws slow circles around her clit, her mouth open as she sighs with pleasure. And then to my surprise she buries two fingers inside her tight wet center, leaving her thumb to play with her clit.

Jesus Christ.

Her body.

She's so fucking sexy.

And I'm so hard if I'm not careful I'm going to blow my load all over her without as much as a single touch. I slide my thumb over the drop of precum and spread it over my head, my eyes rolling back a moment at the silky sensation and the knowledge that my orgasm is looming. This won't take long.

"You are so fucking beautiful like this."

"Feels so good, but my fingers are a far cry from your strong cock inside me. And my thumb is not your tongue."

"Is that what you prefer Baby? My tongue? My cock?"

She moans as her pleasure spikes. "Always." Her eyes lock on my hand wrapped around my cock. "Zeke, you're gripping steel in your palm. You need the relief."

"I'll get it. I promise."

"Zeke," she cries, her eyes calling out to me. "Please. I need you."

Wanting to give her everything she wants and more, I grab her legs and spin her around on the bed so her head hangs off the mattress. "You okay like this?"

"Perfect." She eyes me standing over her and when she realizes just how close my dick is, she licks her lips and tilts her head back. She cups my balls in her hand and then swallows as much of me as she can until I'm hitting the back of her throat.

"Mother fuck, Ada," I gasp. Her tongue swirls around my cock, flicking just under the head and driving me absolutely fucking crazy.

She can only moan in response so I do what I can to join her. Pleasure her. Satisfy her at the same time. I lean forward over her exquisite body, kneading her breasts in my hands.

Pushing.

Pulling.

Sucking.

Biting.

With each little bite of my teeth on her breasts, she sucks me harder, tighter, hollowing her cheeks and fucking hell it is like nothing I've ever felt before.

"Ada you're going to make me come."

I reach my hand between her legs, slipping my fingers inside her and rubbing her slick arousal over her clit. I move my fingers at the same time I slowly thrust my hips forward and back, fucking her face, bottoming out inside her mouth, wondering just what it's going to feel like when I come down her throat.

"Jesus...Ada... You're so fucking incredible. I need to taste you too." I grip her hips and pull them toward me. "Bend your knees, up and around my head, Baby."

She allows her body to be contorted so that her swollen pussy is right in front of my mouth and I devour her like she's my oasis in the middle of the goddamn driest desert. My tongue delving inside her, licking her, swirling over her clit, tasting her.

Ravaging her.

"Zeeeeeke!" She squirms against me but I don't relent. Her teeth slide gently against my cock and if it's even humanly possible, I grow another inch and harden into an iron rod.

"Ada...fuck! I'm going to come." I continue to eat her sweet pussy until she begins to shake and I feel her climax on my tongue.

My breathing erratic, I take one last lick across her warm skin and feel when my balls tighten and my knees go weak. I jerk up in response knowing what's about to come, but I slip out of her mouth and end up blowing my load all over her face.

"Fuck! Ada. Shit. I'm so sorry."

But she's all smiles. Her tongue darting out to lick up what she can. Wiping it down her face and then sucking on her fingers.

This might very well be the hottest thing I've ever watched. But also, I've got to get her cleaned up.

"Ada keep your eyes closed, Babe. If it gets in your eye, it's going to burn."

"I don't even care." She sighs. "That was...amazing."

"We're not done yet, Sweetheart. You're coming with me."

23

ADA

Zeke lifts me in his arms and carries me into his bathroom, only lowering me to my feet once the water is on and it's warm around us.

"Tilt your head back. I need to wash myself off your face."

"I like you on my face." I smile, feeling satisfied yet hungry for so much more.

"Well at least let me get it out of your eyes first."

He helps tip me back into the water, washing away his cum, making sure to wipe it safely from my eyes with a warm washcloth.

"Okay. I think you're good. You can open your eyes."

Slowly, I open my eyes to see Zeke in front of me, his body pressed against mine, his hands smoothing my hair away from my face and then he dips his head and his lips are on mine. It's not a hungry fuck-me kind of kiss. This time is much more tender. Much sweeter, even with his tongue eager and pressing and his fingers fisting in my hair.

This is the kind of kiss women read about. The kind we fantasize about. The kind that knocks us off our feet.

His lips are warm and soft and his hands are possessive but gentle as they come up and around my back. He tries to unhook my red lace lingerie but fails miserably before sighing and smiling against my mouth.

"Fuck it. I'll buy you ten more in its place." That's what he says before he rips the lace with his bare hands until it falls apart and sinks to the ground. He kisses me a few more times, and then pulls back, gazing at me.

All of me.

"Have I ever told you how stunning you are?"

I grin lazily back at him. "You may have mentioned it once or twice."

"You're not like anyone I've ever been with before," he says, his eyes darting between mine and then running up and down my body like I'm a magical creature that will disappear any moment.

"Why are you looking at me like you're about to lose me, Zeke?"

"Because I don't want to lose you, Ada," he responds. "In these few short months, you've woven yourself into this life. My life. Elsie's life. And I've come to love every minute of it. Every moment watching you with Elsie. Every laugh. Every tear. Every shiver of a fever. Every snuggle on the couch. Every sigh from your lips. Every cheer when I'm on the ice. Every moan when my hands are on you. Every kiss, every hug. The feel of your hand in mine. Your body pressed against mine." He turns us so my back is against the shower wall.

"I love all those things too, Zeke. And I promise if your

worry is that I'm going to run away, I promise that thought has never crossed my mind."

"I think I'm trying to say I love you, Ada." Zeke swallows. His eyes never leaving mine.

"You...what?"

"I love you," he says again with a helpless smile. "I've fallen in love with you so fucking hard and now I can't breathe at the thought of you not being here. I'm talking about the forever kind of love. Not the settle until something else comes along. I don't want that, Ada. I want *you*. I don't want to be without you. You're my person. You make me want to try harder to be the absolute best version of myself. You make me want to show you how good a life together could be for all of us. Fuck, Ada, you make me want to put a baby in you so you can truly be the mother of my child because you're so fucking good at it and I need you."

"Uh..." I smile up at him but raise my finger. "Okay so maybe not that fast, though I very much appreciate the compliment," I tease with a wink.

"Sorry," he sighs. "I got ahead of myself."

"That's okay. Your feelings are valid and I love hearing them." I bring my hands to Zeke's cheeks just like Elsie did earlier today when we picked out kitties at the animal shelter. "So, can we focus on that I love you part? Because I love you too, Zeke. So much it hurts sometimes."

His shoulders fall as the tension leaves his body. "You do? It does?"

"Yes and yes."

"I don't ever want to hurt you."

"Nor I you, but that's what love is, right? The constant

ebb and flow of life and knowing that no matter what comes between us, we can solve anything...jump any hurdle as long as we love each other."

"Do you feel like we have hurdles to jump?" he asks me sincerely. "Because I promise you I'll bend over backwards to fix any issue if it means I'll get to have you in my life."

I shake my head. "There are no hurdles, Zeke. You're perfect. Elsie is perfect. This life...it's scarily perfect only because I feel like it's the best dream I've ever had and I'm afraid I'll wake up and this will have all been just that...a dream."

He kisses me again, his hands smoothing up my back to my neck, to my hair. "I love you so fucking much. And if this is a dream, I'm in it too, so I hope neither one of us ever wakes up."

"I think it would be okay with me if you wanted to tell Elsie."

He leans back, searching my eyes. "Are you sure? You're ready to tell her?"

"Are you?"

"Baby I've been ready since the day I interviewed you for the job."

"That's not true," I laugh softly.

"It is true." He nods. "I knew that day you were special. That there was something about you that intrigued me. And every day after that I fell harder. Faster." He slides his hands down my body until he's cupping my breasts in his hands.

"Zeke..."

"I need you. Want you. Right here. Right now."

"Yes. Please."

Like it knows just what to do, my body ignites at his touch, my chest swelling with a peaceful calm that I haven't felt in years. Like knowing the universe is finally putting two lonely souls together has freed me of my anxieties, my fears, my sadness. Like we're to melodies coming together to compose a beautiful masterpiece. An emotionally charged love song.

Zeke lifts me against his body, wrapping my legs around his waist, and then in one slow push he fills me. My head falls back against the shower wall and my jaw drops open at the fullness of him inside me.

"God, Zeke. You feel so good. I'm so full."

"I just want to feel you, Ada. I want to memorize how amazing you feel wrapped around me. How good we are together. How perfect we are. I want to show you how much I love you. Want you. And I need you to let me."

"I would let you do anything. I'm all yours, Zeke."

"Whoa! This a lot of colorful beads!" Elsie dips her hands into the bowl of beads I just placed in a dish on the table.

"You're right. There are lots of colorful beads. And what is the number one rule about touching the beads?"

"Beads do not go in the ears, the nose, or the mouth." She recites my rule back to me verbatim.

"That's right. Good girl." I place another bowl in front of her and pick up a handful to lay out in my hand. "Okay these beads have letters on them. See how each bead has a different letter on it?"

"Yep."

"These are the ones we're going to use to make a message for each bracelet and then we're going to use the colorful ones to decorate the rest of the bracelet. How's that sound?"

"Yeah! I want to make a pink one for Daddy," she says, sitting patiently at the table eager to throw her hand back into the bowl of beads.

"Okay, we can do that. And what would you like Daddy's bracelet to say?"

She crinkles her little face and thinks hard before she finally says, "I love you Daddy."

"Perfect. Here's what I'm going to do." I grab a piece of paper and write out the words I-L-O-V-E-Y-O-U-D-A-D-D-Y so Elsie can recognize each letter and then turn the paper to her. "Here you go. These are the letters we need to be able to spell out what you want to say. So now you get to search for those letters in the bowl and put them on this plate when you find them, okay?"

"Yeah. I can see a D already!" She smiles picking one daintily out of the bowl. "See?"

"Very good, Elsie! So, we need three of those Ds to spell Daddy okay?"

"Okay. I can find more."

"I know you can. You go for it while I cut our string to put the beads on."

Elsie searches for several minutes locating almost every letter needed and I watch her with a calm sense of pride that she can do this task so well. She'll be ready to knock kindergarten out of the park next year.

"What letter do you still need?" I ask her.

"Umm." She looks at the writing in front of her. "I need a L."

As she drags her finger through the bowl of letters, apparently a new thought occurs to her because she asks, "Ada, are you going to marry Daddy?"

Her question catches me off guard. I suppose it's not like I haven't thought about it, but I hadn't yet thought too hard about how Elsie might feel if that were to happen.

"How would that make you feel if Daddy asked me to marry him?"

"I would be happy. Would you be my mom if you marry Daddy?"

"Uh..." I cock my head trying to pick up on her facial expression. "Well, it would make me your stepmom."

"What's a stepmom?"

"Umm, it's kind of like a bonus mommy. I might not be the one who carried you in my tummy or gave birth to you in the hospital, but if I were your stepmom, I would be like a special extra mommy just for you."

"Would you still live here?"

"Of course."

"Would you still make me chocolate milk? And pancakes?"

I smile kindly at her. "You know I would. Nothing would change much if I married your daddy. It would really just mean I would be his wife instead of his girlfriend."

As she considers my words, the doorbell rings. I pick up my phone quickly knowing I'll have a notification from the Ring doorbell so I can see who is at the door before answering it.

Was Zeke expecting a delivery?

Oh no.

His parents?

Did I forget a playdate?

"Who's there, Ada?"

My brows furrowed and my lips pursed, I stare at a picture of a woman standing at the front door. She has long blonde hair and she's wearing what looks like jeans and an oversized sweater with a hat on her head and a scarf around her neck. I've never seen her before, but perhaps Zeke forgot to tell me someone was stopping by for some reason.

Getting up from the table I lay my hand calmly on Elsie's back, not wanting to alert her to the stranger at the door. "Not sure, but I'm going to go check. You stay here and find me that L okay?"

"Yeah," she responds, deeply focused on her letter finding skills.

I quietly make my way to the front door and unlock the deadbolt. With my phone in hand, I open the door and come face to face with the blonde woman. She's taller than I expected her to be from the doorbell camera. With slender features. Her high cheekbones are well defined and her nose is pink from the cold. Her gloved hands are clasped together in front of her but her posture seems stiff and her mouth curls slightly as her eyes rake over me in my leggings and Red Tails hoodie.

For a moment I almost regret not doing my hair and putting on makeup. This was supposed to be a cozy day at home with Elsie.

"Hello," I greet her. "May I help you?"

The look of utter disdain she gives me makes all the

tiny hairs on my body stand at attention. "Who the hell are you?" she spits. A scathing tone to her voice.

What the hell?

Why is she so pissy?

Who is this woman?

"Uh," I scoff. "I'm Ada. And you are...?"

"Who is it, Ada? Who is it? Is it Nana?" Elsie comes flying down the stairs and I watch in horror as the blonde woman's demeanor changes from explicit hatred of me to complete adoration and awe of Elsie.

My heart plummets through my stomach.

Oh shit.

It can't be.

"Elsie! My baby! Oh my gosh, you've grown up. You're such a beautiful little girl."

Lori.

This woman must be Lori.

She opens her arms and steps forward expecting Elsie to run to her arms but she does no such thing, nor will I let her. She grabs onto my leg, holding me tightly, and I maneuver myself in front of her, protecting her at all costs. Without taking my eyes off Lori, I rub Elsie's back and mutter to her, "Elsie, I want you to go back inside and stay there, okay?"

"But I found the L."

"Great job. Why don't you pick out all the pink ones you want to use next, okay?"

"Okay but Ada?"

"Yes, Baby?"

She points to Lori. "Who is that?"

Lori opens her mouth to speak but I beat her to it,

staring her down with all the mama bear vibes I can possibly give off. "She's a stranger, and you don't talk to strangers so you go on back to the table and I'll be there in a minute."

"Okay."

She retreats back inside and I watch as Lori's eyes follow her every move before they come back to me.

"I'm going to guess you're Lori?"

"You have no right to keep me from seeing my daughter," she snarls.

My grip on the door tightens and my heartrate skyrockets because I have no idea what this woman is capable of.

Why is she here?

Zeke said she left and they haven't spoken.

Is she trying to come back into his life?

Does he want that?

Did he know about this?

I know his phone would've gotten the doorbell notification too so the fact he hasn't said anything yet through the speaker tells me he's in the middle of practice.

Fuck.

"You mean the daughter who doesn't even recognize you? The daughter you walked out on and haven't seen since? Who the hell do you think you are?"

"I am her mother and I could say the same to you," she sneers. "What are you? The whore Zeke is cheating on me with?"

Cheating on her?

I rear back. "Excuse me?"

Her nostrils flare and she curls her hands into fists.

293

Go ahead.

Hit me, bitch.

It'll be the last thing you do.

But you'll get to Elsie over my dead body.

"You know when I divorce him and take his money, he won't have much left for you. I wouldn't get used to this big house and whatever other extravagant gifts he buys for you."

"What the fuck are you even talking about?"

She holds up a manilla envelope in her hand. "The divorce papers he sent me."

Divorce papers?

Wait.

My wall breaks and my guard falters when her words slap me in the face.

"Divorce papers?" I mumble. "When did...When did he send you those?"

For the first time since I opened this door, a smirk crosses her face and she looks pleased with herself. "From the surprised look on your face, I'm going to guess he sent them the day after he probably fucked you into submission."

What the hell?

Zeke is married?

He's been married?

All this time?

No.

There has to be another explanation.

Either way I'm done talking to this woman.

"You know what? Fuck you, lady. You don't know me. And you certainly don't know Zeke."

"Well, we'll see about that. Is he here or is he at the damn arena again?"

"Neither," I lie. "You don't need to know where he is."

She narrows her eyes and hollows her cheeks even more than they already are, her tongue moving from cheek to cheek. Finally realizing she's not going to win this battle of the bitches she steps back. "Fine. I'll find him myself. Or rather, my lawyer will be in touch. But you can tell him I don't sign these papers," she says, flaunting them in my face, "until we reach a settlement where I get at least half of his millions."

"Fat chance of that happening," I tell her. "You know damn well he won't give you a dime. You left your family, your own flesh and blood, and never looked back. You deserve absolutely nothing. Now get the fuck out of here and do not come back or I will call the police."

"He won't have a choice." Lori laughs as she backs up to her parked car in the driveway. "I can promise him that. Ta-ta...Ada, was it? If I were you, I'd start packing your bags now, Sweetheart."

It may be below freezing outside but I am sweating as I watch her get into her car and back down the driveway. Careful not to slam it and scare Elsie, I close the door, locking every lock and setting the alarm just in case and then I'm on my phone calling Zeke in an instant. The phone rings several times before it goes to voicemail, which I don't bother leaving knowing a text will be seen before my message would be heard.

> 911 at home. Elsie is fine. Lori showed up.
> I need you.

Knowing he is indeed at the arena and that Lori will most likely come looking for him, I call Carissa. She's the only one who will be able to get to Zeke fast enough to warn him of what's going on.

"Hello?" Carissa's voice on the other end of the line is a comfort to hear.

"Carissa? It's Ada." My clipped tone alerts her without fail.

"What's wrong? Are you okay? Is it Elsie?"

"No," I tell her, my voice shaking from the adrenaline and nerves. "Elsie's fine. Carissa, Lori just showed up at the house."

"Oh fuck."

"She's looking for Zeke and she wanted Elsie but I refused to let her near her. I tried to contact Zeke but he's not picking up and I think he would want to know."

"Good for you. That bitch! The guys are on the ice. I'm on my way down there right now." The clickity clack of her shoes tells me she's making her way to the ice at a slight jog if not a full run.

"Carissa," I breathe. "Did you know?"

"Know what?"

Bile rises in my throat as I force the words out. "Did you know Zeke was still married?"

She gasps. "What? Where on Earth did you hear that?"

"Lori. She had divorce papers with her that apparently Zeke sent to her not too long ago and she said she refused to sign them until they talk." I choke back my tears. "So that means he's married, right? All this time? And he never told me?"

"Noooo. He isn't. There's no way she's telling the truth. That's..."

I expect her to say "Impossible" but that word doesn't come.

"It can't be possible, right?" she asks softly into the phone. "He would've divorced her a long time ago. It's been years."

"But what if..." I try to think of any reason for him to still be married to that vile woman but my mind is such a jumble of all the words that were spoken in the last fifteen minutes, I can't form a coherent thought. "Fuck, Carissa, I don't know. I don't know what I'm supposed to do now."

"Okay, is Elsie safe?"

"Yeah. She's fine."

"And you're safe?" she asks calmly.

"Yeah. A little shaken up but I'm okay."

"Then everything is fine. I'm at the ice. I'll grab Zeke and let him know what's happening. I have no doubt he'll be driving home with his skates on to get to you."

"Thanks Carissa. I really appreciate you."

"Hey, it's no problem. Just breathe. And give me two minutes."

It's not three minutes later that my phone rings and Zeke's number appears on the screen.

"You're still married?" I whisper, surprising myself with how eerily calm the question floats from my mouth.

"What? Fuck!" he murmurs, his voice angry and cold. "Is she still fucking there? Are you alright?"

"No. She's not here. And no, I'm not sure I'm alright," I tell him, my voice shaking. "I told her to get the fuck out and not come back but Zeke, what's going on? She said—"

"What about Elsie? She didn't hurt either of you, did she?"

"Hell no. I would never let her touch Elsie." Anger rises up inside me. I would do anything to protect that little girl. I'd throw my life in front of hers if I had to.

"Thank Christ." I can tell by his silence that he's rubbing his forehead with his fingers trying to decide what to say next. "Ada, listen to me. I love you, okay? I love you. Nothing changes that. Do you understand?"

I'm silent for a moment as well, trying to rein in my thoughts and remain calm. The last thing I want to do is get upset and have Elsie asking all sorts of questions. Like why I'm sobbing in my bedroom or why I'm angrily throwing Zeke's shit out the window.

Or why I'm packing my bags.

"You being married changes everything, Zeke."

"Ada, I'm on my way. I'm driving as fast as I can. Please don't open the door to anyone and for the love of Christ please don't leave."

Why he thinks I would simply walk out of this house leaving a five-year-old alone to fend for herself is a mystery, but what's most disappointing is that somewhere in the deep recesses of his mind he's already assuming I'm going to leave him. So, what does that say for what's going on between him and Lori?

Or him and me?

My heart is shattering into a million little pieces as I

stand here with the phone to my ear. He hasn't denied what I've asked him which can only mean one thing.

It's all true.

He's still married to Lori.

He's been lying to me all this time.

"Zeke..." My voice quakes. "I can't—"

"I promise you, Ada, I'll explain everything when I'm home. Every damn thing. I promise. Please just trust me, okay? I beg you. Please, Ada. I'm almost there."

"Okay, I trust you Zeke," I tell him even though I'm not at all sure I trust anything anyone has said to me in the last half hour. "Please be careful."

"Ada..."

"Goodbye Zeke."

"Ada wait..."

His pleading voice is the last thing I hear before I push the button to end the call. And then I allow my knees to finally go weak and lower myself to the foyer steps.

And wait.

24

ZEKE

"**F**uck! Fucking fuck!" I shout the moment I'm in the car and peeling out of the parking garage. Snow covered roads be damned, because I'm racing home to my girls as fast as humanly possible. It'll be worth any speeding ticket I have to pay. "Ada..."

I want to pound my fists on the goddamn steering wheel.

I want to crash into every moving vehicle on the road out of complete rage toward my...fuck.

She's still my wife.

"What have I done?" I push my hand through my hair, trying as hard as I can to stay calm on these slick roads. The snow is coming down at a faster clip than it was this morning and I remind myself I have to stay focused.

I have to get home.

In one piece.

But the quiver in her voice...

Her resignation...

It destroyed me having to listen to her sound like I just broke her.

Like everything that's happening I'm doing to her on purpose.

Like it was my fucking evil plan.

My phone rings through the car and I tap the steering wheel to answer it.

"Miller."

"Yo, Zeke. It's us," Quinton says through the car speakers. "I've got you on speaker in the locker room. Carissa filled us in. What can we do?"

Tears well in my eyes and I blink them back several times. "I wish I could answer that, but I can't. Pretty sure I just fucked everything up with Ada and if she walks...if she leaves Elsie there..."

"Nah. I'm sure she would never do that," Milo says. "She'll be alright. Have a little faith. She's not Lori. You know that."

"You didn't hear her on the phone. She's gutted. I lied to her guys. You know it and I know it." I shake my head in disbelief. "FUCK! Why did Lori have to fucking show up at the house? Why now?"

"What are you going to do, bro?"

"I'm going to come clean to Ada and pray like hell that she'll forgive me. I'm going to sit her down and explain everything to her in as much detail as I possibly can and then I'm going to leave it up to her because that's all I can do, right? I can't force her to stay with me."

Hawken chimes in, "No, you can't do that."

"Listen, Zeke," Dex adds. "I know it's a little different of a situation but when Tatum was pissed at me, I showed

SUSAN RENEE

up at her place that night and we talked it out. We worked together because deep down we knew we were a team. You love Ada. And she clearly loves you."

"And Elsie," Colby reminds me. "She loves you both. Don't underestimate her. She's stronger than you think. Look what she's been through."

"It's knowing what she's been through that has me scared. She shouldn't have to put up with this kind of bull-shit. The kind I just flung at her out of nowhere. I did this. I did this to her."

"Take a deep breath, Zeke." It's Milo's calming voice again. "We're here for you, alright? Is there anything we can do for you right now?"

"Yeah can you get some snow plows out here because it's a —Shhhhhhhhhhiiiit!" The connection cuts out as I make the left turn and slip on the unplowed roads. I hit the brakes and try like hell to maneuver the car through the slide but it's no use. The back tires slide first to the left and then to the right and before I know it, the car skids into the ditch and rolls to its side and I'm going nowhere fast.

"Ze—you—ay? Wha—out—re? Ze—? The connection to my phone is way too fucked up for me to say anything and I can barely hear what the guys are saying to me.

"Fuck!" I slam my fists on the steering wheel and then take a deep breath and go through any type of mental checklist to make sure my body is okay.

Legs? Check.
Feet? Check.
Back? Check.
Neck? Check.
Arms? Check.

Hands? Fingers? Check. Check.
Head? No bleeding.
I can feel everything. I think I'm good.

Knowing nobody is going to find me out here with the exception of the dog from down the street, I push my door open and climb out into the snowy weather. Fuck the car. It can sit here until I get the mess I'm in figured out.

I was ready to buy another one anyway.

Grabbing my coat from the backseat, I put the driver side window back up and then lock the car and begin my jog home.

Ada.

I just need Ada.

"What on Earth?" Ada exclaims when I push through the front door, a freezing cold mess of a man with snow covered hair and wind-whipped skin. "What happened to you?"

"Lori happened to me," I tell her, pulling her into a massive hug if for no other reason than to simply feel her body against mine. I need her to calm me. "Lori happened and now everything about me feels like it's falling apart and I never meant to hurt you, Ada," I plead with her. "I know I fucked up. I know I didn't keep you in the loop as all this shit was going on and I'm so fucking sorry. I really was trying to make all of this easy for you but somewhere along the line everything blurred and now it's a fucking mess and I need you. God, Ada, I need you to help me. I need to get us through this. For you. For me. For Elsie."

Please. I can't let Lori do this.

"Zeke." She takes my face in her warm soft hands and stares at me, the unshed tears in her wide hazel eyes breaking me all over again. "What happened? Where is the car? Why are you covered in snow? Why are you panting?"

"Accident," I breathe, gesturing with my thumb. "I slid off the road and rolled into a ditch but it's fine. I'm fine. I just needed to get to you."

"Daddy!" Elsie comes around the corner and spots us in the foyer.

"Hi Sweetpea." I try hard to smile at her like nothing is wrong, but she's one perceptive little girl.

"Daddy, why is Ada crying? Did you play in the snow?"

"No, I didn't play in the snow Elsie, but I had to walk in it for a little bit and it's coming down pretty hard. And Ada is crying because I wasn't very nice to her. I did sort of a mean thing even though I didn't mean to and I need to apologize to her."

"Yeah Ms. Cathy tells us at school that if we say we're sorry then everything can be okay."

I nod, hoping to God my little preschooler is right. "You're absolutely right. Do you think if I put on your favorite show to watch you could give Ada and me a minute to talk so I can say I'm sorry?"

Ada shakes her head, her voice soft and resigned as she says, "Zeke, that's not neces—"

"Please, Ada." I give her a pained stare and grasp her hand in mine, bringing it to my lips. "Please. Just five minutes."

She searches my eyes and I'm desperate for her to see

my entire fucking soul. The part of me that burns for her. The part of me that loves her more than anything. The part of me that would do absolutely anything for her. The part of me that shattered into pieces the moment Carissa pulled me off that ice.

She nods silently and I nod back to her thankful she's agreed to let me explain myself. Though we exchange no words, I step aside and lead Elsie into the family room where she can sit and watch her favorite shows while I talk to Ada.

I find Ada in the kitchen a few minutes later stirring hot chocolate for us both reminding myself how fucking blessed I am to have her in my life.

Even if it's only for five more minutes.

"You're married."

She doesn't ask me. She simply states the fact.

"I don't want to be."

Her eyes fall to her drink as she methodically stirs the marshmallows in her mug. She may think I don't notice, but I don't miss the quick swipe of her tears from her cheek. It's killing me that I can't tell what she's thinking.

"Ada..."

"What Zeke?" Her eyes pull up, her features more resolute. "What could you possibly have to say to me that isn't a lie? This whole time. This..." she gestures between us. "Everything we've...everything is a lie."

"None of it is a lie, Ada." My brows pinch together as I grab her hand in mine and squeeze it. "I love you. I love you with my whole self. I'm crazy about you. I would do anything for you, you know that."

"You didn't divorce her," she quips. "She's still your

wife. She's Elsie's mother and I pushed her away even though she does have every legal right to be here."

I shake my head adamantly. "No, she doesn't. Don't you see?"

"See what, Zeke?" She flails her arms. "Did you push her away? Did you leave her and not the other way around? What? Tell me."

"No, Ada. Lori walked out on Elsie and me four years ago. When Elsie was about one."

"Why? What did you do?"

"It's more a question of what I didn't do, I think," I tell her, shoving my hand through my hair. "I knew she wasn't happy but in the middle of the hockey season there wasn't much I could do about it. I didn't have the seniority on the team that I have now. I was still proving myself. I couldn't just take time off. I would've lost everything. I needed Lori to stick around until the end of the season so we could talk and work out our differences but in the end, she wasn't happy. She told me she didn't want to live the hockey wife life anymore. She said she had a much bigger life to live than to be my shadow all the time. She said she didn't want to be bogged down with a kid at home. That..." I choke on my words when I mention the girl I would literally bend over backwards for.

Ada senses my anxiety and my desperation and covers our clasped hands with her other hand, squeezing gently. It means everything to me that she's supporting me through this very raw history of my marriage. "God, I'm sorry." I swallow back the tears and continue softly so Elsie can't hear me.

"She didn't want Elsie, Ada. She didn't want her." I pat my chest. "She didn't want me."

"Oh, Zeke."

Exposing my emotions, I shake my head as a few tears slip down my face. "I could take it, Ada. It sucked, it hurt like a bitch, and I was depressed for a long time. Not because she was gone from my life but because the situation happened to me in the first place. But I'm an adult. I knew in time I would be okay. But she fucking left her child. Her baby. Her little girl. She literally left Elsie sleeping in her crib and grabbed some of her stuff and fucking left."

Ada gasps, her hand clutching her chest. "Oh, my God."

I beat my chest, anger building inside me, my emotions hitting full tilt as I talk about my flesh and blood. "What kind of parent walks out on their partner after having a fucking child because they just decide they don't want to parent anymore?" I ask, my voice shaking with the quiver of my chin. "And what kind of f-f-f-fucking monster leaves their living breathing baby asleep in her crib and just walks away? I'll tell you who, Ada. Lori. That's who."

I shake my head. "I tried so hard to find her for a year after she left. I wanted to divorce her then and press all the charges I possibly could, but nobody could find her. It's like she walked off the face of the Earth. Grady said if she didn't want to be found there were ways she could've hidden herself. For all we knew she was in Europe living her best life avoiding authorities. And she clearly succeeded."

"So, what did you do?"

"There was nothing I could do. Grady told me to give it some time. That maybe after a while she would make a mistake when she didn't know I was looking for her and she would be easy to locate."

"Is that what happened?" Ada asks me, sitting back in her seat and bringing her hot cocoa to her lips. "You finally found her?"

"A few months ago, yeah." I nod. "I'm so sorry, Ada. I kind of forgot that we were still married until you came into my life. I knew I wanted you. I wanted to explore things with you, but I didn't want Lori to be able to say I had cheated on her because I didn't want to lose Elsie. So that's when I called Grady. I begged him to do all he could to find Lori and he did it. He fucking did it and then he served her divorce papers immediately."

I bow my head, sniffling and trying to rein in my overwhelming sadness. "She doesn't love her own child, Ada. She doesn't want her."

"No, she doesn't," Ada says softly. "And I'm so sorry for that. But it's nobody's loss but her own. Elsie had no idea who Lori was when she was here. And I got the vibe she was here for one reason only."

I bring my eyes back up and notice her sympathetic expression. A tiny glimmer of hope flutters inside my chest that maybe, just maybe, she believes me and we can get through this together.

"What did she say?"

Ada leans forward, her elbows on the table. "She said she refuses to sign the divorce papers until she has at least half of your millions."

"Pfft." I scoff. "She can have it all. I don't give two

fucks. I don't care about the money. I care about Elsie. And I care about you. If money is what she wants to get her out of my life forever, she can have it."

"Oooh I don't fucking think so," Ada says scowling at me.

"What?"

"I said absofuckinglutely not, Zeke Miller. You've worked your ass off for that money and she doesn't deserve a dime from you. Not one penny. You owe her nothing. She abandoned you. She abandoned her kid."

"What are you saying?"

"I'm saying if your lawyer knows how to do his job, he should be able to make sure Lori is out of your life for good and walks away from any potential reconciliation with not one more penny to her name."

"So, you believe me?"

She nods slowly, her eyes never leaving mine. "I believe you, Zeke."

I sink back in my chair, my emotions overwhelming me now as tears fall down my face. "Oh, thank Christ."

Ada drops to her knees in front of me and takes my hands in hers. "I believe you and I love you. I'm here for you. I'll fight with you. I'll stand by your side. I'll do whatever I need to do to help you through this."

I lift her up from the ground and wrap my arms around her in the tightest hug I can give her. Allowing myself to revel in the feeling of her warmth, her hope, and her love.

"Thank you, Ada. For understanding. Or for at the very least loving me through this horrible clusterfuck."

"There's nothing we can't get through together," she whispers against my ear. "That's what love is, remember?"

"I swear to God, I'll never forget."

The doorbell rings again and we stiffen in each other's arms. I grab my phone from my pocket to look at the doorbell notification but it's too late. Whoever is at the door is already making themselves known.

"Zeke! Ada! Open up! It's us!"

"The fuck?" I mumble as Ada looks on in confusion. I step toward the foyer and open the door and I'm immediately wrapped in a team hug from Colby, Carissa, Milo, Dex, Hawken, and Quinton.

"What the hell guys?"

"Are you alright man?" Quinton asks.

"Yeah, of course, I'm alright," I answer. "What's going on?"

"Dude, one minute we were talking to you and then we weren't," Colby explains. "You mentioned a snowplow and then bad roads and then we heard you shout and that was it. The line went dead."

Quinton nods. "Yeah so we hopped in Colby's truck and drove out here hoping we wouldn't find you dead in a damn ditch and that's exactly where we found your car."

"Shit, I'm sorry guys. I should've called you. I just...I hit a slick spot and wound up in the ditch but I was fine. And then I was focused on getting back here," I gesture behind me, "to Ada and Elsie."

"We understand. Thank fuck you're alright, man," Dex nearly cries, smacking me on the back in a bear hug.

"Uncle Dex?" Elsie's tiny voice comes from behind us.

"Yeah, Squish?"

"You said the bad fuck word."

25

ZEKE

"Listen to me," Grady tells me from his fancy chair behind his desk. This office gives me the creeps every time I'm in here but only because any time I'm in here it's to discuss a legal issue and those are never fun regardless of what they are. "It's my job to focus on Lori's parenting of Elsie or lack thereof. It's my job to focus on Lori's abandonment of your marriage and of her parental responsibilities. You pay me to do the dirty work, alright?"

I nod. "Yeah. I get it. So, what do I do?"

"You sit back and smother your kid with love and attention. You look like the model parent. Not that you aren't that already. I know you're nervous about this but I guarantee you there is zero need for any anxiety here. When we meet with Lori I'll set her straight. She'll either walk away with nothing or she'll spend years in jail."

"What about statute of limitations? Or proof? I don't have proof that she left Elsie in her crib that day. It's my word against hers."

"No." He shakes his head. "You filed a police report. That's enough. It's on record. I could call the police right now and turn her in except that I don't know where she is at this literal moment. So, this is the best play. Let her think you're giving in. Let her think she'll be on the next flight to dream town with a few million in her pocket. It'll get her in the door and then we'll give her the nasty truth."

"Grady I can't thank you enough for tackling all this."

A slow smile spreads across his face. "That's why you pay me the big bucks, Miller."

"As far as I'm concerned you're worth every penny."

"Are you ready for today?"

Ada circles her finger lazily over my bare chest as we lie in bed together. In order to make sure I had my wits about me to fight Lori, I asked my parents to take Elsie for the weekend so I don't have to worry about her. And then I spent the entirety of last night buried deep inside Ada fucking away all my stress and anxiety and reminding her over and over again, one orgasm after another, how very much I love her. Waking up and realizing she's still here with me, still in my arms...grateful doesn't do my feelings for her justice. She's been a lifeline through all my stress. She willingly unzipped all my baggage and helped me sort the clean from the dirty. She's been my biggest lifeline.

"Actually, yeah. I am." I inhale a deep calming breath and release it, covering her hand with mine. "I feel good.

Grady seems to have everything prepared and with any luck, she'll play right into our hand."

"I have no doubt that's exactly what she'll do," she says. "She's got dollar signs in her eyes. She's not focused on anything else. Her lack of preparation will bite her in the ass for sure."

"I'm sorry you won't be with me today."

God, do I wish she could be sitting next to me in that office.

"You know I can't be there with you in person. It wouldn't be right. But I'll be with you." She taps my chest lightly right over my heart. "In here." Then she reaches up and kisses my temple. "And in here. And then when it's all over, I'll be celebrating with you and about fifty thousand other fans."

"You're coming to the game tonight?"

"I wouldn't miss it. I've got my bedazzled jersey ready just for the occasion."

I turn my body towards her so we're facing each other and wrap an arm around her soft naked body. "Will you let me eat you out after I pull off another shut-out wearing nothing but that jersey?"

A broad smile stretches across her face and she winks at me. "Maybe if you beg."

I roll us over again so I'm hovering above her this time, gazing down at her beautiful hazel eyes. "Sweetheart, I'll spend all night begging if it means I get to fall asleep tonight with the taste of you on my lips."

"Then I guess we have a deal, Mr. Miller." She spanks my bare ass, making me laugh.

She could do that again.

And again.

And again.

"Now get up and get showered. And put your best suit on. Your focus right now is on your freedom. Yours and Elsie's."

I kiss Ada's lips one last time and then reluctantly climb off the bed and head for the shower. She doesn't join me because she knows damn well if she did I would never leave because I'm a sucker for her naked body and a hot steamy shower. So instead, I spend my time under the water thinking about all the encouragement Ada has given me over the last several weeks in regard to my issues with Lori. She had every opportunity to hate me. To be pissed at me for not giving her the whole truth about my marriage to Lori. She could have left and I wouldn't have blamed her. And even just now when she kicked me out of bed, she told me my focus was to be on my freedom. Mine and Elsie's. She said nothing of herself. She didn't include herself.

A month ago, I may have freaked out about her not including herself in my future. I may have worried that she was going to leave me. Leave Elsie. It was my number one fear the day Lori showed up at my door after four years.

But things are different now.

Ada has a whole new confidence in who we are as a couple. She's so fucking strong. The best support system a man like me could ever ask for. I know her focus on me and Elsie isn't because she doesn't want to be a part of my little family. She's not leaving us. It's because in order for our story to have the happy ending she knows I have to fix myself before I can move forward with us. I have to slay the dragon before I save the princess. Or in my case, my queen and my princess.

And I can do this.

I want to do this.

And I can't wait to see Lori's face when she realizes she's the dragon.

And I'm the one with the sword.

I haven't seen her in four years but she looks exactly the same.

Straight blonde hair pulled tight in a high ponytail. She's dressed in a tight black pencil skirt and matching silk blouse with a large bow at the neck. Her blue eyes are vindictive as she smiles at me from across the conference room table, but there's something slightly off about her. Her eyes are bloodshot, and her face gaunt. She doesn't look as healthy as she did when we were together and since I've seen it thousands of times in athletes over the years, I know exactly what I'm looking at.

She's fucking high.

And if she's not high, she wants to get high.

I scoff to myself, shaking my head as her lawyer pulls a chair out for her. She sits down and brings her clasped hands to the table before she finally speaks.

"Hello, Zeke."

Fuck you, Lori.

Drugs? Really?

You're on drugs now?

Is that why you want my money?

To get your next fix?

You deserve nothing but a lifetime of pain and misery in the depths of hell.

Those are all the things I want to say to her in response.

But I don't.

Grady advised me to bite my tongue and say nothing unless absolutely necessary so that he and the mediator can do their jobs. As much as it pains me because I sure as fuck want to rain down the insults and fuck-yous until she begs for mercy, I will do what he suggests. Even if it kills me.

"Right. So, now that we're all here we can get started." Mr. Brookstone, our mediator, opens his folder and clicks his pen. "We're here to settle the terms of divorce between Ezekiel and Lori Miller. I have with me the terms each party has requested." He hands both lawyers a few stapled papers. "I'll give you a moment to go over these and then we'll proceed with any negotiations needed."

Grady doesn't even lift the paper from where it lands in front of him. "Mr. Brookstone there won't be any negotiations from my client this morning."

Lori and her lawyer glance up from the papers in front of them, surprised at Grady's comment.

"Ms. Miller won't be receiving a dime from Zeke."

"WHAT?" Lori's outburst is predictable and I have to bite my cheek not to laugh in her face.

Her lawyer clears his throat and shuffles in his seat. "Uh, I believe as my client has been married to Mr. Miller for seven years, she is indeed entitled to compensation in the form of a percentage of his salary."

"Fifteen million dollars?" Grady laughs. "You really think you're walking out of here an instant millionaire?"

He nods, lifting his chin with a confidence he clearly doesn't have but is trying his best to fake.

Who is this guy?

Is he even a lawyer?

"Fifteen million is half of Zeke's salary. That's common knowledge and should rightfully go to my client."

"Actually, Mr. Price," Mr. Brookstone intervenes. "Illinois is no longer a community property state. I trust you know this. A couple's property or finances are no longer divided equally. If a settlement is not agreed upon in this meeting, a judge can and will allocate funds as he or she sees fit based on particular circumstances."

"I understand that very well." Mr. Price nods, "but even still, my client feels fifteen million is more than fair to compensate for her pain and suffering..."

"Pain and suffering," I scoff with a laugh. Grady nudges my knee with his to stop me from saying something I'll regret. Mr. Price on the other hand, glares at me from across the table and continues.

"It will help her pay off any outstanding debts..."

To her drug supplier you mean.

"And will give her a fair nest egg to aid her in her future endeavors."

"Future endeavors in jail, maybe."

"Excuse me?" Mr. Brookstone asks, his face now pointed at me.

Oops. Did I say that out loud?

"What my client means, Mr. Brookstone," Grady says, covering for me, "is that perhaps Ms. Miller neglected to tell her lawyer that she has a warrant out for her arrest and has for several years for abandoning her one-year-old child the day she walked out on my client."

"That's absurd!" she cries. "I knew Zeke would be home soon. I knew she would be fine."

"You fucking left our baby asleep in her bed and drove the fuck away, Lori! What the hell were you thinking?"

"I..." Her jaw drops and she shakes her head. "It's your word against mine, Zeke. You have no proof. You're making shit up to try to shut me out."

"Oh no?" I shake my head. "So, you didn't know about the warrant then? You've just been traveling the country for four years, hopping from place to place for the hell of it?"

She folds her arms over her chest. "Yes. And there's nothing wrong with that. And besides, you cheated on me."

"I have done no such thing."

"No?" She smirks. "Then who's the little whore who answered the door the other day when I stopped by.

Grady leans forward. "Mrs. Miller, I'm going to assume you're referring to Ada Lewis."

"Yeah. Ada. That was her name."

"Right. She was hired several months ago to be Elsie's nanny as my client was going to need someone who could be around to make sure she could get safely to and from preschool. I assure you several people interviewed her before she was offered the job and she has done an excellent job with Elsie's care since she accepted."

Lori's eyes narrow as she stares me down but she has no recourse, so Grady takes the lull in conversation to continue. "Mrs. Miller we have the video of the day you

318

left on my client's Ring Doorbell. Time stamped. We also have in that video the time my client returned home that day. Three hours later. To a screaming crying child, soiled and wet and laying in her crib."

"But..."

He pulls out a stack of papers from his folder and hands them to Lori's lawyer. "We also have the police report from that night and the note you wrote explaining to my client that you were leaving him."

"But I..."

"Let me tell you how this is going to go, Lori," I seethe. Grady tries to stop me but I'm pissed enough that I don't care anymore.

It's time to slay the fucking dragon and be done with it.

"You're either going to sign these divorce papers and you're going to sign away all of your parental rights to Elsie and walk away with absolutely nothing from either of us except the mercy of my not calling the police to tell them exactly where you are..."

Lori gasps, tears springing to her eyes.

"Or you're going straight to jail." I shake my head. "You will not pass Go. You will not collect two hundred dollars. Or two million dollars or even two cents. You will rot in jail for the rest of your God forsaken sorry ass life for abandoning your child."

"Zeke," she pleads.

"You will have nothing whatsoever to do with Elsie ever again. You will not come near her. You will not touch her. You will not talk to her. You will no longer be her mother. And if I so much as hear a whisper of your whereabouts and it's anywhere close to me or my child, I will make your life miserable. Do you understand me?"

She sits back in her chair, swallowing her words and then looking at her lawyer for guidance. He shrugs his shoulder and shakes his head silently and turns to the mediator.

"Okay, it seems the path is clear here, Mrs. Miller," Mr. Brookstone explains. "If you did in fact intentionally abandon your child for more than a twenty-four-hour period..."

"Try a four-year period," I scoff.

"That is felony in the state of Illinois and you could be looking at significant prison time if convicted. In my legal experience, a mother intentionally abandoning her child never sits well with a judge or jury. If you're looking for my professional opinion—"

"I'm not. I have a lawyer, thank you very much."

Yeah. He's a real winner, Lori.

She chews on the inside of her mouth no doubt pondering how she can get out the mess she's put herself in. Her eyes slide up to meet my cold hard stare and I refuse to look away as I slide the settlement across the table.

"Your choice, Lori. I'd sign the damn papers if I were you." I huff out a laugh. "Though you and I both know I would never be you."

She sits back in her seat and sighs. "You're not willing to give me anything?"

"Not. One. Fucking. Dime."

"Fine," she finally acquiesces. "I'll sign the damn papers."

Fucking right you will.

She grabs a pen from her lawyer and I watch with disdain as she adds her signature to the appropriate forms and slides them back to me. Grady points out exactly where I need to sign and I do so with fervor and then hand them to the mediator.

"It's done." He stands and shakes hands with Grady and Mr. Price. "I'll take care of the rest. Mr. and Mrs. Miller, your divorce will be finalized by the end of the day."

Without saying another word, Lori and her lawyer stand and exit the room and I breathe a huge sigh of relief. "Thank you, Mr. Brookstone," I say, shaking his hand.

"My pleasure, Mr. Miller." He tugs my hand so I lean in a little closer to him and whispers, "And good luck tonight. The Anaheim Stars are a strong team this year."

"Thank you, Sir. And you're right. They'll definitely give us a run for our money, but I'm confident we'll pull out a win."

"I'll definitely be watching."

Grady walks me out of the office building to my car explaining all the tiny details of having everything finalized and reassuring me that I am now a free man.

Free.

That word has never felt so good.

I climb into my car and pull out my phone, sending a text to the one person I've been thinking about all morning.

ME

It's done. We're free! And I love you so damn much.

ADA

YOU'RE free. I'm so damn proud of you, Zeke. And I love you too. So very much.

ME

On my way to the arena. I'll see you tonight. 🩶

ADA

It's a date! 😊

26
ADA

Six Months Later

"**H**appy Birthday, Dear Ada. Happy Birthday to you!" Our friends are gathered around the table as I make a wish and blow out the candles on my cake. With Elsie's help of course. I wouldn't have it any other way.

"Thank you everyone!"

"Ada can we open presents now?" Elsie asks, clapping her hands in excitement and bouncing up and down on my lap.

"How about you give the presents to Ada and she can open them," Zeke suggests to Elsie. "Remember, it's not your birthday. It's Ada's birthday."

"Okay!" She hops down from my lap and grabs the first gift. "This one is from Aunt Kinsley."

"Oooh." I shake the box, bringing it to my ear. "What do you think it could be?"

"Maybe it's another nutsack," Dex suggests.

Colby nods. "Or Nutsack's nutsack."

"Nah, he lost that a long time ago," Kinsley laughs.

I pull back the paper on the box and lift the lid, cackling when I finally see what's inside.

"Oh, my gosh, really? This is really what I think it is?"

"Sure is." She grins as I pull out a crocheted pink penis complete with two little eyes, a mouth, and a sign that reads

Life is like a penis.
Sometimes it's up. Sometimes it's down.
But don't worry, it won't be hard forever.

"That's a far cry from a positive potato," Milo says with a chuckle.

Kinsley nods with an ornery smirk. "Meh. I thought it was time to branch out a little."

"This is fantastic," I tell her. "Thank you so much, Kins. I love it!"

She gives me a wink. "You're welcome."

I open a few other fun gifts from our friends including several adult themed bookish gifts, a new pair of designer sunglasses, and a girls' weekend away for some pampering and shopping at the end of the month before Elsie starts kindergarten and before the next hockey season begins. The perfect time to relax and recharge before the chaos of everyday life ramps up.

"Thank you all so much for all these amazing gifts. I'm truly blessed to have you all in my life. What an amazing day!"

Elsie runs to the small table where gifts were stored and

picks up another box wrapped in red paper with silver ribbons. "Daddy can I give her this one?"

Zeke nods. "Sure, kiddo. Go ahead. This one's from me," he whispers as she brings over the rectangular box and sets it in front of me. I shake this one too but nothing budges.

"Hmm, what could it be?"

Elsie shrugs. "I don't know. Daddy said it's a secret."

I carefully tear off the paper from the box looking for some sort of store logo but the white box is blank. Nothing giving away what could be inside. I rip the tape holding the box down and lift off the lid, a huge smile breaking across my face at what's wrapped within the tissue paper.

"Now THAT is some amazing bedazzle work!" I exclaim as I lift the new Red Tails jersey from the box and unfold it. From the front it looks exactly the same as the one I had made.

"Wait, is this mine? Did you have something new done to it?"

Zeke shakes his head. "No. Turn it around."

I flip the jersey around and gasp as my smile falters and tears well up in my eyes. The jersey I had made had the name MILLER bedazzled across the back. But this one is different. In shiny gemstones across the back shoulder, this jersey says MRS. MILLER.

"Zeke!" I turn my head and find him right by my side, down on one knee, with a diamond ring in his hand.

"Did you bedazzle this ring too?" I tease him even though I'm the one wiping tears from my eyes.

"Yeah." He nods with a laugh. "I sure did. From the best bedazzler in the city."

My shoulders sag and cock my head. "Zeke, this is...are you...do you—"

"I do," he says, stopping me before I can go any further. He slides the ring onto my finger and asks, "Do you?"

"You know I do," I answer him with a tearful smile.

He gazes into my glistening eyes the look of adoration evident in his every expression. "I love you, Ada."

Sniffling, I lean forward and hold his face between my hands. "I love you too, Zeke. I can't wait to marry you." He kisses me as all our friends cheer us on and then wishes us congratulations but then we're interrupted once again by a certain five-year-old little girl.

"Ada, are you going to marry Daddy?"

I crouch down next to her and take her hand in mine. "Is that okay with you?"

"Fucking yes!" she shouts to the amusement of every adult in the room.

"Elsie!" Zeke points to her and then whispers, "You said the bad fuck word."

"But it's Ada's birthday, Daddy and she's going to live here forever!"

"That's right," he says. "Do you think it's time to give Ada your present?"

She gasps, her eyes lighting up with excitement. "YES!" We all watch as she skips over to the table and grabs the flattened box wrapped in pink paper with all sorts of colorful bows on it.

"Oh, my goodness, did you wrap this all by yourself, Elsie?"

"Daddy helped me but I got to pick the bows."

"Well, you did a beautiful job. I love all of them." I take

a bow from the package and stick one on her tummy and then one on her head making her giggle. Then I unwrap the thin box feeling something semi-round inside. I tip the box and watch as a pink and white friendship bracelet falls into my hand, smiling when I see that the letters Elsie chose spells the word M-O-M-M-Y.

"Oh Elsie, this is so special!" My heart tugs in my chest as I give Elsie a great big hug. The thought of being a mother figure for her as she grows up makes me so happy. She is an amazing little girl and I love her with all my heart.

"There's more," Zeke whispers when he catches my glance.

"Oh. There is?"

He nods.

I shove my hand into the box, my hand landing on a paper of some sort. I slide it out and collapse into a fit of tears upon reading the heading.

Certificate Of Adoption - Elsie Jane Miller

My face in my hands, I cry huge ugly yet joyous tears over this special birthday gift. I hear the ladies all starting to cry tears of joy with me and then Zeke's kissing the side of my head. "I hope that's a yes," he whispers in my ear as I sob.

I lift my head, my makeup running everywhere, and bring Elsie to my lap. She holds my face in her little hands and cocks her head. "Did I make you sad?"

I shake my head. "No Elsie." I smooth her pretty curls away from her face. "You made me happier than I think I could ever be in my whole life and I love you so, so, so much."

I slip the Mommy friendship bracelet onto my wrist and hold Elsie's adoption papers to my chest. "I promise I'll be the very best mommy I can be for you." I turn to Zeke. "And the very best wife I can be for you."

He takes my hand and lifts me from my chair, pulling me into a tight hug. "You're already perfect for us, Ada. Happy Birthday, Sweetheart."

"Thank you, Zeke. I love you so much."

"Sooo we've had a wedding in New Orleans, a wedding in Key West, a wedding in our own stadium, and a wedding in Hawaii," Dex counts on his fingers. "Where's this wedding going to be?"

"I don't know." Zeke shrugs. "Maybe we could find somewhere that has a two for one deal."

"Two for one?" Tatum asks bouncing Dex Jr. on her hip. "What do you mea—" Her jaw drops when she sees Dex pull a ring from his pocket and lower himself to one knee. "Oooh, Jesus."

I expect Rory to take the baby from Tatum but when she looks equally as shocked, I step over and pull him from her arms before she goes weak in the knees.

"Tater Tot, you've put up with my shit long enough. I wanted to plan this grand proposal because you deserve the goddamn world and I want to give it to you. But then I got to talking to Zeke a few weeks ago and he said I could share in their special day and fuck, I can't wait anymore. You've already made me the happiest son of a bitch in the world, but I want to make it official. And you deserve it because you've waited so damn long for me to get my act together. Will you marry me, Tate? Please?"

She throws her arms around Dex and he blows out a huge sigh of relief. "Yes! Yes Dex! Of course I'll marry you!" She lets go of her embrace and whacks him in the arm. "Took you long enough!"

"I know, Baby. I know. I promise I'll never make you wait for anything again."

"I think this calls for a celebration all around. I'll be right back." I watch as Zeke steps into the kitchen and a few moments later comes back with a tray of champagne for everyone—including little cups of sparkling grape juice for Elsie and Summer. Once everyone has a glass Zeke wraps an arm around me and raises his glass

"To the Red Tails, without whom none of us would be standing here today with the love of our lives by our side. May we have many more amazing seasons ahead of us."

Everyone raises their glass to toast. "To the Red Tails!"

The end

Want more of Zeke, Ada, and the rest of the Chicago Red Tails?
Visit my website at authorsusanrenee.com

If you loved the Red Tails, stay tuned because we are not out of our hockey era just yet!

The *Anaheim Stars* are coming this fall!

OTHER BOOKS BY SUSAN RENEE

All books are available in Kindle Unlimited

The Chicago Red Tails Series

Off Your Game – Colby Nelson

Unfair Game – Milo Landric

Beyond the Game – Dex Foster

Forbidden Game – Hawken Malone

Saving the Game – Quinton Shay

Bonus Game – Zeke Miller

Remember Colby's brother, Elias Nelson? Here's his story! A spinoff of my Bardstown Series of small town interconnected romances!

NO ONE NEEDS TO KNOW: Accidental Pregnancy

(Elias and Whitney's story)

(Bardstown Series Prequel – Previously entitled SEVEN)

I LOVED YOU THEN

The Bardstown Series

I LIKE ME BETTER: Enemies to Lovers

YOU ARE THE REASON: Second Chance

BEAUTIFUL CRAZY: Friends to Lovers

TAKE YOU HOME: Boss's Daughter

ROMANTIC COMEDIES

Smooch: Arya's Story

Smooches: Hannah's Story

Smooched: Kim's Story

Hole Punched

You Don't Know Jack Schmidt
(The Schmidt Load Novella Book 1)

Schmidt Happens
(The Schmidt Load Novella Book 2)

My Schmidt Smells Like Roses
(The Schmidt Load Novella Book 3)

CONTEMPORARY ROMANCE

The Village series

I'm Fine (The Village Duet #1)

Save Me (The Village Duet #2)

*The Village Duet comes with a content warning.

Please be sure to check out this book's Amazon page before
downloading.

Solving Us

(Big City New Adult Romance)

Surprising Us (a Solving Us novella)

ACKNOWLEDGMENTS

I know writing acknowledgements with every book can sometimes be a little repetitive, but I hope you'll forgive me for a moment as I thank a few people now that the Red Tails series has come to an end. I'm all up in my feelings over here.

Before this series was ever published, I felt like a nobody. Just a mom trying to semi-make it in a world inundated with indie romance authors. It can be a loney world, but I've loved just about every aspect of this job for the past several years. This past year in particular though has been like none other and NONE of it would be happening if it weren't for YOU. The readers!

Colby and Milo sort of slid under the radar but by the time Dex came around, you guys took notice. You started reading like crazy! You bought my books. You talked about them. You made Facebook posts, Instagram posts and Tiktoks! You spread the word and you encouraged me to keep going every step of the way. Your kindness, your love and your encouragement threw the rest of the Red Tails into more best seller lists than I could keep track of! You made me an international bestseller and for that I cannot even express how grateful I am.

You all have changed my life.

Seriously.

You might know my personal story and you might not. One day I'll be brave enough to share it with the world but if you don't know it, please wrap your arm around yourself and give yourself a huge hug and pretend it's from me because my God, YOU HAVE CHANGED MY LIFE and the life of my little family for the BETTER and almost a year later, I'm still crying about it!

Yeah, I'm also waiting for the other shoe to drop. I'm waiting for that moment when all this happiness comes crashing down and I wake up from this dream, but YOU ALL have somehow lifted me up and kept me believing in the GOOD of this world. That good things CAN happen to me and for me. And that I'm not a bad person for accepting the love and living in peace.

So, THANK YOU READERS. From the very bottom of my heart THANK YOU. I hope you realize just how much of an impact you can make on a human being's life, simply by reading a book and talking about it, because you've certainly done it for me. I love you all so very, very, very much!

I would be remiss if I didn't say thank you to my alpha reader team: Kristan, Stephani, Jen, and Jenn. I don't know where I would be without you ladies. Seriously. Thank you for talking every little detail through with me. Thank you for your honesty! Thank you for your encouragement and your laughs and your ideas! YOU make me a better writer and I appreciate you all soooo much!

To Podium Audio, THANK YOU for taking a chance on me and my Red Tails and for helping me bring them to life one book at a time! Gabriel and Stella...I don't even have the words. I love you both for the work you put in to bringing my hockey guys (and gals) to life. You both have done a superb job and I can not WAIT to hear the rest of the series and then work with you again on future projects! THANK YOU for your voices!!!

Brandi, thanks for putting up with my word repetition and for always making me go back and make sure my timelines are correct and for questioning my steamy scene positions 😌 I LOOOOVE working with you. Like, LOVE IT! Seriously!

Phew ok. Now, are we ready for some more hockey because I'm not ready to walk away from the ice just yet. Bring on the ANAHEIM STARS!!!! (coming this fall!)

Special Thanks to my Patreon subscribers for sticking with me in so many aspects of my writing process!

Katie Powell

Dawn Bryant

Betsy Chapman

Lindsay Brewer

Interested in joining my Patreon
visit my website at authorsusanrenee.com

ABOUT THE AUTHOR

Susan Renee wants to live in a world where paint doesn't smell, Hogwarts is open twenty-four/seven, and everything is covered in glitter. An indie romance author, Susan has written about everything from tacos to tow-trucks, loves writing romantic comedies but also enjoys creating an emotional angsty story from time to time. She lives in Ohio with her husband, kids, two dogs and a cat. Susan holds a Bachelor and Master's degree in Sass and Sarcasm and enjoys laughing at memes, speaking in GIFs and spending an entire day jumping down the TikTok rabbit hole. When she's not writing or playing the role of Mom, her favorite activity is doing the Care Bear stare with her closest friends.

facebook.com/authorsusanrenee

x.com/indiesusanrenee

instagram.com/authorsusanrenee

tiktok.com/@authorsusanrenee

amazon.com/author/susanrenee

goodreads.com/susanrenee

bookbub.com/authors/susan-renee

patreon.com/RomanceReadersandWishfulWriters

Made in United States
North Haven, CT
15 June 2024

53684892R10192